CONCEALED JUDGEMENT

CONCEALED JUDGEMENT

Stacey
Enjoy !
Barb Dimich

Barb Dimich

To order additional copies of this book, contact:
Xlibris Corporation
1-888-7-XLIBRIS
www.Xlibris.com
Orders@Xlibris.com

CONTENTS

In loving memory of my nephew, Sammy 1976 - 1997

CHAPTER ONE

Explicit directions to the blue neon sign in Masquerade were accurate. Ann Longworth parked in front of the coffee shop facing Crypt Lake. *Masquerade, Crypt Lake*, the names sounded like a scene from a mystery novel. The Kozy Kafé didn't coincide with any part of the theory.

Weary and worn out, Ann gradually slid out of her Trans AM stepping out onto a graveled parking lot. A glaring sun reflecting off the lake blinded her into a squint. Though bright, it welcomed her from her obvious doom and the gloomy, gray skies she'd left in St. Paul. Ann looked across the boundless lake following the horizon. Fishing boats spotted the lazy scene and Masquerade cut a figure of peaceful auras.

Ann strolled into the Kozy Kafé scanning the large room inside. The smell of greasy hamburgers and fries competed with the scent of freshly baked sweet rolls and bred a new form of nausea inside her stomach. She observed six people who were scattered throughout the room sitting on fifties style barstools at the counter and tables. Large windows facing the lake exposed a magnificent view and doubled the lighting inside the café. Classic Chevy's and Fords, The Four Seasons, Beach Boys and Annette and Frankie from their beach day movies lined the walls in the form of replica poster pictures. Green Coke bottles roosted on shelving in back of the counter along side vintage, model cars. A modern day song played on a nostalgic jukebox amusing the patrons though contradictory to the decor.

Ann approached the counter and waited while a teenager do'd with a ponytail and wearing a red, camp-shirt and gathered, dirndl skirt tended to a coffee drinker. The girl then be-bopped toward her in the era popular black and white saddle shoes over white Bobby socks. After a brief exchange of words, Ann was directed to chose one of numerous, deserted tables.

Significantly overdressed in heels and a linen suit, Ann nodded as each guest stole a peek at her. Difficult to ignore their staring eyes, she wondered what prompted the Fifties décor in a restaurant near a lake presumed to be a fisherman's haven. Not wanting to tip anyone off, Mrs. Franklin had chosen this place to meet. Too late, Ann jeered silently her suit was a dead giveaway. She was unmistakably a stranger in town, and not here to fish.

Sitting down at a table with her back to the wall, Ann contemplated Friday's meeting in the AG's office. Working with the Attorney General's office for the State of Minnesota, Ann investigated fraud. An amazing fact was the sinister ways people created as a means to sham state and federal funds. Last Friday, Ann had been assigned this case along with Madison Baker who was one of four Deputy Attorney Generals in the AG's office. Ann's job involved a compilation of endless paper trails and interviews to discover how the thefts occurred and who the culprits were behind the stealing. Madison prosecuted when sufficient evidence warranted charging out a criminal complaint. The state auditor's report had hinted in the direction of a Board member, or employees of the boarding school's involvement in the embezzlement. Either way, nearly a million dollars of allocated funding to the county-run facility in Masquerade were presently unaccounted for.

Madison, officially a Juris Doctorate grad, had been unusually quiet during the discussion of this case. The two women always had an embedded trust for each other and Madison frequently bragged about Ann's *sixth sense*. Ann rarely thought or spoke of her second sight despite being plagued with the bothersome obstacle since she was a child. Deliberating over the very idea of having insights to *feel* something was going to happen hardly ever meant it would turn out good.

After their meeting that day, she and Madison met alone in Madison's office as they normally did to discuss their procedure and approach to the case. Caught off guard by Madison's cat-like, green eyes when they widened with fury, an argument between them ensued. Madison's aggressive personality exploded like a stud in heat and she told Ann she wanted her to work with a new investigator the state had hired. Admittedly, Ann didn't know about the rookie, but found it odd Madison was pairing her up. *Why now, when none of the investigators had ever worked with partners?*

Friday's argument, once again, exposed Madison's sufficiently vicious attitude. She attacked, flinging hurtful words. Ann didn't understand the anger behind Madison's verbal assault on her, or why she seemed irritated when the AG had thrown this mess into their laps. Following the verbal attack, Ann left Madison's office without reaching any sort of agreement of how to proceed. The problem at the moment wasn't how to handle an investigation. She'd been doing this job for what felt like eternity. The problem was the argument between her and Madison appeared to be an intentional distraction and proposed some mighty suspicious groundwork. Why would Madison deliberately try to distract her is what puzzled Ann.

Hearing the jingle of bells on the door, Ann looked up as an esteemed-looking woman strolled into the coffee shop. The six customers, and the waitress, all greeted the woman calling her Angela. She smiled generously acknowledging each person with a brief conversation that was followed by laughter.

Ann concluded this must be Mrs. Franklin. During brief en-counters with each patron, 'Angela' made direct eye contact and affectionately touched an arm or a shoulder of the individual she spoke with before strolling onto the next one. Ann watched a wispy confidence unfurl with each movement from the woman's deli-cate, thin features. She had beaming, blue eyes that retained sheen of purpose and sparkled against her flawless, milky-white skin. Both characteristics actually praised her snow-white hair and though she was impeccably dressed in a conservative, cotton blouse and navy slacks, Mrs. Franklin's attire didn't stand out nearly as

much as Ann's suit did. Looking at Ann, the woman graciously
walked toward the table.

"Ann Longworth?"

"Yes."

"I'm Mrs. Franklin."

Smoothly, Mrs. Franklin slid out a chair and sat down. Ann
noted Mrs. Franklin still graced with ease and confidence, momentarily examined Ann similar to the way Ann had studied her.

The young waitress skipped over to their table breaking the
concentration between both women and coffee was ordered.

"Ms. Longworth, have you been waiting long?"

"Not at all. Your directions were perfect and I arrived a couple
of minutes before you."

Moments later, coffee was served in Fiesta-style cups on matching saucers, another symbol marking the fifties era. Mrs. Franklin
diverted her attention from the waitress ignoring a curious look
forming on the young girl's face. The teenybopper missed the obvious hint and Mrs. Franklin spoke deliberately.

"Jeannie, is there something you need?"

The teenager's face recreated shades of apple-red as Jeannie
clumsily spun around and stumbled away from the table.

"Mrs. Franklin, as I explained over the phone I will be con-
ducting interviews, talking with people and looking over the reports where the State Auditor found discrepancies. Why don't you
tell me what you know at this point."

"I'm in charge of the orphanage here in Masquerade."

Ann's head came up from her report file and she looked at
Mrs. Franklin. "I thought you were on the County Family Coun-
cil Board."

"Yes, I am, but I am also in charge of the boarding school, or
Agency as we sometimes refer to it. Anyway, Minnesota lawmakers
passed a law to fund this county-run boarding school, the only
one of it's kind in the state. Its purpose is to house and educate the
children of poor families and troubled neighborhoods, as well as
orphans in the State of Minnesota."

"Yes, I'm aware of the program. It was designed by the Legislature to help the communities support families move from welfare to work."

Mrs. Franklin nodded and continued, "We're the first state to return to the old-fashioned notion of providing public funding for living and schooling, calling it an orphanage. It's intended for children who have been neither jailed, nor removed from an abusive home. Three years ago the Federal Government funded over fourteen million dollars, and the State provided an excess of seven million to insure the program's success. The building was constructed and we opened almost two years ago. The day the auditor arrived, one of my employees, Mandi Marriano, did not show up for work and has since been reported missing to the police. This occurred a month ago."

"Missing as in she ran away, or missing as in foul play?"

"Dare I say, she most likely found a permanent address in the Caribbean, or somewhere else, since the auditor discovered in the vicinity of one million dollars snatched from our account. I don't know how she managed to do it, however."

"And, you think this Mandi . . ."

"Marriano."

". . . stole the money?"

"Ms. Longworth, I'm not sure what to think. Mandi Marriano was . . . I'm sorry, *is* a beautiful woman." Letting out an exasperated sigh, she continued, "Yes. I believe she stole the money. But the woman is a dolt and couldn't possibly have done it alone. In fact, I'm certain she had help. Someone big, someone in a high position with direct access to the funds has their hands in this."

"You still believe someone is accessing the account now?"

"I honestly don't know."

Ann watched Mrs. Franklin. Her clear, blue eyes had lost some of their radiance as she muttered her last statement. Ann saw metamorphose unfurl into presumed failure. No doubt about it, Mrs. Franklin had experienced betrayal by an employee she had trusted.

"You're telling me someone on the Board, or possibly a higher up within the agency helped Mandi Marriano?"

"I can assure you no one on the Board is involved in this theft."

"Mrs. Franklin, sometimes what we are quite familiar with isn't always how it appears. Now, I'd like to ask you a few questions."

"Very well," she responded and slowly sipped her coffee.

Ann flipped the page of her yellow tablet fully aware Mrs. Franklin didn't care for the implication. "How long has Mandi worked for you?"

"When the facility opened, Mandi was one of the first employees the Board and I hired."

"What kind of education and experience did she have."

"High school and her work experience was limited since she's only twenty-three now. There was something very sad about that girl when I met her and empathy convinced all the Board members to hire her as our accounting secretary."

"Does Mandi have any relatives or family here in Masquerade?"

"None that I'm aware of. She came to us seeking a job. At the time, she told me she was from a suburb in the Twin Cities."

"Did she make friends easily?"

"Not necessarily at the Agency. However, as I mentioned, she is a beautiful, young woman and I believe she met and made several male friends upon getting settled in here."

"Do you know any of those male friends?"

"Ms. Longworth, this town thrives on tourism. I know the people who are year-round residents since we are a small community. Nevertheless, I can't possible meet and know the thousands who parade through here during the course of a year."

The waitress returned filling both coffee cups and Ann jotted down additional notes as Mrs. Franklin continued after the waitress left without delay.

"You know there was one gentleman who frequently called Mandi while she was at work. I don't know his name and I never heard Mandi mention him. Now that I think about it, he hasn't called at the Agency since her disappearance."

"How would you know about the phone calls?"

"I make it my business to know everything that's going on within the agency."

That didn't surprise Ann considering Mrs. Franklin's approach to their meeting thus far. "Is there anyone else who might know who this guy is or what his relationship is to Mandi?"

"I can't say for sure, but I'll check with some of my employees and see if anyone knew his name, or who he was. Wait a minute, Susan might know. She and Mandi did seem to hit off."

"Who's Susan?"

"Susan Bradford supervises the payroll and accounting department for the agency."

"Tell me about her," Ann said writing the name in her tablet.

"She's another one who didn't originate from this area. Came up from the Cities and has also been with me since the school opened. She has no family from here that I'm aware of, but she's smart as a whip with a bachelor's degree in accounting. The poor thing has been simply distraught since the auditor found a large sum of money missing. She takes a lot of pride in her work."

Ann was beginning to recognize a pattern with Angela's employees. Two key employees appeared to be lonesome doves either seeking a better way of life, or hiding from the hawk that would surely devour a dove. "Mrs. Franklin, did you hire anyone from this area that you already knew?"

"There's something you need to understand, Ms. Longworth. Most people who already live here are affiliated with the resorts and tourism enterprise. Before the school opened I had to advertise statewide in order to fill positions for a twenty-four hour day. So, to answer your question, no, I haven't hired anyone on a full time basis from this area. Yes, I've had a couple of part timers, but they often leave for higher paying jobs in the Minneapolis, St. Paul area."

Ann stopped writing and looked up. "Weren't you the least

bit curious why these two women came up here from the Twin Cities job hunting, then?"

"Not really. I never gave it much thought."

"Have you noticed any unusual spending habits or outrageous purchases either has made?"

"Mandi loves expensive jewelry. Whether or not she can afford it, I couldn't say. Though what she wears isn't costume, it certainly isn't astronomically priced, either. Susan, loves clothes, but what woman doesn't?"

"So what you're telling me is that you know of no large purchases like a new car," Ann glanced out the window toward the lake, "recreational vehicles or lavish vacations by either of them?"

"I can't say one way or the other. As well as I know my employees on the job, I don't make it my business to intrude in their personal lives."

"How many employees do you have?"

"Since we are a twenty-four-seven facility which means we operate twenty-four hours a day, seven days a week, I have a total of one hundred and fifty people working for the Agency. I'd like to make you an offer, Ms. Longworth."

Ann finished scribbling her notes and looked at Mrs. Franklin. "What kind of offer?"

"I believe it would be in everyone's best interest if you stayed at my house during your investigation. I will concoct a story you're a friend of the family and here for a visit. Then we can discuss this case freely and no one will be the wiser."

Ann admitted to herself the similarities between Mrs. Franklin and Madison Baker could take one's breath away. Self-imposed needs to control the situation hit the top of what Ann thought could become a long list. "That won't work, Mrs. Franklin. I may have a partner working with me."

"I have plenty of room in my house. Your partner can stay there as well."

Reflecting on Mrs. Franklin's persistence Ann withheld an urge to go buy a pack of cigarettes from the machine near the door. The older woman's desperation was reflected in the tone of her voice. However impossible the thought seemed to be one of her employees might be corrupt, Mrs. Franklin knew what she wanted and Ann believed she successfully obtained her goals at measurable cost. Ann made direct eye contact with Mrs. Franklin's blue eyes. "As generous as your offer is, I can not accept. I don't know that I will be spending that much time here in Masquerade."

"Quite frankly, Ms. Longworth, I think you will soon discover I have access to everything you will need to know. It would be in your best interest to spend as much time here as is humanly possibly and deal with this situation."

Mrs. Franklin was downright staunch. For the second time, Ann glanced through the window facing the lake and contemplated several options. Admittedly, she loved the investigative part of her job furnishing time away from the office, time away from Madison and her demands. Ann also believed Angela Franklin and Madison Baker were equally determined. And the last thing she absolutely wanted to do was share a house with Mrs. Franklin. Especially when these days Ann's desires bordered on isolation. Ann looked back at Mrs. Franklin and told her, "If I spend any time in Masquerade I will stay in a hotel, but thank you for your offer."

Mrs. Franklin leaned across the table with frantic, blue eyes prepared to negotiate. Ann debated whether the telltale panic was at all related to the obvious loneliness showering her unguarded eyes. It seemed rather unusual for a stranger to invite another stranger to stay in one's home. Trained or inborn, Ann studied Mrs. Franklin and briefly considered the possibility the woman may be hiding something. Instantly, she recognized the genuine loneliness in her eyes.

"Ms. Longworth—"

"Please, call me Ann."

"All right then. Ann, if you can find Mandi and the missing money, you will have saved the taxpayers an enormous amount. I feel the least I can do is give you free room and board in return."

The jangle of bells across the room diverted Ann's attention. The door opened signaling another customer had entered the café and Ann's jaw dropped. She gaped at the mass of male dominating the entrance. He had stopped just inside the door, his body chopping the light from the sunshine pouring in. He'd wakened the echoes of a lazy afternoon with his intimidating stance as he scanned the room seeking someone out. With deliberate motion he removed a pair of sunglasses and checked things out again. His search ended when his eyes met Ann's stare and he strutted in the direction of their table. Ann recognized the secret expression oozing from his dark eyes and she felt her heart thump out a couple of extra beats. She knew trouble when she saw it.

She swallowed hard paying close attention to his chiseled features that coupled with rippling, bronze muscles and boiled over a tank top in a bothersome way. Jet-black and brush-like hair mated his rounded mustache and he was eyeballing her with intensity. She'd never seen or met this man before this second, or even in her lifetime. Out of the corner of her eye, Ann saw Mrs. Franklin turn and look at who had entered the café.

"Oh my God! Oh good Lord in heaven! Chase!"

Next to her sudden outburst, the table moved and Ann quickly grabbed her coffee cup before it spilled into her lap. All eyes in the café heard the commotion and now gawked at the three of them. The mystery man had supplied Mrs. Franklin with a look of disgust as she rushed over and flung her arms around him.

"Oh my God! Chase, what are . . . when did you . . . why didn't you call me?"

"Mother. I felt like surprising you."

"You certainly did that," she clucked. "Ann Longworth, meet my son, Chase Franklin."

Taking obvious liberty and purposely scanning her figure, Chase calculated there wasn't a damn thing connected with this woman, or to any woman, that could in all likelihood be safe. Musing over the way her clothing hinted provocatively of hidden motivation and spelled trouble with a capital *T*. She had one of those perfect oval faces that nipped him hard every time by catching him off guard the way it seduced a man. She had submissive-looking blue eyes, no, smoke blue, he corrected, which were crammed full of catastrophic mischief and grief. The longer he stared at her the more she looked vaguely familiar, suspicious even. "Have we met somewhere before?"

Ann recognized arrogance and how his earlier expressions had been replaced with a menacing glare. A sarcastic, menacing glare, Ann thought. "Mr. Franklin, I think I would have remembered if we had met."

Neither gestured a handshake.

"Chase Edward Franklin," Angela clucked again, "how could you possibly know Ann? And what brings you home for the first time since . . . without calling first?"

Chase gave his mother a long stare. Home for only one reason, he was faced with telling her he had accepted an overseas transfer. The sooner he told her, the sooner he could leave. Looking back at Ann Longworth, something familiar about this female disturbed him. He couldn't think of it now, however in time he would remember where he'd met her. After an ugly incident with another woman, nothing would ever convince him women were worth their weight in gold. *She* had been the reason he volunteered for the overseas assignment. With certain urgency, he had to remove himself from the torment of her memory, and faced his mother who'd sat back down. "I need to talk to you, Mother." Looking at Ann Longworth, he said, "It's personal."

A quick pinch gripped Ann's throat and she assumed, like mother, like son. He'd spoken with the same distinct tone exercising his bewitching power to control everyone in his path. Hell, she thought, he did more than dominate with his power, he convincingly displayed how he without fear of reprisal manipulated anyone and everyone. Something told Ann by the way Chase Franklin stood here physically unmoving, all strong and supreme, she definitely stood in his way at this moment.

"Chase, I hope you're planning on sticking around for awhile.

It's been five years since I last saw you."

Ann looked at Mrs. Franklin, then shot a disbelieving look at Chase. *How could anyone ignore his or her family?*

Chase yanked out a chair and sat down at the table. *He was sure he knew this woman.* Unbending, he faced his mother and responded, "A week. How long is this going to take you?"

"Chase, we'll talk at home later."

In a defiant manner, Chase tipped his chair backward crossing his arms in front of his chest. His mother's annoying practice told him he was being disruptive and to run along. God, how he remembered the connotations in her voice. And he despised their implications. Like he'd tried guessing many times before, Chase wondered again why, if his mother didn't want children did she bother to have the one child she did? Way to many times he'd vacillated on the potential reasons she'd gone to all the trouble? Without retort, Chase stood up and left the café.

Ann had watched and witnessed the ruin of a man she wouldn't have given two cents to know. She waited as Mrs. Franklin's morose eyes followed her son. Quickly, Ann perceived the reckless alienation between the two of them.

"I'm sorry for the interruption. Now, where were we?"

Ann wasn't sure whether to blow up or express sorrow and thirsted for knowledge on how blood relatives found fault in each other.

"I believe we were discussing your accommodations."

Ann shoved the grievous thoughts from her mind. "Yes we were and as I told you I will be staying in a hotel." 'Angela's' eyes remained fixed and unshakable and she had assumed a posture of superiority. The same posture, after regaining her composure, she used on her son. Funny Ann just realized, Chase Franklin didn't have his mother's eyes.

"You consider me a suspect, don't you?"

Her muscles twitched at the accusation. "At the moment, I consider you a source of information. It isn't apropos for me to stay in your home, Mrs. Franklin."

"On the contrary, it's quite fitting. It would give you the freedom to do your investigation without raising suspicion. I already told you I can easily explain you're a friend of the family."

Ann hated to admit it, but Mrs. Franklin raised a valid point. The biggest problem with investigating was the standard custom in which information always leaked out. People talked, particularly after they had been interviewed. "I'll be returning to the Cities and be in touch with you."

"When are you coming back? This problem isn't something you can just put on hold."

"I have no intention of delaying my investigation, Mrs. Franklin. I'll call you tomorrow and let you know where things stand after speaking with my supervisor. When I return, I'd like to interview Susan Bradford as well as other employees. I will also need a list of all people affiliated with the orphanage and those who have access to the agency's books. I'll be speaking with the police concerning the missing person report on Mandi Marriano. And Mrs. Franklin, as I'm sure you are aware, not a word of my investigation is to be mentioned to anyone."

Mrs. Franklin acknowledged with a nod and both women left the Kozy Kafé after paying for their coffee.

CHAPTER TWO

Leaving the Kozy Kafé, Chase felt every blasted one of the umteen million emotions of all the dysfunctional people in the world. His level of anger had risen a notch or two because his mother never wanted him, and confusion. God, how she loved confusing him keeping the old wounds festering in his head. *And we wouldn't want to leave out hopelessness.* An irrevocable need that filled him with a hideous requirement for her love. He couldn't forget his own hatred cavorting through his mind at this moment like a fleeing criminal in one of his capers. The end result simmered down to irritating guilt and unwanted resentment towards his mother. He couldn't take it anymore. Something needed to be done and he'd done it. Chase had vowed to himself, his decision to leave the country was the right one. *Wasn't it?*

Shifting his gaze to his surroundings, Chase had counted upon the changes here in Masquerade since his last return home. He masked his surprise this moment when the only change he saw was the manner in which some habitation had deteriorated and appeared neglected. Though his visits had been infrequent, coming home to see his father had definitely provided satisfaction. And it didn't matter where in the world his job took him, Chase always called his dad weekly. Now weighted down with longing, he missed those chats and the attachment he'd developed with his dad could never be replaced.

A distant insensibility surrounded him concerning his mother who had more or less cast him aside. Her obvious interest lied in the children of welfare. In a habit he didn't understand, her dedication to helping the needy became the driving force bonding him with his father. Angela Franklin would forever do for others and his mother would never fill the emptiness that had consumed him since his father up and died.

Chase hadn't prepared himself, hell he hadn't given any consideration to the idea. But, significant aging signs had definitely selected Angela Franklin as its next victim of evolution. Wrinkled skin and crows feet near the corners of her eyes had done horrible things to her admirable features and were just other facets leading to the ultimate ending. Her ghostly hair actually scared him, but not as much as her eyes did today. The sparkle he remembered lacked a familiar brilliance and his mother had aged fiercely in just a few short years.

Chase's muscles tightened as he dwelled on how to explain his reason for coming home to Masquerade. Trev had insisted he couldn't announce his transfer over the phone. Chase's heart pumped out a few extra beats as he marched along Cozy Cove Road. *What the hell did he care what his mother thought about his transfer?* Neither of them needed the other and his chest heaved laboriously with each catapulting step. Chase smacked his lips and clenched his teeth together. He *would* leave the country as soon as the papers came through. Volunteering for the relocation, he and his partner each had opposing reasons. Jack Trevor fancied being closer to a woman, and his own urgency necessitated *him* getting away from the recent memory of one. Two women, he corrected as he looked back at the Kozy Kafé.

Chase kept walking and mulled over the latest assignment he and Trev had been given. Prior to the current case at hand, his trip home had been planned and cleared with the boss. Since their transfer papers hadn't shown up on the boss' desk, they were handed this case as their grand finale in the United States.

Continuing along Cozy Cove Road, Chase's stride slowed to an amble gait. The snowman old man Anderson had carved in the trunk of a sawed off pine years ago still snickered at him with an extravagant black smile. Years later and not a child anymore, he muttered, "Damn thing doesn't even look like a snowman."

Looking out across the water, fishing and recreational boats speckled the lake. This place had always served as his lifeline, but now it tugged unmercifully on his heart prompting memories from his past and reminding him of something that was gone forever. Chase secretly envied the contented fisherman tinkering around with their rods and reels and he'd give anything to return to those good old days. A string of luck always seemed to follow him after fishing with his dad. Not to mention, in a boat on Crypt Lake was where he and his father solved most problems whether they talked or not. He watched the boaters with envy knowing some of the fishermen took a case out and polished it off never having an itch to drop a line in the water. Others with their sons had cases of dead serious skin tingling competition for the largest catch of the day.

Chase sniffed and the moist air combined with the stale smell of fish twisted his gut into *bete noire*. He couldn't remember the stench ever becoming an object of hate in his younger days and he picked up his pace.

Hearing his name, Chase stopped and turned around. His mood perked up. "Well hell, if ain't Scotty Welston as I live and breathe."

Scott shook hands and both exchanged a male's version of slugging, ducking and feigned clenched-fists blows as though they were boys once more.

"Chase-man, what're you doing back?"

"Schmoozin', you? The pros keeping you busy?"

"Not busy enough. You know I'd play year round if they'd let me."

"Yeah," Chase nodded. "Damn, Scotty, it's been a long time. You remember as kids, we couldn't wait to get out of here?"

"Yet, we always seem to find our way back, don't we?"

Chase studied Scott for a moment reliving flashbacks of high school spent together and disputing any truth to what he said. "You know, I've never missed Sunday's when the job isn't interfering. Scotty, old man, you still got it."

Scott grinned and feigned throwing a pass.

"Remember the high school championship?"

Scott stopped short, coming to a standstill. "How the hell could I forget that? You're the reason I completed my pass. That guy didn't know you were on his ass until you clobbered him. It's also what got me my scholarship followed by the big times. Hell yeah, I remember!"

Lost in some distant trophy, Chase muttered, "Those days are sweet memories."

"Damn straight they were."

"Do you remember the party after the game that night? It was our first drunken binge."

Scott laughed reminding Chase, "It was our first time drinking and I think caroming the walls sums it up. My first, cheap hang-over worsened when Uncle Max cussed until my frickin' toes curled."

Chase vividly recalled their companionable drinking amongst rowdy shouts of the rest of their teammates. "I never told you, but I woke up the next morning running for the bathroom where I began praying to the god of toilets."

"Chase-man, I'm still trying to forget the fact I puked my guts out on three-two."

"And all this time I thought you could hold your own."

"Ditto."

Both men looked at each other then broke into jovial laughter.

Chase remembered like it happened yesterday and said, "Dad found me at the point my guts hit the dry heaves. Took one look at me and called mom upstairs."

"Bet they all thought we'd been to a green paint party."

"I expected my mother's wrath to end all mankind that morning. Never have figured out how she knew. *"Ballsy of us* is what she called it."

"No way! Your mom really said *ballsy?*"

Chase nodded as laughter floated up from his throat.

"I believe we can thank Uncle Max for that one."

"How is Max anyway?"

"I'm running errands for him. The old he-goat's got a burr stuck up his you-know-what with pre-prep for the Fourth. How's your mom?"

"You know mom, same as always."

"Gotta go, catch ya later," and Scott jogged away.

"Hey, Scott!"

He swung around, jogging in place, "Yeah?"

"Go for the ring next year."

Scott raised both thumbs up, then took off.

Chase continued checking out the town, not ready to face his mother again, and neared the high school football field. Some of the best times of his life were here playing ball with Scott. Their lives daunted with changes then and now, Chase was well aware of Scott's passion for football. It had become his saving grace after the tragic death of Scott's parents. Max had pushed him to play the game to keep his mind occupied. The sport got him to hammer out his misery on a field instead of brooding over his loss. It paid off since Scott did make the pros as a quarterback. Chase also remembered how Scott had longed to play for the Minnesota Vikings, but it wasn't in the cards.

For whatever reason, the woman with his mother, what was her name? Ann Longworth his mother had said. Her familiar face kept surfacing in his conscious mind. Chase still couldn't remember how he knew her, but he'd stake his transfer on the fact they had met somewhere else before today.

***

Tuesday morning upon returning to her office, Ann met with and reported her findings to the Chief Deputy in the AG's office. Madison had reported in sick and wasn't answering her phone at home. Ann then met the rookie, Christie Madera and spent the rest of her day briefing the new investigator. She still didn't fully comprehend the new procedure, but the Chief Deputy told her if Madison had requested the training, then she must abide by the decision to teach the rookie. Next week, Christie would follow Ann to Masquerade.

Wednesday morning Ann packed her laptop and suitcases into her car and drove back to Masquerade. Pleasantly surprised, she observed spring's beauty consuming the once virgin trees bordering the highway. The branches were regaining their shades of green foliage from the barren winter as bright sunrays flared out from a dazzling, blue sky. A fresh breeze blowing in through her driver's window smelled clean and pure and rejuvenated her senses for the first time since that horrid night.

Ann reached for her purse and pulled out a pack of cigarettes. A lot of tantrums, a shit load of support, nine months, two weeks, three days and ten pounds later, Ann had conquered her habit. And ever since, not a day slipped by without craving the euphoria. Now she longed to inhale the nicotine. She frowned thinking how she had given them up because *he* had asked her to. *He* also had reduced her freedom because she let him move in with her. Not that she did much socializing, but everything revolved around *him*. She gave up a lot of things because *he* had asked her to. Last night, she gave in to her craving and bought cigarettes on her way home. *It didn't make any difference anyway.* The car lighter popped and Ann inhaled the menthol, thinking it was better than any sex she'd ever had.

Signs referencing Masquerade began showing themselves around two in the afternoon. Alert the second time to a sharp curve in the highway, and introducing the gigantic Crypt Lake, Ann drove her car into a roadside rest facing the lake. The majestic view overpowered her. Striking blue sky met with fresh water making it impossible to define where one ended and the other began. The picture reminded Ann of her life. There was no beginning or ending, just endless boundaries of nothing. She listened as water slapping gently on the shore played serene music and gulls sailed and screeched overhead. Today the first calmness in several months challenged her to forget everything.

A soft sigh slithered out and Ann didn't want to be late arriv-

ing at Angela's house. The unknown energy pulling on her to stay
and be as lazy as the slow-rolling waves seemed far more enticing
than being stuck in a stuffy office. With major regret, Ann gained
entrance into her car and left the rest area headed for Masquerade.

Upon entering the city limits, Ann hadn't noticed the first
time how the town stretched out across either side of the four-lane
highway west of Crypt Lake. An informational sign, and Angela's
second set of directions, indicated one more turn near the lake and
Ann nipped the corner abruptly with her Trans Am.

The street sign, Cozy Cove Road come into sight seconds prior
to a quick downward dip. Instinctively, Ann slammed her foot on
the brakes and her jaw dropped as air piled upward from inside
her lungs. When several shocking seconds passed, tranquility
penetrated her veins and Ann exhaled the air that had stuck in her
throat. The enormous body of water sprawled out in front of her
and was just a tad to close for comfort. She'd almost driven into
the glistening, blue liquid near the edge of the road. The lake was
actually bigger than life, yet it was quaintly capable of washing
away some of her hidden pain. The swaying waves rolled into the
bank here as well and persuaded the release of her pent-up feelings
of defeat. A mild wind blew into her car and furnished Ann with
unusual potential for renewing the shitty outlook she had taken
towards life.

Ann reread Mrs. Franklin's instructions to the house aware she
was on the correct street. She drove following the narrow road
bordering the shore. Lofty birches with white bark, strapping elms,
and various panoramic pines scattered themselves near both sides
of the tarred road. One pine, angled and growing parallel to the
lake compelled her foot to slam on the brakes for the second time.
Ann stared at the tree bowed and growing close to the water out of
what appeared a need for survival. The tree's needled branches had
a unique jagged shape and were darker green than the other pines.
Though the tree looked positively healthy, it's form fringed on a
parallel line to her shaky past. It didn't belong with the others and

reminded Ann of a Japanese Bonsai, but it truly was a loner of the Minnesota pine.

Driving a bit further, Ann located Mrs. Franklin's address and gaped in disbelief at the house. Perched high upon the only hill overlooking the water, the two-story contemporary revealed ceremonious flaunting being the largest home on Cozy Cove Road. A breezeway porch joined the two-car garage to the house in what looked like a nuptial knot. A massive, pine-treated deck preceded a stone entrance behind well-kept greenery and herbage. Mrs. Franklin most likely heard Ann arrive since she stood waiting just inside the screen door.

Ann shut the engine off and slipped out of her vehicle. They greeted each other with generous smiles in the middle of the deck.

"I'm relieved you agreed to stay here. This is going to make our working together much easier. Since Mr. Franklin passed away, this house is nothing but a desolate monstrosity."

"How fortunate for the taxpayers its summer and every hotel was booked."

"Pish-posh," she smirked gesturing a wave of her thin hand for Ann to come inside.

Upon entering the house, a spacious foyer welcomed Ann and nearly duplicated the size of her apartment kitchen. An arched entry preceded the living room to the left with French glass doors filling the entire front wall. As Ann took a peek, a glorious view to the lake added to the capacious room. Sunshine penetrating the French windows, highlighted honey finished wood throughout the living area. An oak mantle sitting above a brick fireplace homed in as the central point of the room and was surrounded by gleaming, wood floors. A baby grand sat in one corner and contemporary furniture hunkered around the fireplace on a Persian rug.

Ann observed Mrs. Franklin's relaxed manner. She didn't seem marked by her original concern for etiquette and good form in her own home. "Mrs. Franklin, this room is quite charming and tastefully done."

"Thank you, but please, do call me Angela. Mrs. Franklin is

for my employees. Speaking of which, I thought you were bringing a partner with you."

"She'll be arriving next week."

"Ann, I've got two rooms upstairs all ready for both you and your partner. Chase is around town somewhere. I'll have him bring in your suitcases when he comes home."

"That won't be necessary. I can take care of them myself. I'd like to get my clothes hung up and my laptop running. Then we can get to work."

"I'm afraid Susan Bradford isn't available for that interview you requested. I completely forgot she's on vacation this week. I didn't know if you wanted me to speak with anyone else, so I've compiled the books since the agency opened and I brought them home with me."

Ann followed another wave of Angela's hand. She had in deed lugged home two full boxes for her to delve into. "Good, I'll get started and take a look at them and compare what I find to the auditor's report."

Digging into the Agency's accounts would consume long, tedious hours. Since being burdened with a partner for the first time in her career, hopefully the *rook* would have the background knowledge to assist.

CHAPTER THREE

Unusually warm for June, the humidity levels were soaring to extreme discomfort. Ann stepped outside of Angela's house after changing from church clothing and eased herself into a pillow-covered lounge on the deck. She stretched her bare legs to soak up the sun's rays. Totally relaxed and sipping coffee on the serene Sunday, she mulled over the past four days. She'd waded through the first six months of the Boarding School's business expenses and found nothing. Throughout her diligence of adding debits and credits, Ann quickly perceived Angela liked to chatter.

She didn't think it right listening to stories while the State paid her for what imitated a vacation. Angela spoke of her life experiences and being born here, she had lived in Masquerade her entire life. She married her high school sweetheart, Duke, had one child, Chase, and donated her entire life to helping people in need. Angela didn't have to explain to Ann why her eyes manifested permanent disappointment in her son. Since meeting the brusque man, Ann couldn't really blame Angela either.

Although the chatting had taken place while discussing facts on the case, the complete episode still suggested unethical behavior for a state employee. And for that reason, Ann felt guilty taking a day off to bask in the sun.

She heard Angela moving about inside the house and mentally blocked out the mild disturbance. Indisputably, since meeting Angela Franklin at the Kozy Kafé, this woman knew her business and assumed a real concern connected with the welfare of the children and *her community* as she called it. The orphanage ran like a finely oiled machine. Ann had to recant her previous assumption and comparison of Angela to Madison. While having identical wants and needs, the two women were extreme opposites in their styles and approach to any situation.

Angela wasn't bossy nor did she rule with an iron reign. She didn't have Madison's cynical and condescending nature. Since meeting Angela, Ann had discovered her delightful charm to be almost magical. Her captivating powers influenced others and sweet compassion accompanied Mrs. Franklin's affable manner. She not only knew what she wanted, but knew how to achieve her goals without hurting or destroying people. Ann realized the potential groundwork being put into place for an important friendship to form between the two of them. And not the type where Christmas cards became the only exchange.

Lying back in the lounge, she cast her thoughts aside and took pleasure in the lake's magnificent view and extreme calm. A windowpane appearance had replaced the rippled waves from yesterday. Trees and houses cozied in along the banks mirrored themselves in the glasslike surface. A jay with its bright blue back and gray belly flew by whistling to his partner.

Ann shaded her eyes with a pair of sunglasses before closing them. Singing robins competed with a single cardinal drowning out the soothing hum of highway traffic located distantly behind Angela's house. All were just enough to put Ann at ease and indulge in a nap. Considering the late morning hour, Ann hadn't grasped until this week the exhaustion she'd suffered throughout the last several months.

Her mind veered sharply to the unforgettable night of her fiancé's death. Accepting the fact her life was destined for emptiness didn't come easy. The only two cares she had in the world had turned into lost causes. She felt cheated by the circumstances and well past anger over her loss. Almost four months had slipped away since that horrendous evening preceded her wedding by one month.

The day she was supposed to exchange vows replayed in her mind like an overdone newscast. Sitting on the apartment floor with dry eyes, Ann had shredded her wedding gown to bits with the violence of a cattle stampede. After three hundred delicately, strung pearls had been ripped from the bodice flying and bouncing off of walls, Ann stood up and kicked the heaping mass of lace and satin across the floor. She recalled the pounding rain that day and how the drop-covered window served as tears for her waterless eyes.

Today, Ann choked back a dire urge to scream. Falling instantly in love with *him* had been easy. With his charming grin, the love of Ann's life had taught her how to laugh on her worst days and he had unsheathed her hidden qualities on her best days. He'd taught her to liberate her stored-up anger and relish life.

The last night of her fiancé's life, he'd been with a friend and called from his cell phone wanting to surprise her with new information on her father. Next thing she knew, he was dead, gone forever. She would never find out what he had uncovered. In fact, she didn't even know where the two of them had gone that day. How could he have been so selfish not to tell her what he had learned? He *knew* the significance she'd placed on finding the father who had abandoned her. Vials of wrath rose inside of her right now and Ann took in a long breath needing to get a grip.

Orphaned since birth and hardened by fate's destruction, Ann had vowed years ago, she'd never cry. Instead, the day of the funeral, she sat rigid and stiff on the hard pew staring at his closed casket. The authorities had refused to let her look at him, claiming his severely burned body would be a morbid sight for her to see. The loss had drained her heart and mind and she might just as well have been dead herself. The day she destroyed her gown, Ann also slid the marquis diamond from her finger for the first time since their engagement. Strange as it seemed, she hadn't felt anything when she removed her ring. Opening her eyes to stare at her stripped left hand, Ann wondered if her heart would forever feel like stone?

No matter how hard she tried to forget everything, the death of her fiancé and her father's abandonment continued to dominate her sleep in the form of hellish dreams. The same frightful nightmare worsened each night. Ann would wake up alone and scared, soaked in sweat with eerie feelings of being trapped and tied up in darkness.

The past was over and done, gone forever. There wasn't a damn thing she could do about any of the circumstances, if she could just stop the nightmare, if only they would cease. She needed to seek out the hidden source and analyze it.

Ann shoved it all to the back of her mind and speculated on thoughts of Angela's son. Chase Franklin had made himself scarce since they met earlier this week and something was definitely awry between mother and son. She'd never understand their hostility and dozed off under the glow of sunrays.

***

Back home a few days, Chase already missed the exhilaration of his fast paced world. His job in New York City took him everywhere tracking down criminals. He had a killer instinct to capture the bad guys. And it became enhanced by a wild thrill that consumed him after a big arrest. He thrived on those gushing adrenaline forces of his racing heart. It was a *high* he couldn't eliminate from his life. Unfortunately, he also knew those same thrills that excited him were the reason relationships failed. He had learned the hard way women didn't share the same excitement. He'd sworn them off forever on account of the exposed facts.

Chase grunted as he headed toward the inevitable showdown with his mother. When he came within sight of the Franklin house, he took advantage of the scenery. He hadn't seen her since Monday and figured if women were going to display themselves, he'd damn well reap the benefits. She wore red jogging shorts with a white tank top clinging to the heart of her breasts. She wasn't ordinary by any sense of the word, still Chase hadn't figured out how he knew Ann Longworth. Set in motion with confidence, he neared the deck checking out the firm muscles of her trim legs.

He stood near the bottom step and recalled every squeak and moan in the deck stairs before soundlessly making his way to the top. Leaning against a wood railing, Chase took in every inch of her curving figure as his mouth began to water. Soft ivory shoulders turning pink from the sun beckoned to him and so did the jutting tips beneath the ribbed tank top. Her slinky shorts preceded what, he thought, were exceptionally pleasing legs turning red from the sun's rays. The more he stared, the more he had to confess the sun wasn't the only thing heating up outside.

He pushed away from the deck railing inching closer and said, "You're gonna look like a lobster if you're out here much longer."

Ann didn't move but had been watching him through her dark glasses. As he ambled in her direction, his broad shoulders took over and concealed and blocked the sun. A devious grin lined his lips beneath his mustache. Ann had heard his rugged breathing as he lurked his way up the stairs and she lazily asked, "Mr. Franklin, do you make it a habit to sneak up on unsuspecting ladies?"

"Only when they expose themselves publicly."

Ann lifted her head fixing her eyes on Chase. His lofty physique reminded her of one of the far-stretching pines. His dark hair glistened in the sunlight and although straight was trimmed excessively short. Ann privately resented a natural tan covering every inch of his exposed flesh, as it seemed to glow under a coating of his sweat. She scorned herself for the tingling feeling in the pit of her stomach and without any warning, her face filled with heat from the ideas commencing inside her head. She was both excited and aggravated. "Mr. Franklin, there's a law in the Cities against men who ogle women."

He hadn't removed his sunglasses and basked in the arrogance he'd become well known for. The color of her face bared her thoughts and without hesitation Chase stepped closer. "There's also a law against indecent exposure."

Ann sprang upward and scrupulously glanced at the clothing covering her body. When she looked upward, his lips had parted into a first-class grin exposing flawless teeth below his erotically appealing mustache. No reasonable answer could explain why her pulse had increased as their covered eyes stared at each other. She assumed by the very way this man stood in front of her he was a man who had made it. At what, she had no clue. Ann's tank top was sticking to her sun-baked skin, but it was Chase's gaze-covered eyes sucking the air out of her lungs. All of a sudden, she felt her face drive out a wave of heat remembering she hadn't put on a bra.

"Mr. Franklin, if you're assuming I'm indecently exposed you're a very hard-up man desperately in need of a woman's attention."

Chase felt the sweat forming on his neck and across his forehead. Little did she know the accuracy of her statement. He also felt what every man did—excitement and mistakes of the addiction—she was a very attractive woman. He'd better change the subject. "Ms. Longworth, what've you discovered on your case?"

Her heart skipped a beat and jiggled inside her chest. A craving appetite in the pit of her stomach mixed with puzzlement over his interest. She gathered Angela had broken her vow and told him about the embezzlement. Ann exerted efforts to thwart the flow of juices racing in her blood as Chase deliberately moved in on her. It had to be the sun beating down causing beads of perspiration to drain from the pores of her skin. He wasn't threatening, but Ann certainly felt thrilled by the forthright manner in which he was staring her down behind his covered eyes. She also knew Chase Franklin was a presumptuous shit and taunting the hell out of her. Instead of shooting the words off her tongue out of frustration she met his boldness with demure calmness. "Why would you care about my case?"

Chase discovered something particularly different about Ann Longworth from other women he'd known. Little scared her and she seemed to prompt inviting the competition of his little escapade. Intentionally adhering to his latest self-imposed principle towards women, Chase saturated his words with sarcasm. "Soon, Ms. Longworth, you'll discover, all things I care about pertain to the law."

Removing her sunglasses, Ann eyeballed Chase Franklin with

a critical squint. Heaping mounds of smugness protruded from his massive body and she was going to offer him a shovel, but asked with sedate quietness, "And why is that, Mr. Franklin?"

He carefully eyed her as if capturing her on film. A clandestine longing occupied her smoke-colored eyes and he believed oodles of secrets lay hidden in them. As if out of control, his gaze journeyed across her face and down to her breasts until an unwanted interest well on the verge of developing, treaded dangerous ground. Quickly as if she saw where his gaze went he shifted and couldn't stop thinking she had to be concealing something. "My mother obviously hasn't told you."

"Told me what?"

"I'm an FBI Agent and every part of the law interests me."

Ann stood up as if facing off with Mr. Superiority. "Well whoop-de-fricking-do!"

Chase instantly stiffened when the little tigress blew him off. If he hadn't known better, he'd have thought she'd just swung a two by four at him and he forgot to duck. She'd rendered him speechless and he swore it wouldn't happen a second time.

Ann quickly dodged his broad figure and scuttled into the house through an open French door.

Irritable and hostile, he realized the brazen little snot definitely wasn't typical. Nor did she fear him like most he encountered. In fact, he thought, Ann Longworth reminded him of a hotheaded blonde he once knew and that notion *really* scorched his blood. He assured himself she wouldn't get a second chance to flaunt herself in his face.

His draw back had caused her to suck in short breaths of air to calm her guts and Ann smirked once inside knowing she'd gotten the last word. Ann had barely set foot inside the house when Angela glanced up from her seat on the couch.

"Come here, dear. I have pictures of my husband I want to show you. I'd forgotten how handsome he was in our early years."

Angela handed the picture to her as Ann inched closer. She took the picture and studied the black and white photo. The se-

nior Mr. Franklin was a statuesque man in excellent physical shape
like his son. His black hair stood out from a softened face and dark
eyes in the faded black and white photograph. A thick, black mustache lined his upper lip curving toward the corners of his mouth.
If Ann hadn't known better, she would have sworn the man she
was looking at was Chase.

"It seems like only yesterday that big lug of a teddybear was
stumbling around here."

Ann listened to Angela watching her eyes varnish over staring
nowhere in particular. Unmistakable emptiness had gathered. *Was
it any wonder with a son like Chase* she snipped silently.

"I still remember the first time I saw Duke. I looked into those
big, brown eyes of his and saw his entire world, all his hopes,
dreams and everything I would ever want or need in the profun-
dity of his gaze."

Ann gaped in stunned quiet as Angela relived her first meeting
with Duke. She had discovered her soul mate the first time she
ever looked into her lover's eyes. Of all things Ann would've thought,
love at first sight wasn't one of them.

Glancing again at the picture, Ann spoke with a subdued yearning. "He looks very kind and gentle. Was he?"

"Oh, my dear child, if Duke heard you say that, he'd turn
over in his grave this instant. Although, he couldn't fool me no
matter how hard he tried. He was the most caring, loving man I
would ever want or need."

Ann didn't respond, simply because she never felt the love for
her fiancé Angela had carefully articulated. The sudden awareness
enclosed her in a bleak, wintry feeling.

"I don't mind telling you, I miss Duke. I miss how he used to
follow me everywhere and more than I care to admit. Some days
his attentiveness felt like a thorn in my side. It drove me crazy
until he wasn't here doing it anymore."

Deep in her own thoughts Ann wondered what her handsome, tawny-gold haired man saw in her? She had unappealing
looks, nondescript said it best about her figure. And her ropy hair

pretty much did what it wanted to. Ann never understood what her fiancé had found so appealing. Certainly others with far more striking beauty would have flocked and fallen at his feet.

"I could always tell when Duke was watching me. His eyes had a way of penetrating into my soul."

Lost in a distant trance and impassioned by envious twinges toward Angela for having found her soul mate, the perfect being you never knew was missing until you found him, Ann believed for the first time marriage would have been a drastic error in her judgement. She felt shivers penetrate her sun-baked skin and Ann sucked in several deep breaths before gulping hard. It was possible, she supposed that his charm and her particular need had blinded her into assuming she was in love with him.

"I could see through Duke's facade. His eyes held enormous amounts of love. My fear of dying first vanished, of course. But I always felt he wouldn't survive without me."

Ann swallowed hard a second time before her bottom lip frantically rolled between her teeth. She couldn't stop the thrashing floodwaters in her belly disguising its face as guilt. She was actually worse than Madison ever thought of being. She had deceitfully used *him* for personal gain.

Glancing sideways at Ann, Angela reeled with astonishment. "Oh my dear child, I've said something to upset you." Angela guessed the wounded look she saw in Ann's eyes was a sure sign of a broken heart. "Ann, I'm really sorry."

Squirming uneasily, she said, "No, it's nothing." She didn't want to talk about the guilt she didn't know how to take responsibility for. Ann wondered if fate had singularly prevented her from adding to a serious mistake. The afterthought was too much of a burden to dwell on especially if Angela's description of true love were real. It indeed appeared her love stemmed from a personal need and had been selfish. But, she recalled, *wasn't he the one who pushed her into the engagement?*

Angela quickly changed the subject. "Let's go sight-seeing and stop for a bite to eat. It's a nice Sunday and I, for one, could use some fresh air. You've been working hard and deserve to relax as well," she'd said while picking up the photo album and pictures.

"That'd be nice."

"Then we'll leave in an hour."

As Angela stood up, a picture of Duke slipped from the album and fell to the floor. Ann stooped to pick it up. As she handed it back, mountains of grief shuffled lines across Angela's face. Her eyes clamped shut blocking the droplets of her tears. "Are you okay?"

"I will be in a minute. This picture was taken the day Duke proposed marriage." As if releasing her private sobs of anguish, Angela told her, "Duke was the best thing that ever happened to me and I miss him too much some days. I hadn't thought much about him until Chase showed up here this week. We never forget the memories. They always find their way back whether we want them to or not."

She'd fingered through more pictures, sniveled and wiped her nose.

"We both wanted a large family. But after my third miscarriage, the doctors advised against it. That precious little miracle of mine happened unexpectedly when we found out I was pregnant again. I had our only child at the age of thirty-two. I can't begin to explain to you how Chase's birth provided Duke and I with enormous amounts of happiness. He was the second best thing to happen to me in my life."

Some how the tormenting ache of guilt gnawing away at her heart had lessened. Angela had wiped away her tears of sadness and was now negotiating with a smile.

"I know Duke loved and cherished Chase. Some days their male bonding could be quite irritating. But, I know Duke taught Chase proprieties in life and I'm positive my son learned the difference between right and wrong."

Angela's blue eyes brightened as she spoke reverently of Chase. Ann wondered where he had disappeared too and glanced outside through the French doors.

"I'm probably being a foolish old woman. But there are way too many days I know Chase doesn't care. This is the first time he's been home since his father's funeral." She wiped her eyes blurring over with tears again. "Chase has made his decision to stay away for whatever reason. In some ways, I know I'm to blame for it." Angela blotted away another round of tears with a hanky. "I think sightseeing is exactly what we both need. I've learned not to think of either my past or Chase. I'll be ready in an hour."

Nodding in agreement, Ann left the room shelving her own dilemma. She peeked out the windows scanning the area a second time, but didn't see Chase anywhere.

CHAPTER FOUR

He leaned against the outside wall in between the windows allowing the shock of his mother's words to settle. The sun beating against the house blistered his sweltering skin. He was stunned and couldn't blink for the longest moment, not that it would have made any difference. He'd never seen his mother cry. He didn't know his mother had miscarried three times either, or that she wanted a large family. What did she call him? *Her precious little miracle?*

He waited until both women left the room and silently slipped into the kitchen. He needed a cold beer and was grateful he'd stocked his mother's frig a few days before. Chase grabbed two cans guzzling the first in one long swallow. He crushed the can in his fist and hurled it into the garbage. Marching to his father's den in the back of the house, he carried the second cold beer with him.

Chase settled himself into the worn leather chair behind a marred, cherry-stained desk. This room provided another place where he and Duke Franklin shared immeasurable hours talking out anything and everything. He glanced up at the mounted fish hanging on the wall. The ten-pound walleye was the first one he ever caught with his father. Today, Chase couldn't decide which of them had been more excited about the catch. He lifted the can to his mouth wishing he had his old friend *Jim Beam* here to soothe the raw feeling stabbing his gut. Instead of the slither-down-your-throat smooth taste of bourbon, Chase settled for a Lucky Strike cigarette and lit up, inhaling methodically. He glanced at the short smoke and always believed he'd quit sooner or later.

When the phone rang, Chase belched loudly before answering.

"Chase-man, Trevor here."

Chase grunted out another burp hearing his partner's voice. Jack Trevor was an extremely intelligent man and loved his work. A man with a bachelor's in political science and a master's in criminal justice, Jack seriously lacked the obligation it would take to receive any kind of diploma in English. Inarguably, Jack Trevor declared his lingo was an intentional camouflage. Chase couldn't argue the point when as a matter of fact it worked to their advantage in the field. "What'd you find out?"

"The twenty-three year old, Mandi Marriano been 'ported missin' from Masq'rade, Minnie'ota?"

"What?"

"The Minnie'ota police reported her missing on second of May."

"Damn it, Jack! This state has more than one police department. Was she reported missing by the Masquerade police, or some other department? And who reported it?"

"You ain't gonna like what's I learned. Your mother made the report there in Masq'rade, Minnie'ota."

Chase sprung forward in the chair, "The hell you say," and burped, "are you sure?"

"Pos'tive. Seems the victim didn't show up for work one day, so's your mother called the popo seeing as the victim ain't from Masq'rade, Minnie'ota."

"For chrissake, Trev," he knew Jack was intentionally demolishing the hell out of the words to antagonize him. "It's Mask-a-rade and it's not Minnie-ota, it's Minn-a-so-ta!" Chase felt his blood pressure rising because Jack also referred to any law enforcement agency that wasn't Federal as *popo*. Chase swore if it weren't for the color of Jack's pure white ass he could pass as a black man. He then said, "I'll call you back."

"Hang on, I gots more."

Chase grunted, wondering how much worse this day could get. "I'm listening."

"Seems the victim was seeing some guy named Daniel Garcia.

He's outta the Minnieapple area there. Owns a few Cessna's solo since his partner died. I's checking further in it."

"Is that it?"

"Dem la'ents we found on the money belonged to Madison Baker."

"I already knew that."

"Yabut wha'cha didn't know is she works for the State of Minnie'ota."

Chase was almost afraid to ask. "Doing what?"

"Dunno, yet. Boss sez since you's there, might as well put you back on the clock."

"Did you notify Masquerade PD, yet?"

"Figured you could."

"I'll call you back within the hour," and Chase slammed the handset back into its cradle.

He stood, guzzled the remnants of his beer and crumbling the can, he angrily stubbed out the butt of his cigarette. Chase marched out of his father's den first belching, then bellowing. "Mother!"

He met her half way up the stairs of the two-story.

"Chase, what's wrong? Who was on the phone?" She took one look at him. "You've been drinking, and smoking!"

Ignoring the implied guilt trip she routinely sent him on, Chase demanded, "Did you report Mandi Marriano missing to the police?"

"Yes, but how would you know that? Why would you even care?"

He ignored her questions. "How the hell did you know Mandi Marriano?"

"She works for me. Why are you yelling at me . . ." then staring at her son, asked, "what do you mean, *did* I know?"

Chase never discussed much of anything with anyone let alone information on active cases. He saw the startled look in his mother's eyes. The image of that poor kid's body stopped him from divulging her death. The locals could tell her.

"Chase who was that on the phone?"

The wheels in his mind were spinning out of control. Jack told him latents came back to a female who worked for the state. This was becoming all too coincidental. Scrutinizing Ann's features for clues, he figured he'd try something out and weigh the reaction. "Ann, do you know anyone working in the State offices by the name of Madison Baker?" She tilted her head slightly and he watched one eyebrow crimp upward in a questioning slant.

"Yes, I do. Why?"

Believing this lady was way to smooth for his liking, he continued grilling, "How do you know her?"

"Are you asking in an official capacity?"

Smart lady, one trick to good investigative work was, answering questions with a question.

"Chase Edward Franklin, that will be just about enough of your third degree. Ann is a guest in my home and as I've already explained to you, she's inquiring about missing money from the orphanage. Now what's this all about anyway."

"My office just called, I have to return to New York immediately."

"Chase, you just got here. I don't see why they can't do without you for awhile. Didn't you tell me there was something you needed to discuss with me?"

Brushing past his mother, he said, "It'll have to wait. I'll call you." He didn't give her a chance to respond as he bolted up the stairs to pack and change his plane ticket.

Ann eyed him with acute awareness, wondering why he wanted to know about Madison. "I need to call my office."

"The phone's in the kitchen."

"Don't need it, I'll use my cell phone." She bolted to the bedroom where she had set up a temporary office.

***

An hour later following her goodbye to Chase, Angela met Ann in the foyer and both agreed to walk. Ann completely understood the defeated look on Angela's face being abandonment was a constant issue in her own life and very well known. She wanted to explain to Angela everyone deals with the hopelessness of being alone at some point in his or her life. The only problem with speaking her mind was Ann could easily have started an argument with Angela because of the distance between mother and son. Instead, Ann kept her observations to herself and listened while Angela talked up a storm.

She explained how the resorts dominated the highway's east side near Crypt lake. Across the highway were Masquerade's business district and a large majority of residential living. Masquerade had a small airport as well as an area for seaplanes to take off from the water.

As they strolled, Ann's interest veered to the housing on their left. Each structure had been personalized to suit the owner's taste. She could see some were lived in year round and a few were used seasonally. The various styles and colors, sizes and shapes weren't uniformed like areas in the Cities. Brand new homes rested near old ones and over time certain earlier homes revealed rundown living conditions. Whatever the style of each house, all had one identical characteristic. They'd been built with windows. Tons of windows. Square, round, oval and rectangle shaped windows as well as sliding glass doors tended to the front of each structure. And every window had one exclusive purpose, to view the lake from every room within.

"Did you know, Masquerade was established over seventy years ago with a single resort by a distant relative of Max Phelps?"

"No, I didn't."

"Max is a good friend of mine. We've helped each other through several situations in life. People of all nationalities have migrated here without any particular predominance. Those permanently living here have survived on the tourist business. Of course, the main attraction is the lake with several well-established resorts keeping the community in business year round."

Ann heard honking horns and prating conversations from the majority of men anxious to cast off. Mixed in with all the clamoring, Ann also heard deep devotion in Angela's voice for her *good friend* Max. Angela's pitch variation to change the subject and continue speaking had definitely geared up to a wordy mode. Barely taking in a spare breath, she expertly drowned out the other noises. But, Ann thought, Angela hadn't drowned out her earlier disappointment and she began to interpret Angela's chatter covered and replaced personal frustration.

"Max owns Devils Point, the largest resort located on the north end of town. Cozy Cove Road ends just up there beyond Max's resort. Before my Duke passed away, Max and Duke were partners at Devils Point. The resort still employs close to two hundred people."

"What did Duke die of?"

"Emphysema."

Ann immediately understood Angela's comment to Chase about smoking and decided against divulging her own weakness in starting the habit again. Without skipping a beat, Angela's speech kept time with her vigorous gait giving one the impression she were selling Masquerade as an ad agency.

"Just north of Max's resort there's an old run down, two-story dance hall. Duke and I loved to dance. On Saturday nights, a band played on each floor. A makeshift trailer attached to the side of the old place was turned into a kitchen. Patrons ate dinner and finished off the evening with dancing to music of their choice. The owner passed away years ago and no one ever did anything with the property. Being out of sight, I suppose people don't care."

There was appreciation in the method with which Angela doted on her fond memories of candlelight dinners and slow dances with her lover. Ann pictured the scene clearly in her mind. With an instrumental band, women wore old-fashioned dresses and men were outfitted in wide lapel suits of the original era. In those days, Ann could visualize men and women being appropriately devoted to each other. As Angela dwelled on the past, Ann noticed she spoke with a romantic notion of her experiences and knew those memories were seemingly difficult for her to part with.

"Max's ancestors named this town."

"They did?"

"It's a fact. Apparently they wanted to bewitch people with the mystique and keep Masquerade a secret from the chaos of the world. Over the years, it backfired and has now become an advertising slogan to attract tourists."

Angela glanced at Ann. "All in the name of money, my dear. It's unknown how the lake obtained the name Crypt, but Max has always believed the town and lake names are synonymous. Rumors floated around before Masquerade became an official town that Crypt Lake was a burial ground. They say our immigrants used to dump the coffins of their dead into the middle of the lake."

"You can't be serous?"

"Oh heavens, no, it's never been proven. Personally, I think it was started to keep people away from here. Now, it has the opposite effect. People come out of curiosity."

"On the contrary, I'd be well on my way in ten seconds flat if it were true."

They reached Devils Point where a large kumquat-shaped sign rising above their heads preceded the entrance. The symbol commendably flaunted Crypt Lake's shape.

"You hungry?"

"Yes, I'm starving."

"Let's eat here and you can meet Max."

Upon walking through the drive-in entrance, the vast resort stretched endlessly. Numerous cabins graciously spaced, afforded privacy for the occupants. Two enormous log cabins centralized to the rentals advertised a restaurant, dancing, gift shops and various indoor activities. There was even a small grocery store.

Both women turned when a man called out.

"Angie, you're looking lovely as ever."

"Max, I was hoping we'd find you. This is Ann Longworth. Ann, this is the man who owns Devils Point and exploits the crazy stories I've filled your head with."

Once very attractive, Ann clearly saw how the weather elements had altered Max's handsome features. Standing only an inch or two taller than Angela, his wrinkled and parched skin implied aging and actually complimented his abundant gray hair and brows. Upon the introduction, Max took Ann's hand and held it between both of his.

"Ann, how very nice to meet you. How long are you staying in our fine community?"

Truly cavalier, Ann thought as Max's dry callused hands kindly squeezed hers. His touch bore gentleness along with vibes of erratic excitement. A twittering commotion building in Ann's chest shocked her. Her palms moistened and the small hairs on the back of her neck perked up as chills spiraled down her back. She saw something flicker in Max' eyes and felt her heart thump out a few extra beats. Ann marched her composure back into place and said, "I'm not sure. I needed some R and R away from the Cities."

"Ah, a city girl and a pretty one at that."

Ann responded, "City girl, yes. Pretty, I don't think so."

"Never reject a compliment given with sincerity. And let me assure you this is a wonderful place in which to relax and enjoy the outdoors. If you need anything, all you have to do is ask."

She felt her face flush and as quickly as her heart had thumped out extra beats, Ann sensed an easy tide washing over her. Max's gray eyes had crinkled mirthfully and his face inflated with enthusiasm. "Of course, Max, thank you. I have to say Masquerade does seem like a very peaceful town."

At that moment all three turned when a second man's voice yelled Max's name from across the resort.

"And that would be Scott. He's home for the summer trying his hand at the upkeep of a resort. And, I'm afraid his agility is strictly limited to a football field."

"Max, I didn't know Scott was coming home." Angela then asked, "When did he get here?"

"Last week." Max turned to face Scott as he approached.

"Max, we got a problem in cabin eighteen. Toilet's backed up."

"Discretion was never your best suit, young man. Scott, you remember Angie. And this lovely young lady with her is a friend, Ann Longworth. Ann, this is my nephew, Scott Welston."

"Angela, good to see you again. I ran into Chase earlier this morning. Ann, nice to meet you," and Scott shook hands with her.

Scott had eyed her momentarily before speaking and Ann could see by their facial features the two men were related. Scott had Max's buoyant smile but towered well above him.

Angela moved toward Scott with her arms outstretched. "Scott, come here and give me a hug. My gosh it's been too many years."

Hugging Angela, he said, "You're still as pretty as I remember."

"Scott, you're still quite handsome yourself and just as full of it as you ever were."

"You are beautiful, Angela, but Chase and I never could con you," and winking at Ann Scott added, "Chase and I were just discussing the very subject earlier. By the way, I forgot to ask Chase when I saw him, how long he was home for."

Ann's insides curdled waiting for Angela to answer. How would the respected Mrs. Franklin conceal Chase's ill-mannered behavior?

"Scott, I'm afraid Chase had to return to New York. His office called needing him back there immediately."

"That's too bad. I figured the two of us could raise some ruckus again."

Cocking an eyebrow, Angela bantered, "I hope nothing like the stunt the two of you pulled the night of your high school championship. You were both pistachio sick with hangovers for three days."

"Tell me, would either you or Uncle Max have known if we hadn't exposed our insides?"

"Oh Lord, Scott," Angela clucked, "the entire town knew of the plans your team had made long before any of you ever acted them out."

"You mean Uncle Max didn't rat on us?"

Max smirked, "And you call yourself educated."

"Dear Scott, once you have your own, you'll always know what they're doing and when they're doing it.

Ann turned and covered her mouth with a cough to hide laughter as Max and Angela tap-danced on Scott's ego.

"Angie, are you ladies hungry? The chef has prepared one of his finer meals and I'm buying if you both have time."

"As a matter of fact, we came by here to eat. I haven't told Ann how good the food is yet. Can either of you join us?"

"I better take care of cabin eighteen as I'm pretty sure this one here doesn't have a clue what he's doing. Kids! Bring 'em into the world, feed and clothe them, send them off to get one of them college degrees and they return not knowing a blasted thing."

"Ann, don't let this old goat scare you off. He's really quite harmless and jealous he can't share lunch with two very lovely women."

"Angie, on that note, I'm outta here before I show this kid just how harmless I can be. Ann, good to meet you. Enjoy your stay."

"Thank you, I will."

"Well ladies, I have an arm for each of you. Where would you like to sit in there?"

"Near the windows. Ann might enjoy watching all the water activity."

Scott extended each elbow and said, "Come with me."

After Scott assisted both women, he sat down and said, "Ann, tell me what it is you do and how you found us."

"I work in the Attorney Generals office in St. Paul." Ann left it at that redirecting, "I heard Max mention you play football. Did he mean professionally?

"Oh Lord, Ann. Do not get him started on that subject."

Scott laughed and responded, "Angela thinks what I do is barbaric. I keep telling her the only thing barbaric is when my offense doesn't do their job and I get cremated by the defense."

"You're a quarterback, then." Ann noticed for the first time,

Scott was wearing a Super Bowl ring on his left hand. "And I see you've won the big one."

He nodded, asking, "Do you like football?"

"I'm afraid I've never paid much attention so I can't really say whether I enjoy the game or not. I know my fiancé used to watch it faithfully."

"You're engaged?" Angela clucked.

Unknown what had prompted her to bring up the subject, Ann said, "Not anymore," and told Angela and Scott of her fiancé's untimely death.

"I'm sorry," they both expressed in unison.

Ann didn't know where the comfort had come from that wormed its way into her soul, but she divulged the trials of her life to both of them. The more she told, the easier it became and she heard herself blurting out words to explain the uncertainty of being raised in an orphanage. Carefully, because it didn't seem to matter anymore, Ann had avoided informing either of her lifelong search to find her father.

An hour later they had finished eating and Angela boasted, "Scott, that chef has done it again."

"Max has always had a way of finding and choosing the best." Scott looked at Ann, "I feel like a swim, how about you?"

"We can't swim after eating. Besides, I ate too much and feel more like a nap."

"By the time you go back . . . where are you staying anyway?"

"She's staying with me. I met Ann while doing business for the orphanage and invited her up here."

"Even better. Once you go back, change into your suit and return, an hour will have passed. But, you could always lay on the beach and sleep it off if you don't feel like swimming."

Thinking about Scott's offer momentarily, Ann especially wanted to learn more about Max, and Scott too. Her sixth sense had begun working overtime and had kicked in with strong vibes during their introductions. She needed to figure out why. "Tell you what, I didn't bring a swimsuit, but I wouldn't mind a little tanning."

"Great. I've got a few things to take care of for Max and I'll meet you on the beach in about an hour."

Angela and Ann left Scott and walked out of the restaurant. Both stopped and looked around searching the area surrounding them.

"That was strange," Angela said.

"You felt it too?"

"Yes. I'm positive someone was watching us."

They both turned around a second time, but saw no one.

***

After saturating herself with suntan lotion and changing into cut-offs and a spaghetti-strapped shirt, Ann returned to the beach at Devils Point. Elated laughter spilled from the mouths of children fabricating sandcastles. She smiled watching teenage girls squeal and jump out of the lake as boys displayed their taunting affections from down under the cool depths of the jade-colored water. Several mothers were dousing their babes with lotion and oil in an effort to impede the sun from toasting their delicate skin. Lifeguards, one in a tower, one walking along the shore and one in a boat kept vigilant eyes on everyone.

Ann glanced down the beach when she heard a man shout, "Hey, beautiful. Annie, down here."

Ann removed her sandals and began walking along the shoreline toward Scott. Wearing boxer style swimming trunks, he lifted himself out of Crypt Lake and greeted her with a big smile, dripping water and spraying droplets with each stride.

"How is it you happened to come to a resort town and forgot to bring your swimsuit."

Averting her eyes toward various boats on the water, Ann sighed, "I didn't forget. I've never owned a swimsuit."

"One of the shops up at the cabin sports some intriguing bikinis. Let's go get you one right now."

"Um, I don't think so."

"Why not?"

"I never learned how to swim. I'm content to just kick back and watch everyone else."

"I'll teach you. There's nothing to it and the water feels great."

Ann had to admit splashing around in the cool wetness had appeal under the blaze of the sun. "Not today, but I might take a rain check."

"A rain check it is, Annie. I brought a blanket and I've got a spot for us near a tree so you won't burn up out here."

"Excellent," she said as Scott single handedly guided her to a shaded area. "I brought along a book to read."

"Anything interesting?"

"Not unless you enjoy happily-ever-after in a sizzling romance novel."

"Not the dreaded fantasy fiction!"

Ann exploded with bubbling laughter when Scott feigned a swooning damsel and collapsed to his knees.

"But, Rhett, I do love you," Scott toppled backward spreading his arms out. "I'll worry about that tomorrow."

Her laughter came from a place in her belly Ann never knew existed. In between her giggles, she dropped to her knees along side Scott and said, "I see you're not completely adverse to reading romance."

"*Gone With The Wind* is a seriously boring, but epic novel," Scott sat up, "and I'll stick to memorizing the stats of my competition, thank you very much. Hey. Max gave me strict instructions that if you're still in town I'm supposed to invite you to the annual Fourth of July barbecue next week. And even if you're not, you can always drive back up here."

Ann peered at Scott. "With fireworks and everything?"

Seriousness occupied her face and he said, "Oh, come on, Annie, don't tell me you've never seen fireworks?"

"Just on TV."

"Then, I guess you'll have to stay at least another week because Devils Point makes quite a celebration out of the Fourth. There's contests, games, barbecued pig, burgers and brats and more food than you'll see in a lifetime, a live band with dancing and all finished off with our monumental display of fireworks. We always take a pontoon out and watch them from the water."

"You sound like a billboard ad."

"So, you gonna hang around?"

"I'll certainly give it some thought, and tell Max thanks."

Since he'd met her a few hours ago the haunted inner pain in her eyes had grabbed him. Though she revealed her recent loss, Scott felt pulled to Ann. The pull was full of strength, and comfortable. "Annie, what is it about you?"

Her lips parted in surprise. "Sorta like we've known each other our entire lives?"

"Exactly. Yet we just met a few hours ago."

"Scott, what did Max mean about raising you?"

Watching a sailboat tottering in the wake of two jet-skis squirting by a bit closely, he told her, "My parents were killed in a boating accident when I was twelve."

"Oh, Scott, I really am sorry."

Facing her, he added, "Max is my mom's brother and became my legal guardian."

Ann selfishly brooded at least he had someone.

"Angela was always there for me throughout high school. I remember the first time I wanted to ask a girl out to a high school dance. Chase had a date and wanted us to double. I'd never really had any guidance in that area and, well, Angela pulled me aside one day and told me how to ask and what girls liked to hear. I'm sure Chase probably said something to her about my having cold feet. He always understood things even when the words hadn't been spoken. It's like he could read my mind half the time."

"Really?"

Scott nodded. "Yeah. Chase really is one of the good guys in the world, Annie. I can say without a doubt he's a man whose actions put other men to shame. He's definitely never given women any reason to hate men the way most of our specie does."

Ann was stunned and asked, "What do you mean?"

Scott looked at her. "Annie, he'll never lie or cheat on women because he has a too much respect for them."

"Meaning?"

"Meaning more than I've got, but then I've met some pretty brassy females in my career. I also know Chase will never admit he really wants to get married and start a family. He just hasn't met the one who's worthy of him. Unfortunately, his job runs interference for him."

"How so?"

Scott stared out across the water with his arms resting on his propped up knees. "He needs a woman who can tolerate the ugliness of his job even though he'll never talk openly about it. A woman who will put up with his long hours away from home and though she'll worry every time he's working a case, she won't let her fear come between them." He looked at Ann. "He also needs a strong woman who can and will stand up to him, a woman who can love him in spit of his flaws."

"Flaws is putting it mildly."

Scott laughed. "I can tell you've already had a run in with Chase Franklin and his pig-headedness."

Ann wasn't about to discuss her opinion of Chase with Scott and asked, "Did your mother have any other brothers or sisters?"

"Not that I'm aware of and Max has never mentioned anyone."

"And you have no siblings?"

Scott shook his head.

"Was Max ever married?"

"Yah, until his wife passed away a few years ago after a bout with breast cancer. Aunt Betty was the best and so were her chocolate chip cookies. They have one daughter, Karen who lives here. You'll meet her and Pete along with *the brat* on the Fourth."

Ann slugged him in the arm. "Scott!"

Rubbing his shoulder, he grinned and said, "Jake's really my little buddy and maybe one day I'll have a kid just like him."

Ann readjusted her body to face him. "You know, Angela was right. You are very handsome and I'm wondering now how you've avoided the clinches of matrimony yourself."

"Annie, you're also a beautiful sight for sore eyes," and flashing her another smile, said, "I've been practicing all my life avoiding clinches and sacks. I am the master!"

Fighting back a second bought of laughter, Ann said, "Angela was right about one thing. You're full of shit."

"Angela never said shit."

"No, she didn't but the meaning was well implied and you are most definitely full of *it*."

"You're a pretty gutsy lady, you know that?" He stood up. "And I think, before I find myself wading in *it*, I'm going for a dunk. You sure you don't want to try out one of them sexy little two pieces from the shop?"

"Not a chance! Your testosterone levels are in overdrive and you can take a dunk with the blonde who's been eyeing you ever since I got here."

Scott spun around to look. "Where?"

"Men. You're all so subtle. Right there, in the water wearing that skimpy blue thing. I'll sit here and read my 'fantasy fiction'."

Ann pushed back the single tuft of hair that continually harassed her and slid on her sunglasses. She watched Scott maneuver around several ducks towards the blonde and leaned against the birch tree. Scott hadn't given her anything to curb her feelings about Max, but he sure did amaze her with what he had to say about Chase. Ann recalled the first day she met Chase Franklin. He had given her the impression everyone else was beneath him. Now she wondered if that was his approach to people in general. As her eyelids began drooping, the children's laughter along with blue jays and robins lulled her into sleep.

***

They were chasing her, getting closer as she ran into the shadowy opening. Suddenly, darkness loomed toward her and Ann was trapped in a dead end alley surrounded by towering brick buildings. Panic drained her when she turned to run back the way she had come and saw two men with masked faces. One brandished a knife. In a last ditch effort Ann let out a scream that would have woke the dead. One called her name and laughed then told her it was time. Time for what? Water rushed in around her and she pleaded for her life, but it was too late as the air rapidly seeped out of her lungs. Their hands clutched her shoulders and held her under. Ann fought and struggled to break free of their grasp.

"Annie, wake up. It's Scott, wake up."

Ann opened her eyes and liberated another scream. His hands were gripping her shoulders as water dripped from his wet torso.

"Damn, you scared me."

She stared wide-eyed at him, gasping for air.

"I was out there swimming when you started screaming. I think you were having a bad dream. Are you okay?"

Beads of dampness rolled down her temples and her skin felt cold and clammy under the scorching sun. Before long shakes and trembles converged on her body.

Scott wrapped his arms around her. "Hey, kiddo, you're gonna be okay. It was just a bad dream."

Yeah right, just a bad dream. When would they end?

CHAPTER FIVE

Chase sat at his desk in his New York office staring at the evidence. Sealed in an FBI evidence bag, one hundred thousand dollars splattered with dried blood had been dusted over with white residue from the lab's fingerprinting.

He lit a cigarette as a distraction from his twitching muscles. He couldn't erase the vivid picture of the girl's mutilated body lying on the apartment floor clothed in nothing but a blood-soaked t-shirt. The twenty-three year old was too young to suffer brutality, much less death. The coroner's report said he had counted twenty-seven punctures and lacerations to her neck, chest, abdomen and extremities. He also noted the slice to her neck alone would have killed her and the stab wounds were done with a large, wide-blade knife. Chase averted his eyes from the paperwork curious about the murder weapon authorities didn't find.

Inhaling his cigarette, he still couldn't blot out the images molded and engrained in his memory. The poor girl's murder had been committed by a psychopath, someone provoked easily by anger. The act, he thought, was pure mutilation.

He snubbed out the cigarette and digested the only two reasons for anyone to act out with this kind of violent nature. The unimaginable rage was either to inflict revenge, or to leave a message to those who discovered the body. The bloody scene in that miniature, geometric room told Chase raging revenge was the cause. He assumed the money he stared at had been left behind because the crime had been interrupted. NYPD was called when an unknown neighbor reported hearing screams coming from apartment twenty-two. So *why* revenge and *who* sought the revenge on this young woman? The background checks on Mandi Marriano came back clean telling them nothing.

One puzzling factor came when the coroner confirmed two different people had stabbed Mandi Marriano. Entry wounds indicated one suspect was left handed, and one was right. Madison Baker's prints had been identified on the plastic they found the money wrapped in. Her prints were also on file through her job with the State of Minnesota. Fingerprints discovered on one singular bill were identified as a guy named Geoffrey Doyle. Blood smears in the apartment gave no clear prints.

Identification of Mandi's body came once additional information had been entered into the NCIC computer by the Masquerade PD. As of today, they still hadn't located any living relatives of the victim. Chase had contacted the Masquerade PD from Minneapolis advising Chief Casimir Mandi Marriano's name could be removed from the computer. Caz told him, he'd learned Mandi had made a dental appointment for an abscessed tooth. The dentist had taken x-rays and their department had just attached the dental records to her missing person record the previous week. Caz also mentioned his own mother had reported Mandi missing a little over four weeks ago. Odd, Chase thought, she hadn't been murdered until ten days ago. Caz hadn't been made aware of any relatives the victim had either.

Jack had run criminal checks on both Baker and Doyle. Up to this point, neither had any past criminal history. Doyle died almost five months ago according to the Minnesota State patrol handling the accident and that, Chase thought, eliminated him as a murder suspect. The trooper said Doyle wasn't driving the car and no drugs or alcohol were involved. The surviving driver was a guy named Daniel Garcia. How did Doyle's one print get on the money? Unless, of course, he really had been involved and the accident just took him out of the picture before his time.

Chase also learned from the trooper Geoffrey Doyle owned a small airline called Doyle Airlines with Daniel Garcia. Until his death, Doyle had controlling interest in the business since financing it seven years ago. Now, Garcia maintained sole ownership. Jack ascertained both were pilots in the Air Force and went into business after honorable discharges from the service, opting not to re-enlist. *Ten bucks says this guy, Garcia, is involved up to his eyeballs.*

Chase wondered why the hell Jack was late, again. Trevor, who was supposed to be here thirty minutes ago, was working on any connections that might tie Baker, Doyle and Garcia and the victim together.

Upon driving from Masquerade to the Cities, Chase delayed flying back to New York and got a hotel room. He wanted to talk with Baker and went to her office in downtown St. Paul, only to discover she wasn't in town. Her secretary wouldn't disclose where Baker had gone, or when she would return. What he did learn while roaming the halls of the Attorney General's office, is Madison Baker was a Deputy Attorney General and primarily Ann Longworth's boss. It was shortly after overhearing the buzzwords he met with the Attorney General who confirmed the information. During their meeting he didn't divulge his suspicions and informed the AG they would be in touch.

Since arriving back in New York a few hours ago, Chase didn't have information on Ann Longworth yet, but he would very soon. He was still positive he knew her from somewhere and wondered why he didn't think to get her prints while he was home.

Home, he mused wondering if his mother's life was being jeopardized. He'd learned a long time ago there were far better causes to win than an argument with Angela Franklin. When she told him she invited Ann Longworth to stay at the house during the investigation, he lost it and they both exploded into a heated match. As much as he wanted to be wrong, he instantly surmised Mandi's murder was related to the stolen money from the agency where his mother worked. This case was becoming too involved for an expedient close.

He looked up when he heard the glass door open fretting with edginess Jack was forty-five minutes late. Through the maze of Special Agents and their desks, he saw her feline grace. Chase wondered how the hell she got in here? His chest tightened into a mixture of suffering and fury. That voluptuous sway is what first attracted him. He watched as she batted her lashes at the stares and Chase gritted his teeth to suppress his rage. It had been six weeks since their sudden demise. Good ol' Jim Beam had definitely been his best friend that week. She reached his desk and stood in front of him wearing her favorite color, *sexy red* she called it. Her blonde hair was pinned up on top of her head and her pale, begging eyes told him why she was here.

"What do you want, Cindy?"

"Chase, we need to talk about this."

"There's nothing to talk about. You made a decision and now we're done."

"How many times do I have to apologize before you'll forgive me?"

He'd been shuffling papers on his desk from one pile to another avoiding those damn teary eyes of hers. Abruptly he stood up, pushing his chair backward and looked directly at Cindy. "You just don't get it. What you did is unforgivable."

"Chase, please, give me another chance."

She was gonna start it again. He watched wetness spill over from her eyes, recalling how many times had it been those same phony tears misled him through five years of agony. She'd cried to him so many times connected with stuff he couldn't begin to comprehend, he'd learned to accept her tears as part of her daily routine. Cindy had used him and maybe in some ways he had used her to deplete the formerly recent void in his life. Looking at her with disgust right this minute, Chase doubted he could ever have been in love with her. He tried to remember what about Cindy he had once been fascinated by and didn't have an answer.

"Chase, I still love you. You have to give me a chance to make it up to you."

"To bad you didn't remember how much you loved me six weeks ago. I'm late for a meeting."

"Please, can't we talk about it? At least try and work it out."

"It's over. There is no second chance, Cindy. Now leave or I'll have you escorted out of the building."

The words hissed out of her mouth. "What did you expect me to do? For five years you've been staked out somewhere, anywhere, but with me. You were never home and I was lonely."

He shuffled files on his desk again feeling the sting of guilt. He spoke with deceptive calm, "You should've gotten a dog."

"You bastard!"

Chase had motioned another agent to his desk. "Sid, get her outta the building for me."

He watched as Sid took Cindy's arm nudging her toward the door. She turned and spat the words at him, "You son-of-a-bitch, you'll pay for this!"

Chase heard Sid tell her, "Lady, threatening an FBI agent is a crime. Now you gonna go quietly or would you like me to book that pretty little ass of yours in the Gray Bar Motel?"

Chase saw Trev enter as Sid escorted Cindy out. Jack's humongous figure nearly made up an entire defensive line. He lumbered around desks and other agents awkwardly and Chase snickered as some ducked out of Trevor's way. The man's size wasn't Jack's only intimidating factor. One glance at his onyx-colored eyes and shaved head discouraged a felon's tendency to run. Chase definitely liked having Jack's ominous presence in the field.

He waited until Jack had stuffed himself into a chair behind his desk facing Chase's desk. Chase hated the office layout because partners were already joined at the hip for long hours. Why did they have to stare at their ugly, mutt-faced partners in the office as well? "You settled yet?"

"Baker's in Mexico."

Chase heard him, familiar with Jack's stubbornness and assumed his determination had paid off again. His persistent hunches were seldom wrong. Silent a moment longer, Chase asked, "What's Baker doing in Mexico?"

"Still workin' on it, but there's somethin' else."

"Yah, what?"

"Our boys in Revenue want this bizness."

"Doyle Airlines? Why?"

"Rights now I'm working on possible connection in San Luis, but seems they ain't been paying their taxes."

Chase new Jack never revealed information until he could prove it. "You mean San Luis? Down in Mexico? As in Bastide?"

Jack's familiar grunt was also the way he answered yes.

"Franklin, Trevor, in my office now."

Both Agents stood and ambled into John Caleb's office.

"What have you got so far? And I want Franklin to tell me since I can't understand a fricking thing you ever say, Trevor."

Chase smirked looking first at Jack, then at their aging, black boss.

"It goes something like this. The victim was reported missing in Masq-a-rade, Minn-a-so-ta," Chase emphasized for Jack, "four weeks ago and is found murdered over on hunder' and ninth along with one hundred thousand dollars. Forensics matched one set of prints found on the money to a Madison Baker who ironically works in the AG's office in Minnesota."

John nodded.

"They also found one print belonging to a Geoffrey Doyle who just happens to have died in a car accident and also lived in the Minneapolis area. The accident occurred months before the missing person report was filed on the victim. Which by the way, my mother reported. The victim was her employee."

"Judas Priest! You got any other back home connections, Franklin?"

Chase shook his head. "But there's more."

"I'm listening."

"During an audit at the orphanage my mother works for, a state auditor discovered a million bucks missing and reported it to the AG's office. A woman, Ann Longworth, is investigating and just happens to work with Madison Baker in the AG's office."

Agent Caleb rolled his eyes.

"Trev, here, learned Baker's in Mexico and the Revenue boys

desperately want Doyle Airlines owned by Doyle and one, Daniel Garcia. Now we believe there's a connection to Angle de la Bastide."

"Bastide's involved? Have you contacted the boys over at DEA?" Chase answered, "I will when we're done."

Jack added, "I axed my 'formant and he tells me it's gospel."

"Trevor, if you can't speak English, shut the hell up. I don't wanna listen to your backwoods shit."

"Takes the cotton outs your ears. It ain't backwoods *sheet*."

"You're right! It's a mockery to my race and you're intentionally trying to antagonize me."

"I ain't mockin' you."

"The hell you ain't!"

Chase knew he had a better relationship with his forty-five than John Caleb and Jack Trevor had with each other. They called it nuptial convenience. Their bantering flowed like diarrhea and Chase lit a cigarette waiting for their repartee to end. Slouching back in the chair, his thoughts veered to Ann Longworth. He was still waiting for George's report. It's too bad, he mused, such a lovely creature had involved herself in the criminal elements of life.

"Well, looks like you two are going to Minnesota. I'll have your flights and tickets within the hour."

Chase and Jack stood, "John, make the flights later in the evening, I'm waiting on a report from our computer genius."

"How late?"

"I need several hours." Both men left John's office.

***

Two hours later Chase was deep into Ann Longworth's life thanks to George their computer whiz kid. He didn't believe for one second, she was innocent. With George's amazing capabilities, he'd prove it. He continued reading. Real name, Annarose Leigh Longworth born in July, thirty years ago, or, he recanted, she would be thirty on the tenth of next month. Orphaned from birth she'd been raised, rather, bounced from one foster care family to another. Six to be exact due to *defiance and disobedience* were the words quoted in print. Chase took great satisfaction in knowing he was right as he read more about the numerous fist-a-cuffs Ann engaged herself in with her foster siblings and fellow students all through school. At the age of sixteen she had petitioned the court to become her own legal guardian which the judge granted. From there she lived on her own renting an apartment, working and going to school.

The first surprise came when Chase read Ann Longworth had put herself through college *twice*, obtaining a bachelor's in accounting and a master's in psychology. She had the background and intelligence to pull off the embezzlement, he reflected. Continuing to read, he swore George had magic fingers and could get his *analytical engine* to spit out how many times the president took a crap in the course of a day.

Ann's first and only real job began with the State of Minnesota, in the AG's office working fraud. The second surprise came when Chase read about her finances. Both her bank and credit accounts were impeccable. She owed nothing with an exceptional credit history and had a comfortable figure in savings. Her bills were paid on time and she'd never overdrawn, overdone or gone under on anything in her life. There wasn't a speck of criminal activity, let alone a parking ticket. In fact, she'd never been anywhere except Chicago and Minnesota.

"You's about ready to go?"

"Give me a minute."

"We ain't gots a minute."

Chase was wrapped up in the report and didn't look up. "Gimme my ticket and I'll meet you there."

"Gots us another problem."

Out of the corner of his eye he saw Jack drop an envelope on his desk and asked, "What?"

"Hotels are all filled in Masq'rade."

Chase stopped reading and looked up. "I'll get a cabin at Devils Point," and he went back to the report he held in his hands.

"Plane leaves in ninety minutes. You's can read on the plane as well as at your desk."

He felt his eyes widen, and said, "I knew it! Jack, take a look at this." Chase couldn't believe what he was reading and handed the page to Trev. Chase had his connection and he was gonna bring Ann Longworth down with the rest of them. Now he had to figure out a way to protect his mother.

CHAPTER SIX

The slender blonde had striking beauty and Ann refused to endorse her feelings of envy when Christie's voluptuous sway carried her up the stairs. She had gorgeous long hair plunging downward from a ponytail and had dressed casually in a white jeans skirt and emerald green v-neck shirt with white tennis shoes. Ann would have guessed Christie's age to be five years younger than thirty-two despite Madison committing a professional faux pas. She'd mentioned the age after their heated argument and at the time Ann had been too distracted by their quarrel to care.

Ann introduced Christie to Angela who then took her upstairs to unpack. Later, she went over the facts of the case and put Christie to work on another set of books. Ann then left with Angela and both went to the Agency to conduct the scheduled interviews.

***

Ann sat at a table in Angela's office surrounded by accounting books and bank statements while Angela sat quietly behind her desk. Both waited for Susan Bradford's arrival.

Ann suspected Angela's prolonged silence came after the police had called and informed her Mandi Marriano was found dead in New York. If the police had additional information, they weren't sharing. Ann realized Chase's involvement was a result of Mandi's kidnapping going across state lines followed by her murder. The homicide also explained the last conversation Ann witnessed between Chase and Angela. What puzzled Ann was not having the answer to why Chase wanted to know about Madison. Ann had called the office and discovered Madison was out of town indefinitely. The why, hadn't been disclosed.

Without looking up, Ann asked, "Angela, who has control over the bank accounts for the orphanage?"

Angela looked across the office at Ann. "Well, that depends. Only the board has knowledge of the total amount of the Agency's funding. Three people, besides me, have access to the books."

"What about the payroll checks and billing?"

"That falls under Susan's department."

"Does Susan have the authority to sign checks and authorize payment."

"Yes, why?"

"After I interview her, I'll decide, but I've got an idea that might help move this along."

"What's that?

"Have you hired anyone to replace Mandi?"

"Good Lord, no! I hadn't really thought about it. I've been more worried about . . . well, you know. Why? What are you thinking?"

Ann saw grief pass through Angela's eyes. Her customary enthusiasm had dissipated and Angela seemed to close herself off with the distance between them. "I know how hard it must be to understand why or how anyone can commit criminal acts, but you can't take responsibility for other's peoples actions."

"Oh, I don't. It's just that . . ."

"You want to be able to trust your employees."

"Yes, I do." Angela leaned backward in her chair closing her eyes. A moment later, she opened them and looked at Ann. "What were you thinking?"

"It would help us considerably if Christie took over Mandi's job."

"Are you crazy," Angela clucked, "how can she possibly do that?"

"Think about it for a minute. Christie just arrived this morning. No one knows she's in town. We'd have someone on the inside," Ann hesitated, "sort of spying for us."

"Is that really necessary?"

A knock at the door stopped Ann from continuing and Angela stood and went over to open her office door. Ann closed the books and files and stacked them. She kept a yellow-rule tablet in front of her.

When Ann looked up, she didn't know what she thought she'd expected to see when Susan Bradford came into the office. But what she saw wasn't at all what she expected. *How the hell could she afford Armani suits?* Angela was right about one thing. Susan's expensive taste was a result of her love of clothes. Ann had no clue, where in the land of ten thousand lakes you could purchase the over priced designer's name.

"Susan, thank you for coming in to speak with Ms. Longworth. We both appreciate any help you might be able to offer."

"No problem, Misus Franklin."

"Susan, this is Ms. Longworth."

Susan's poppy red coloring was a bad dye job and her hairstyle reminded Ann of Cleopatra. Her drawl had been as casual as her walk. Susan's above-average height and designer outfit screened a few excess pounds. Unusually brown skin, almost a molasses coloring, tainted every ounce of exposed flesh. Ann immediately noticed Susan had one blue, and one brown eye.

"Hello, Susan. Thank you for coming. Hopefully, this won't take too long. You can have a seat here at the table."

Casually stepping forward, Susan said, "Okay," and pulled out a chair to sit down.

"It looks like you spent your vacation in the sun. Did you enjoy your time off?"

"Yes. I flew to Mexico."

"I bet it was really hot down there this time of year."

Susan nodded.

"Well let's get started. First, I want to explain to you, I'll be recording our conversation as well as jotting down a few notes. I

rely on the tapes since I've got a terrible memory. My problem is
my boss expects me to be able to re-write every word spoken during an interview, so don't let the recorder or what I'm doing bother
you." Ann started the miniature recorder and spoke into it stating
names, dates and the time.

"Am I under arrest?"

Ann examined Susan momentarily. She'd started a drum roll
with her fingers on the table. Ann carefully thought over her words
before answering and said, "Not at all. Within the confines of my
job, I don't have the authority to arrest anyone. I'm only seeking
out information regarding misplaced monies for the Agency and
anything you can tell me will be a great deal of help."

"Okay."

"Good. Now Susan, for the record, and speak toward the recorder, tell me your full name and date of birth."

"Susan Alba Bradford. I was born September twenty-fifth."

"The year?"

"Do I have to? I'd rather just give my age of thirty-six."

"Okay. Now, Mrs. Franklin told me that you are head of the
accounting department. Is that correct?"

"I supervise seven people in both the accounting and payroll
department, yes."

"Is that seven total between both departments?"

She nodded her head.

"I need you to give me a verbal answer, please." Smiling, Ann
informed her, "The recorder can't hear your head nodding."

"Okay. Yes, seven between both departments. Three work with
payroll, three work with the accounts, and one secretary. That was
Mandi."

"How long have you been a supervisor?"

"Since the agency opened almost two years ago."

"In the time since you began working for the Agency, have
you ever noticed any of your subordinates acting strangely or brag-
ging outrageously of materialistic purchases?"

"What do you mean?"

"Have any of your employees ever talked of outlandish shopping sprees they've gone on?" Susan's perpetually drum roll on the table drew Ann's attention to her long, Cajun spice nails. The color clashed with the rest of her.

"Not that I can recall. And I wouldn't have any idea what they may have bought for themselves."

"Do you ever associate with any of the employees under your supervision, or within the Agency, outside of work?"

"No, except when Mrs. Franklin has her annual picnic for everyone in the summer."

"Okay. Tell me in your own words what your job involves." The monotonous finger tapping stopped and Susan stared blankly at Ann.

"Why do you wanna know that?"

Stress lines had formed across Susan's brow and a haggard worried look surfaced on her face. "It's for the record."

"Well, as the supervisor, I make sure that all the bills for the agency are paid. We issue payroll checks and keep the books recording our debits and credits."

"Are the records kept in just these books," Ann picked up one accounting book, "or do you also enter them into a computer."

"We do both. Mrs. Franklin wants a back-up system in case the computers ever crash. Once the information is entered, we print it off and put it in the book."

"Is there anyway that the printouts don't match what the computer says."

"I generally go over the figures every week on Friday and I've never found any mistakes that weren't corrected. Meaning I haven't discovered any mistakes *after* it's too late. The printouts are also dated and timed which normally is on Friday after I've approved them."

"How do you know which printouts match what the computer says?"

"The program we use dates and times every page. So when the

printout is complete, it shows two of each. The date and time I authorized it and the date and time it was printed."

"Wow. I didn't know computers could do that."

"It's just one of several designs we had implicated in the program."

Ann looked at Susan who had assumed a superior posture indicative of her confidence. "And you said you do this every week on Friday?"

"Yes."

"Why every week?

"We're paid weekly and it was just simpler to keep everything the same."

"Do you actually pay the bills weekly?"

"No. We just have various due dates throughout the entire month."

"And nothing goes out without your approval?"

"That's right."

"What about your quarterly reports?"

"Those are integrated into this program and we just punch in a few changes before printing off the book's record."

Ann pointed, "This same book I asked you about earlier?"

"Yes."

"Then you also make quarterly tax payments and such?"

"Just on the employees payroll since this is a nonprofit agency. But, we pay the state, federal and social security taxes for the employees on a quarterly basis. Our medical and other insurance plans are paid every six months."

"Okay. Which one of your employees actually makes out the checks for the employee's payroll?"

"The computer actually prints out the employees checks."

"And you sign them, or does Mrs. Franklin sign them."

"Not exactly. We have a stamp with Mrs. Franklin's signature for issuing checks on bills, and *stuff.* The payroll checks are pre-stamped with the County Commissioner's signature. Those checks are kept locked in the vault we have in the office. Mrs. Franklin's stamp is used on quarterly checks."

"Who enters new employee status into the computer so the payroll checks can be printed?"

"I do."

Susan had forced a smile before answering and her tan had paled slightly. "Do any others have access to this process?"

"No."

"How many people have access to Mrs. Franklin's stamp?"

"Just me and Mandi when I'm not available to stamp them."

"Who took care of signing the checks while you were on vacation?"

"Well, Ken did since . . . you know. But, Mandi always did it before."

Ann detected a rise in Susan's voice and looked up from her notes. "Then, Mandi wasn't the only one with access to stamping the checks, was she?"

"But she always did it before and it was just this one time Ken did it on account of her taking off and me being on vacation. I just can't believe she could do something this wrong. I guess she had all of us fooled."

Ann glanced up from her notes again when Susan unconcernedly blamed and concluded Mandi's guilt. "Have you ever noticed the check numbering sequence out of order?"

"No."

"What about the payroll checks? Who has access to those?"

"Everyone in payroll does including Maryann Johnson, Ken Fredrickson and myself."

"Anyone else."

"Yes, obviously, Mandi. I just can't believe she'd do something like this."

"Susan, how well did you know Mandi Marriano?" Ann watched a dignified look spread over Susan's face.

"I was her supervisor. I thought I knew her better than I did. Mandi loved to talk. Sometimes it was almost a distraction to the others in the office. I know she wasn't from here and she seemed lonely."

"Did she have any family?"

"I don't really know."

"Where was she from?"

"She was hired at the same time I was and I thought she told me she had been living in the Cities."

"But you're not sure?"

Susan shook her head.

"Answer for the recorder."

"No, I'm not sure."

"You are also from the St. Paul, Minneapolis area, right?"

"Yes."

"Had you ever met Mandi before coming to Masquerade?"

"No."

"Do you know if Mandi was seeing anyone? You know, a boyfriend, or if she had anyone special?"

"Danny called her frequently. But I don't think they were boyfriend, girlfriend."

"Who's Danny?" Ann jotted down more notes as Susan's nails nervously tapped the table once again.

"Someone she knew from the Cities."

"Do you know Danny's last name?"

"No."

"Did you ever meet Dan?"

"Danny."

"Excuse me, Danny."

"She didn't bring him to work with her and I already said I didn't associate with anyone outside of work."

Ann said, "Okay," noting Susan's rising voice and the avoidance of a direct answer. "Is there anything you can tell me about this, Danny?"

"My gut feeling is Mandi wanted a man real bad. I think she wanted a permanent relationship with him. I got the impression the man couldn't be tied down."

"Okay. Susan, is there anything else you can think of that might be of help to us?"

"No."

"All right. I'm also going to be talking with the rest of your staff one by one. None of you are permitted to discuss what you have told me since this is a confidential investigation. Thank you Susan for your assistance." Ann added a verbal notation concluding the interview and shut the recorder off.

Angela stood up from her desk. "Susan, I'll be working quickly on a replacement for Mandi. I think, since I know you need a secretary, we'll utilize the temp agency until you and I can hire someone full time."

"That sure would help. We're getting behind. I've had to authorize some overtime."

"All right, I'll call them this afternoon."

Susan left the office and Angela closed her door. "Well, what do you think?"

"I think we need to find out who *Danny* is. Is there anyone that works here that you think might know him?"

Angela said, "Come in," when someone knocked on her door a second time.

Susan opened the door and stepped inside. "Ms. Longworth, I just remembered something Mandi told me some time ago. She mentioned she'd gone flying one weekend with Danny."

"Flying, as in airplanes?"

"Yes."

"You mean he took her flying, or she took lessons from him?"

"I think he gave her lessons. She wanted her pilot's license real bad."

"How long ago was that?"

"I know this is stretching, but it was sometime last summer. I remember because she was really excited about flying in a seaplane off of Crypt Lake."

"What bearing do you think this might have?"

"Well you wanted to know about expensive habits and I know

flying lessons are terribly expensive."

"Thank you Susan, I'm sure we can check the records with their office."

"You're welcome." Susan left the office and closed the door behind her.

"Ann, the seaplanes operate out of Devils Point. I'll call Max."

Ann was a master at reading people and honestly didn't know if it came naturally like her *sixth sense,* or if somewhere through the years she had subconsciously perfected the ability. "Angela, I think we better keep our eye on that one."

"Why?"

"You wanted to know what I thought. Well, I think Susan Bradford is lying through her teeth."

Angela shot Ann a stunned look and clucked, "How do you know that?"

"You told me she was very upset when the auditors found the discrepancies. Susan's not tormented or even worried like you are about unfaithful employees. That woman is upset because she's involved up to her mismatched eyeballs and she knows I'm onto her."

"Ann, I don't believe you. I can confirm everything she told you today."

Ann picked up her tablet. "Can you confirm what the checks were written for that she said she issued on 'stuff' using your stamped signature?"

"I'd have to see them first, but most likely yes."

"The other thing that hit me during the interview was when she said you're a non-profit agency."

"Ann, we are a non-profit agency."

Ann opened the book she'd been working on before Susan Bradford came in. "Angela, come here and look at this. Why would a non-profit agency be donating money to another non-profit agency?"

Angela went to the table and quickly glanced at the figures. "You believe Susan did this instead of Mandi?"

"As a matter-of-fact I do. I want to see the cancelled checks for both billing and payroll."

"We'll have to request them from the bank. They aren't returned anymore unless we ask. I'll take care of it this afternoon for you." Angela had flipped through several more pages and spoke with hardness, "Let's call her back in here right now and we can find out."

"No, don't."

"Why not?"

"I need to find tangible proof she's the one who put your signature on anything that wasn't related to Agency business. Right now, all I can do is implicate you since it's your signature on those checks."

"You don't really think I'm involved in this, do you?"

"No I don't. I want to speak to," Ann looked at her notes again, "Ken first, then Maryann. Will you call Ken in here for me?"

Ken came to Angela's office and Ann repeated her routine explanation, then turned on the recorder.

"For the record, Ken tell me your full name and date of birth."

"Kenneth Michael Fredrickson, October twelfth, nineteen sixty."

"Ken, describe in your own words what your job entails?"

"I work in billing and receiving. I keep the computerized records of all bills received and paid out for the Community Family Agency."

"How long have you worked for the agency?"

"Eighteen months since the Agency first opened its doors."

"So what your job involves is that you basically keep the records and issue the checks."

"Not exactly. I keep the records and issue an invoice for Maryann to cut a check."

"Then you don't actually make out the checks, or rather print the checks off on the computer?"

"Correct."

"What are the invoices used for?"

"They're just another back-up system. I issue an invoice to make payment. Maryann cuts a check and gives it back to me to verify against the bill. I then give it to Susan to authorize and sign."

"How often are bills paid?"

"We have the standard monthly bills, utilities like gas, heat and electrical, the Agency's vehicle maintenance, anything that's required on a monthly basis. Then there's our quarterly and semi-annual bills."

"What's paid out quarterly?"

"We have a contract with our food and medical vendors to pay them quarterly."

"And semi-annually?"

"Since it costs more to pay quarterly premiums than it does semi-annually, all our insurance plans are paid every six months."

Ann asked several more routine questions and repeated the need not to discuss the interview with anyone else. She finished up with Ken and questioned Maryann next who backed up what Ken and Susan had already told her.

After Maryann left, Angela said, "I contacted the bank and they said I could pick up copies of the checks tomorrow."

"Sounds good. This evening I'm gonna go over the payroll books with Christie and will have her work on them while I continue interviews with the others."

"You think money's missing from the payroll account, as well?"

"I won't know until I look over everything. Are you convinced Christie should be on the inside?"

"Yes. Unfortunately, I have no other choices at the moment."

CHAPTER SEVEN

Ann shot upright in bed shifting her eyes erratically around the moonlit room. The same nightmare had taken possession of her one more time as her heart beat out the words 'I'll get you my pretty'. In the dream, she was being chased, then caught, then faced her own death. Wiping the sweat from her brow with the top sheet, Ann chewed her bottom lip and turned on the bedside lamp. It was three in the morning. Scanning the room was becoming a ritual and Ann had a strong urge to look under the Eastlake style bed and open the closet doors. Plainly, she could see no one hid under the tufted, velvet sofa sitting beneath a pair of pantaloon curtains hanging on the closed window. A round table near the end of the footboard was covered with a floor length, mauve cloth and white Battenburg lace. A porcelain tea set hand painted with roses, and sitting on top, would certainly have been disturbed if someone were hiding underneath the table.

Slowly, Ann inched out of the high bed, went to her purse and removed a pack of cigarettes. Putting on a lightweight robe and tiptoeing downstairs, she opened a single French door and stepped outside. A gentle wind ruffled along in the warm night air and Ann lit a cigarette, inhaling deeply. Something was eating away at her insides and she couldn't figure out what. She did know if the ugliness haunting her sleep didn't stop, she'd collapse from sheer exhaustion.

With the unknown desperate feelings of fear, Ann believed any future restful nights were certainly out of the question. The night breeze softly fingered her heated skin. Ann slipped quietly inside the house, retrieved a Pepsi and returned outside.

Her heart stopped. In less than the second it took to release a scream, the large figure stood motionless in front of her. Instantly, a firm hand covered her mouth cutting off her air supply. She fought as his free arm wrapped around her waist snugly and she felt the barrel of a gun awkwardly jab her in the stomach. The can of pop fell from her hand and landed on her bare foot before rolling across the deck and her scream was muffled by the man's hand.

"Dammit," he growled, "stop screaming, Annarose! It's Chase."

Her heart was racing faster than cars in the Indy 500. Though, she couldn't see his face, his commanding voice was one she knew she'd never forget. Her eyes had squeezed shut from the horror and Ann ceased struggling upon slowly opening one eye and peeking. Throbbing pain in her foot preceded her outburst when he let go of her.

"You son-of-a-bitch! You scared the shit out of me. Just what in the hell are you doing sneaking around anyway? I thought you went back to New York."

His vision had adjusted to the dark and clearly fright had surfaced in her eyes. He calmly answered, "I saw the glow of your cigarette and decided to check it out."

"With a fricking gun? What the hell are you doing out in the middle of the night anyway?" She glanced neurotically around for the cigarette she had dropped.

She'd almost slipped away from him. Her silk robe hanging mid thigh did things to his manhood he hadn't expected. "I'm on a twenty-four hour clock. When I can't sleep I walk." Gazing at her now, the moonlight created golden highlights in her dark hair. He noticed her hands shook vehemently as she tried to light another cigarette. Chase took the matches lighting one and cupped Ann's hands between his until a fire burned on the tip of the cigarette. He stepped on the cigarette lying on the deck, then lit one for himself and handed her the can of pop she'd dropped.

"I wouldn't open that right now. Let me get you another one, or would your prefer a beer?"

Ann inhaled the cigarette in an attempt to restrain her trembling fingers. "Maybe a beer would help."

"Help what?"

"Just the same nightmare I keep having."

Chase studied her for a moment before ducking inside the house.

Ann slithered into the lawn chair. God, her heart was still thrashing around inside her chest. Exactly what she needed after that damn nightmare was to be scared out of her fricking skin.

Chase stepped outside on the deck, opened both beers and handed one to Ann.

"Thank you, I think. What are you doing back here? Did you just get in town? Does your mother know you came back?"

I

Chase propped his butt against the railing. "Annarose, you ask too many questions."

Her mouth fell open. "How'd you know my name was Annarose?" Ann waited as a cynical grin formed below his mustache.

"You'll soon discover I know everything."

Her fingers were still trembling and Ann took a slug of her beer, then inhaled on her cigarette. With her vote cast, he really was an arrogant SOB.

Chase felt an odd twinge of guilt when the moonlight exposed stress lines across her face. "Are you always this nervous?"

"Only when I'm attacked in the dark."

"I didn't attack you. I merely stopped you from waking up the entire neighborhood."

A wave of heat slowly rose from her neck to her cheeks. His dark eyes were shaded by the night, but she felt them drilling into her soul and draining what little spirit she had left as he leaned against the railing smugly examining her. "Why are you staring at me like that?"

"Another question," he said just to provoke her. Since the day they met, the secrets she kept hidden in her eyes continued to annoy him.

His voice was deceptively smooth like velvet. Ann saw a disturbance in his eyes as his head turned. She suspected Chase was deliberately trying to irk her and recanted, "Maybe if you'd answer my questions, I wouldn't have to ask so many?"

Chase inhaled the last of his cigarette and dropped it into his beer crushing the can in his fist. "You wanna another beer?"

"No." Ann put out her cigarette and immediately lit another. She gulped beer from the can wishing he'd go away.

Chase stepped outside and plopped himself into the lounge next to the chair Ann sat in. He didn't miss the way she flinched. "How long have you known Madison Baker."

"Why do you care?"

"I wish just once you'd answer my question without asking a

question. I know what you're up to, Annarose."

"And just what exactly would that be?"

Chase withheld an urge to lash out. "Just answer the question. How long have you known Madison Baker?"

"Ten years. Why?"

"How long where you engaged to Geoffrey Doyle?"

Ann felt her jaw drop after her skin had peeled away from her body. "How'd you . . . you're investigating me?"

Chase rewarded her with a vainglorious grin. "Still a question, but you catch on quickly, Annarose."

Once her initial shock had passed, Ann tried to redirect her emotions. She had to regain control of those emotions, which were so far out of whack at the moment she couldn't think. "Chase, I have no idea what you're assuming I might be involved in, so why don't you tell me and I'll tell you what I know."

He smirked and thought over her request. She was one clever lady. And other than he scared the crap out of her, Annarose Longworth was confidently poised in a sensuous package. Reasoning, it might be a smart move on his part to enlighten her. It'd definitely be easier to keep an eye on her if he had her trust. He lit another cigarette swearing to God he was smoking too much. Chase sat up and faced her. "Yes, you're right, Ann. I am checking you out."

"Why?"

"Too many coincidences. A state auditor finds financial discrepancies the same day Mandi Marriano turns up dead in New York."

"Wait a minute. How do you know Mandi was killed the same day the State did an audit?"

"I had a meeting with your Attorney General. The day Mandi *is* found murdered, we find a hundred thousand dollars that I'm betting my life on came from the agency my mother works for. Low and behold Baker's prints are identified on the outside packaging of the money. We find one print of your fiancé, Geoffrey Doyle, on the inside. All of a sudden you're handling the investigation of the missing money? Doesn't take a rocket scientist to see the correlation."

Chase watched her expression unmask shock, then still and nurture seriousness.

"You're lying! Geoffrey was killed in a car accident long before Mandi ever disappeared. In fact, one month to the day before we were supposed to be married."

He watched the way her frame stiffened thinking she certainly had a daring and bold spirit about her. Chase wasn't sure what he thought about the other info. "That I didn't know. But, I do intend to find out how you're involved in this."

"How can Geoffrey's prints be found on money four months, almost five, after he's dead? I don't believe you."

"I can't explain why we only found *one* print. Doyle obviously had his hands on it before he died. Mark my words, your fiancé *was* involved."

Keeping her jitters rapped taut, Ann said with quiet calm, "I'm not involved, Chase." Her imagination rolled over a million different theories. The least important, her concern with what Chase thought of her. Without a doubt her future had a bleak ending in view of her engagement to Geoffrey. Chase had already assumed she surely had to be up to her neck in a sea of fraud and embezzling because of it. At this moment, Ann needed to harness her rage. She just couldn't believe, or accept, Geoffrey's fingerprints were found on stolen money. It had to be a mistake and Ann drained her beer can. *If* what Chase said were true, how long had Geoffrey been entangled in corruption? How could she not have known? *How could she have been so stupid?* No, she thought, Chase was wrong.

He'd been watching every breath she took and quirk she made. Her heavy lashes shadowed her cheeks in the moonlight. To his interested amazement, her voice sounded guiltless. For the moment, the secret expression in her eyes had been replaced with quandary. "Tell me what you've learned in your investigation."

She heard the change in his voice. It was oddly gentle, still mistrusting. Unmistakably, it was in her best interest to cooperate with the FBI. "I don't have tangible evidence yet. However, after going through some of the books, I've discovered several hundred thousand dollars written out to non-profit agencies. I'm positive a supervisor is behind it but I need to check out a few more things."

The report George had put together for him had told him plenty, but he'd lay odds she wasn't telling him everything. "What's the supervisors name?"

"Susan Bradford. So far, she and Mandi were the only ones with access to these checks."

"These checks?"

"Yes. There are two sets, one for payroll and one for bill payment. Anyway, I know Susan's lying about Mandi and how the money is being embezzled. I didn't come right out and ask her because I didn't want her fleeing on us. The odd thing was the way she indirectly implicated Mandi in the theft."

"How so?"

"Well, she's definitely covered her tracks, but all her answers lead back to Mandi. Then she fabricates the name of some guy Mandi was supposed to be in love with, but the guy wasn't interested."

"What's his name?"

"Danny somebody who may live in the Cities and gives flying lessons."

Chase muttered, "Garcia."

Ann sprung forward on the edge of the lawn chair. "Who did you say?"

She'd met his gaze with a wide-eyed stared? "Daniel Garcia."

"It can't be!"

"Why not? He *was* business partners with your fiancée."

His voice had hardened into sarcasm. Ann thought about the coy way Susan had returned to inform her and Angela about the seaplane. "Geezus, no wonder you suspect me. Except you've overlooked one small detail. Doyle Airlines doesn't give flying lessens. They deal strictly with cargo."

Chase finished off his second beer and lit another cigarette leaning backward. "So prove me wrong, Annarose Leigh Longworth."

When she didn't respond to him he turned and looked at her. Her face had paled to chalky white and she looked deathly ill under the night sky. "Ann, are you alright?"

Ann hefted herself from the chair and ran to the deck railing. She leaned forward spewing her guts over the side. She heard Chase groan and didn't care until he'd placed his hand on her back. With his other hand he held her hair away from her face.

Chase waited. She'd puked about three times before the dry heaves started. Through the silky layer of her robe, he felt the bones of her spine and it did something to him. Something he wasn't prepared for. He couldn't ignore how her bones seemed to penetrate through her skin and clothing. When she'd finished, he let go of her, went inside and returned with a glass of water and a wet towel to wipe her face. "Here, drink this."

Ann took the glass and reached for the towel when he gently began dabbing her face. The moist towel felt cool against her warm skin. His touch felt so contrary to their clashing personalities. When he finished her face, he continued wiping perspiration off her brow and neck. Then, he smoothed her hair with his other hand. Something in her stomach fluttered about even though she had no idea what could still be left inside. Upon opening her eyes, he was staring at her. His hand came down cupping her chin tenderly.

"Can't hold your liquor, can you?"

"Generally, yes." She drank more water when her stomach contracted again. Moment's later Ann went back to the lawn chair and sat down. "Thanks for helping me."

"Remind me of this the next time I offer you a beer." Chase jaunted down the stairs and pulled out a hose to wash the vomit away.

Ann watched him with mild interest. She didn't understand the sinking feeling in her chest when he switched back to his cantankerous nature. Under the inception of the dawn sky, minor flexing in his muscles moved in rhythm with the rest of his body. Without being obvious, Ann sat in the chair following Chase's every move. With long strides, he replaced the hose, took the stairs two at a time and plopped into the lounge. "Chase, are you going to tell your mother any of this?"

"No! And I'd appreciate it, if you didn't either. So help me God if anything happens to her because of you, I'll make damn sure you never see the light of day."

Ann didn't feel threatened by his words. Actually, confusion filled her mind with the changed feelings he expressed for his mother. One thing about Chase Franklin rang clear—everything Scott had told her seemed to contain some truth. "Where's your car?"

"I'm staying in a cabin at Devils Point."

"I'd have thought it would be easier to stay here. I mean after all, I am a suspect and you could keep me under close scrutiny."

That one bit hard. He assumed he deserved it and didn't respond to her sarcasm. "Tell me about life as an orphan."

Ann wasn't surprised. If he knew about her engagement, he'd know about her orphan status. "Not much to tell. My mother died in childbirth and my father didn't bother to hang around. I'm beginning to have my doubts as to why I've spent my entire life looking for him. I guess because I've always had a need to belong somewhere, to have roots."

"Sun's gonna be peaking over the water's edge soon. How's your stomach?"

"Better." Now if she could just get her mind to cooperate.

"Well, I make a superb omelet if you're up to it."

Ann stared blankly, at what, she couldn't have told anyone. A loon's cry scared the daylights out of her and woke birds in a tree hanging over her head that chirped good morning to the world.

"A little jumpy, are we?"

"Why are you being so nice to me?"

"Little Orphan Annie, you ask way too many questions."

"Tell me, is there anything you don't know about me at this

point?"

He stared at her, then burst out laughing. "You really are something. Watch," he said pointing at the lake. "It's one of the amazing wonders of the world. To sit quietly and watch the sun rise off the water."

The amazing wonder, she mused, was how a man could go from one extreme to the other with the quickness of a jackrabbit.

"Look, here it comes."

The glitter caught her eye taking her breath away. Bright orange slipped above the waterline raising the fireball into the aurora sky. The orange quickly transformed to golden yellow and gleamed brilliantly across the smooth, water surface. The moon paling with the brightening sky winked at the sun as if saying goodnight and Ann had never seen a sunrise, much less anything this radiant.

Chase recalled many mornings like this one sitting here with his father. Dad had taught him how to make those fantastic omelets stuffed with onions, green peppers and ham and lots of cheddar melted on top, on the side, a perfectly toasted English muffin. Right now, his mouth watered in anticipation. They'd sit here watching the sun come up and eating breakfast. Then, pack up a cooler and traipse down to the calm water before anyone else was up, take out a boat and go fishing. He looked out of the corner of his eye. The sun had transposed Ann's face into a golden shine. He was actually surprised. Her expression was one of amazement, no, he thought, reverence described it better. He couldn't do anything but dismiss his suspicions . . . he sorta liked sitting here with Annarose, *his number one suspect*. Incredible, he thought, how the epitome contradicted her personality.

Chase stood up abruptly chucking his last image. "You want breakfast now."

He'd interrupted a brief lull of chirping birds. "Yeah, maybe I'll feel better if I eat something."

Chase skirted around Ann's chair at the moment his heart performed tremors in his chest. "Coming right up," he muttered.

Ann stood up. "I'll help. I need some coffee."

"I don't need any help. I'll bring it out." Chase needed to put some distance between the two of them and added, "Too many cooks spool the stew."

Ann toppled into the cushioned chaise. If she dared, she could almost fall asleep. Her vision was hazy and her eyes felt layered with sand from fatigue. She also felt trapped like the unsuspecting gnats caught in a spider's web located in the deck's corner wood post. Ann confessed silently, even she was convinced of her guilt with the facts Chase had presented. At this moment, she had to believe in the system no matter how cruel it had been to her as a child growing up. No, she mused, her problem fell under wrath, and the hatred rising in her stomach like the puke did a short time ago. Her fury was rumbling toward eruption thinking her own boss might be involved in the theft of all that money. And what about the murder of that poor girl? Could Madison and Daniel really have done that? What about Geoffrey? Why did the FBI find his single print on money almost four months after his death? How did Susan fit into the scenario? She'd been asking herself the same questions over and over. And why did Chase tell her what he knew? The FBI never divulged anything. Ann made her mind up. She'd scour those books with a fine-tooth comb, and she'd re-interview everyone as many times as necessary. She wasn't going down for this crime.

***

Someone watched her. God, she just wanted to sleep, she needed the rest desperately. The staring forced Ann to open her eyes and look around. The umbrella on the table was open and shaded her from the sun. She saw Chase in a chair with his back to her. A baseball cap covered his face. He wore no shirt and had changed into a pair of cutoffs. He was sprawled out nicely under the sun's rays. Ann assumed she'd fallen asleep for a few minutes and the stares were part of the dream. She sat up. "What time is it?"

Lazily, Chase removed the cap covering his face and looked over his shoulder at her. "Around ten in the morning. I came out with coffee and breakfast and you'd fallen asleep."

Ann noticed he'd rearranged the patio furniture to protect her from the glaring sun. Another contradicting quirk of his turbulent behavior she didn't trust. Maybe he just vacillated on those quirks to keep her off guard.

Lifting himself out of the chair, Chase wanted to know if the color of the red robe Ann wore, was *her* favorite color. He'd figured out while eating both omelets, the red she routinely wore is what reminded him of Cindy, and he hated the suggestion. At the point of his realization, he remembered the day he met Ann Longworth. She'd been wearing a light colored suit with a red blouse. Once figuring it out, Chase saw Annarose differently and hadn't completely been convinced the similarity is why he believed he knew her.

"Figured since I contributed to your lack of sleep last night, you probably needed the rest. My mother and that partner of yours went off somewhere."

"Shit! They shouldn't be seen together."

Chase regarded her critically. To a certain degree he was beginning to understand her shameless spirit.

Ann's heart did that little riffling thing when Chase sent her one of his faultfinding stares. Nevertheless, Ann had forgotten Christie's arrival and she'd slipped up by not warning them. Her eyes shifted and gawking at Chase's bare chest and legs, Ann felt commotion, spine tingling commotion. His wide shoulders tapered toward his corded stomach muscles. There had been plenty of disturbances in her life, but nothing like what this man could do to her with his eyes and now his body.

"The way I see it, those two being together is the least of your problems, Annie."

She saw the witch-hunting thoughts filling his stubbled face.

"You suspect Christie, too? She just started her job last week and can't possibly be on your list of suspects."

He stepped under the umbrella's shade to protect his bare feet from the scorched deck. He couldn't resist and slipped his hand up the side of Ann's arm brushing a finger along her cheek.

At first she flinched whiffing tobacco mixed with sweat and breakfast. Suddenly, the touch of his hand was tender, soothing, and Ann gulped.

"I have to go Orphan Annie."

The wistful expression in his dark brown eyes seemed to be pleading for a truce. He turned to go and Ann said, "Chase?"

He looked back and what Chase saw shocked him. Innocence wrapped in red. *How could she be innocent when all the evidence pointed to her?*

"Thank you for . . . you know."

He nodded and left.

CHAPTER EIGHT

The only noteworthy incident during the past week was the way Masquerade prepared for their celebration of the Fourth. A carnival came to town Thursday night and would stay through Sunday. The festivities would begin with contests for all ages, followed by a parade. Max's barbecue was planned to start in the afternoon with a band and dancing later and topped off in the late evening hours before an amazing fireworks display. Everyone had Friday off since Saturday was the Fourth of July. Christie made plans with her boyfriend in the Cities and Angela had gone to Devils Point to assist in preparations for tomorrow.

Ann hadn't seen hide nor hair of Chase since the previous weekend. She honestly didn't know if it was good or bad. Faithfully, Ann informed the Chief Deputy of her findings since Madison still had not returned. A tug of indecision regarding Chase's suspicions pulled her in several directions. Should she inform the Chief Deputy and implicate herself? The whole difficulty went to proof she wasn't implicated in this crime. Though the paper trail she'd started had facts, it was all circumstantial evidence of *who* had stamped those checks.

After unresolved deliberation, Ann decided a walk along the lakeshore might untangle everything. She dressed in lightweight clothes and locked the house. Soaring humidity and rising temperatures clobbered her as she stepped outside. A good storm would be the only resolution to blow out the mounting pressure.

Ann headed north on Cozy Cove Road towards Devils Point watching people cluster. Boaters and fishermen were lined up clogging the boat landings. Some waited patiently to dock, others not so diligent expelled unpleasantries in the clammy atmosphere. The peaceful greeting her first day in Masquerade had dissolved into jumbled communications, laughter and enormous amounts of boat traffic. Though confusing, these activities would remain lively and brisk the entire three-day weekend.

Upon reaching the beach at Devils Point where she and Scott had shared a few hours, Ann thought of Scott or Max who she hadn't seen since their introduction either. Spotting a vacant bench under a tree, Ann plopped down on the wooden slats. She could have sworn the temperature advanced another ten degrees since leaving the house. Stillness had replaced a light breeze. Sailboats sat stationary and Ann wondered what they did without a wind.

The sticky air lingered and smothered, while the cotton shirt she wore clung to her gummy skin. Ann removed her sandals and kept walking until the sun-baked sand burned her bare feet and she bolted for the water. The warm water felt like a hot bath but soothed the bottoms of her feet and Ann continued in the shallow depths northbound past Devils Point.

Some time later, whether it was hunger pains in her stomach or a movement catching her eye, Ann shifted neurotically. Looming directly in front of her stood a rundown building. Ann felt her knees weaken and believed they could have been stirred with a spoon on account of the eerie looking building. The growling in the pit of her stomach had been caused from not eating since the evening before. Nervously, she wanted to be convinced the movement she swears she saw had been a squirrel or a rabbit. The uneasy feeling sent creepy chills along her spine in the humid warmth. Fixed and immobile, the deserted building fit the description Angela had given her of the old dance hall. No trespassing signs were posted and proceeding further only invited trouble.

Barely seconds had passed and without warning the universe turned gravely dark. Thunder rumbled overhead and Ann swiftly turned on the ball of her foot running in panic. Black clouds rolled briskly in front of a brewing storm. Parallel lines of nasty white caps grew and surged toward the shoreline. Powerful and windy gusts blustered and bowed the frail birches and branches of elm trees like rubber bands. Gulls and ducks had disappeared under the moaning echoes of the wind.

The threatening storm wasn't the only thing frightening the crap out of Ann. Goosebumps now merged with beads of sweat as an unknown presence produced rising levels of anxiety. Ann didn't make it to shelter before large drops of rain fell from the blackened sky.

Her pounding heart competed with each rumble of thunder and crack of lightening as she kept running. Ann reached the vacant beach at Devils Point and the clouds discharged rain in buckets while the winds raced at a pretty good clip. She'd heard stories of being near the water during severe storms and with the lightening, she knew trees were forbidden. Now blinded by torrents of rain, her intuition told her to seek shelter immediately. Ann continued running for the cabin where her and Angela had eaten lunch.

Sirens sounded at the second Ann smacked into a powerful force. Her scream became lost in the roar of the wind and she felt a man's powerful hand grab her arm. He knocked her to the ground shoving her under a cemented-down table.

Filled with horror, Ann covered her head and squeezed her eyes shut. The siren and wails of the wind drowned out her words as Ann begged the man not to hurt her.

"Ann, stay down!"

She heard her name over the howling wind and accompanied with shivers and tremors, Ann opened her eyes and saw Scott. He shouted at her above the wind's drawn-out shrieking cry, but the only word she heard, was tornado.

***

The tornado left as quickly as it had bashed the shores of Devils Point. The damage had left downed trees, missing shingles on rooftops, broken windows and overturned boats and picnic tables. One vacant house, along with several campers had been demolished and tourists thanked God it hadn't been worse. Power had gone out, but auspiciously no one had been injured. The excitable buzz circulated astonishment and pulled strangers together for the first time. All wondered if the disaster would halt their weekend's commemoration.

Ann sat alone inside the unlit cabin where Scott left her after the tornado had passed. He'd given her a towel to wipe herself dry and soon after taking care of her, went to tend to others in need. Her muscles twitched and trembled, coating her skin with chills. She moved restlessly wanting a cigarette and hoped Angela was unharmed. As a distraction from her own discomfort, Ann watched people in the unlit room. Although they were pumped up with anxiety, they listened patiently to Max and Scott promise everything would be fine.

The rain continued outside and took Ann back to the day she shredded her wedding gown. The incident seemed to have occurred in another lifetime. On that tragic occasion, her feelings were remorse and grief. This second, fear mixed with anger and permeated her veins. She came close to dying today and tried to decide if the pouring rain and being under a picnic table were related to her dream of being trapped inside and drowning. She really believed someone had been watching her from that condemned structure and the feeling was as real as her nightmares. It couldn't have been the property owner. Angela said he passed away years ago. Ann heard the whisk of a match nearby and glanced up.

"You look like you need this as much as you need dry clothes."

Ann took the cigarette Chase handed her and inhaled, receiving minimal relief from her internal alarm.

Chase had been watching Ann since he saw Scott shove her under the table. Now she distanced herself apart from the others. Next to the numerous victims, her face appeared normal. To him, she conveyed emotions running so deeply, he questioned if she even knew they existed.

"Orphan Annie," he brushed her cheek with his finger, "do you make a habit of getting caught in the middle of tornadoes?"

His voice held an infinitely compassionate tone. It calmed as well as probed her. His touch prompted summersaults inside her stomach. Why did he always seem to appear at the worst moments in her life? "Not generally," she answered, "but it's typical of my shit magnet life." *And she wished he'd stop calling her Orphan Annie.*

He'd been lighting a cigarette for himself when laughter floated up from his throat. All he could do was repeat her words, "Shit magnet life."

"Have you checked on your mother?"

"Always with the questions. She's fine and around her somewhere. I'm sure, helping the less fortunate."

Ann expelled a burst of air from her lungs feeling inward relief. "What about her house?"

He was acutely intrigued with the secrets behind those large, smoky eyes. Chase wondered if she knew what her eyes did to him. Lately, he'd found himself debating what her lips would taste like, as well. "Orphan Annie, will you ever stop asking so many questions?"

Jumping to her feet, her mood veered sharply to anger. "Stop calling me that!" As if all her emotions had boiled over, she shouted at him, "Call me Ann!"

Chase reached, grabbing her arm before she could flee. Unable to resist her fiery defiance, he pulled Ann close and smacked his lips to hers.

Ann thrust her fists into his chest and pulled away rubbing her mouth with the back of her hand. His driving kiss had invaded. Ann flinched and shifted in reverse when Chase reached for her again. She spun quickly and bolted out of the cabin into the pouring rain.

Chase smashed out his cigarette and stormed out of the cabin through the opposite door. Annie had gotten to him like a bad rash. The very thought froze in his brain. He didn't know if he could ever trust a woman again.

He had a short-lived engagement, one that wasn't even long enough to tell his mother. Cindy, his blonde goddess, had promised him a lifetime together. He'd trusted her and deeply relied on her love, maybe even depended on her. It took five years until she finally accepted his marriage proposal. They moved in together and maybe that had been the mistake. Though he doubted it.

Chase still couldn't get the image of that morning out of his mind. After an all night stakeout, he came home exhausted and walked in on Cindy with another man.

They'd only been in the new apartment a month. Cindy was a whiner. His place was too masculine, he told her to redecorate. His place was too dreary, he told her she could paint. When she complained about the neighbors, he conceded and they moved into a new place. *Dammit!* He would have given Cindy the world served on a silver platter in exchange for her love.

Upon finding Cindy in bed with another man, he went bizerk yelling and threatening. He physically threw both their naked bodies into the hallway, slammed the door and he and *Jim Beam* got real acquainted. Anonymously, he called the police to report a nude male and female in the hallway. He reneged the following month on the apartment lease and had to pay the entire year's rent in order to get out of the written agreement. He just couldn't live there when all he saw was Cindy naked in bed with others. Since, he still had many sleepless nights wondering how many others there had been. She'd been a fifteen thousand dollar mistake and he hadn't been with another woman since. How could he?

***

Max had been standing on the opposite end of the cabin tending to victims when he heard Ann yell. He witnessed the kiss and Ann's fists hitting Chase. His jaw fell open and he stared blankly after Ann shouted at Chase and scrambled out of the cabin. Those words, the pitch and God, he thought, the emphasis of those three little words, *call me Ann*, sent him back to his withered past. If he hadn't watched it with his own eyes, his ears would have deceived him into believing the voice belonged to Letitia. He'd always called her 'Letty' and she hated it as well. Letty would become angry just

the way Ann did, and she'd yell at him, 'call me Letitia' just the
way Ann did. It just couldn't be he mourned silently.

***

If Jack's snoring hadn't kept him awake, the firecrackers certainly would have. Obviously, the tornado that passed through
Masquerade less than twenty-four hours earlier didn't impede an
early celebration.

Chase looked up in time to catch a hazy sun nosing its ball
over the horizon. The storm yesterday hadn't lessened the heat or
the humidity. If anything, it was worse and power still hadn't be
restored to Masquerade.

Chase looked down again. He'd been reading paperwork since
four in the morning with a flashlight. Specifically, the report George
had provided for him on Ann. Something didn't jive. Once a shock
to him, the facts didn't appear quite as guilty now. Ann and Doyle
were engaged for eleven months and had a joint safety deposit box
at a bank in the Cities. Every other account Ann or Doyle had,
had been independent of the other. The dirty bastard died a month
before her wedding she'd told him. At the time, he couldn't identify the weird sensation the info gave him.

George was amazing Chase mused as he continued reading.
His digging had retrieved the name of Ann's real father, Harlan
Longworth, who died twenty-seven years ago in Topeka, Kansas.
Since Ann's mother didn't survive childbirth at the age of twenty-
seven, Chase wondered why Ann's father had deserted either of
them. Her biological parents never married and he could only
guess why her mother would give Ann her father's name. The scum
had skipped out when he learned of the pregnancy.

Chase rested his elbow on the table and propped his head in
his hand. He popped the top of a warm beer with his free hand
and swallowed, then he choked. The name screamed loudly from
the paperwork lying in front of him. He set the can down and
grabbed the piece of paper reading the report a second time. How

in the hell had these names escaped his scrutiny? *Letitia Marie Phelps, born Minnesota, May 29, 1933, died Illinois, July 10, 1960. Preceded in death by one sister, Annaleigh Rose Phelps. No other living relatives.* Chase had read over the information rather quickly trying to ascertain Ann's guilt, the other names had all been ignored.

Slumping back in the chair, his orphan continued to capture him off guard. Annaleigh Rose Phelps was Max Phelps sister. Making Max Phelps Ann's uncle. He'd missed the name Annaleigh Phelps simply because everyone referred to her as Annie. Referred to, as in Annie Welston, Scott's mother. He washed his hands over his face, muttering, "Shit."

Chase now knew why he thought he'd met Ann. She was the spittin' image of Scott's mother, especially her eyes. What was it she told him, she'd spent her entire life looking for her father. No wonder she couldn't find him. His little orphan wasn't completely a lost soul. What puzzled him over and above the case, was why Max had never mentioned Letitia. For the life of him Chase couldn't remember Scotty having an aunt. What he did know is he and Scott were six when Ann was born in Chicago. Did Scott know about Letitia? What would they all say if they found out Ann was his number one suspect? They wouldn't say anything. They'd just kill him and put him out of his misery, and slowly he thought.

Chase touched his mouth remembering how Ann had tasted honeyed. Waves of shock collided inside his entire body when he kissed her. He'd seen the way Scott pulled Ann under the table yesterday when the tornado hit. Seeing her himself, he was going out the door to do the same thing. In one split second, Scott had beat him to it. It really had bugged him watching Scott shelter Ann the way he held her, all protective like.

Chase stood up abruptly, ignoring the *sleeping beauty* and trying to comprehend how Trev could sleep through all the noise. Campers were waking up early anticipating the day's events and the resort would be in full swing within the hour. Chase headed for the shower to scrub away his mounting frustration in cold water.

***

Scott greeted Angela and Ann inside the main cabin. Candles brought out during the night hours had been blown out as the sun lightened the room.

"Scott, did you get everyone taken care of yesterday?"

"Sure did, *Mom*." Scott laughed then added, "We were lucky nobody was hurt and the few that lost their campers have been put up in spare cabins."

Angela asked, "Who owns the house that was smashed?"

"Not sure, but the place was only used in the winter for ice fishing. No harm done."

"Where's Max? I'm gonna check and see if he needs any help."

"Haven't seen him. He's been acting like a lost soul since yesterday."

"I wonder why. I'll go look for him."

"Catch ya, later." Scott put an arm around Ann's shoulder and said, "So what kind of destruction can I save thee fair damsel from today?"

"Nothing if I have anything to say about it. Scott, I never had a chance yesterday to say it, but thank you."

"No problem, kiddo. So, are you ready for some football?"

Without knowledge, Ann's face became expressionless.

"You know, Monday night football, the theme song, let's have some fun?"

Ann shrugged her shoulders to hide her confusion.

"Oh, man do you need to learn what's important in life."

"And I'm sure you'll fly home in between touchdown passes just to teach me."

Scott looked down at Ann and said, "Absolutely." He removed his arm, and yelled, "Hey, Chase-man, over here."

Ann gulped trying to steady her erratic pulse. She'd left Chase standing near this very spot yesterday after she yelled at him and he responded by kissing her, rather harshly she recalled.

For a moment, Chase studied them both indignantly. Her

little figure was clothed in a snappy outfit of white shorts and a red shirt. A red shirt caressing her nice. She wore a white, baseball style cap with matching tennis shoes and her hair had been pushed up under the cap. He sauntered in their direction and saw it clearly now with the two of them standing side by side. Their dark, wavy hair and smoke blue eyes were just the beginning of the similarities. He wondered if anyone else saw what he could see so plainly this second. "Scotty, how's it goin?"

"Gonna be a hot one today, but I doubt anyone will mind with everything we've got planned. Annie says you've met."

"That we have." Chase drank her up with his eyes. "Ann."

He'd spoke her name with quiet emphasis. So quietly, Ann doubted Scott noticed the tension between the two of them. Ann deliberated whether Scott saw the private message Chase had sent her.

"Wanna raise a little hell later?"

"Might as well," Chase said, "you, me and good old Jim Beam."

"Already anticipated it," Scott confessed. "Max conned me into starting the kids races first and Ann here, kindly volunteered her services. You wanna join us?

"Not my style, I'll catch up."

"Can you believe this gorgeous lady has never seen live fireworks?"

"Scott, nothing surprises me."

"I've promised her a day she'll never forget. We'll be at the parade following the races, come back over here and then you and I can do some serious carousing."

"Later, Scotty."

Scott faced Ann, and said, "Follow me, beautiful."

Chase gritted his teeth knowing his internal annoyance was preposterous. He watched them leave together telling himself his irritation made no sense.

***

To see their heightened and excited faces, hear their silly laughter and even the cries, arranged a smile on Ann's face. As she watched the parade from the sidelines, the children made her speculate about her own biological clock running out. In six days she would be thirty. True, she knew there was still time. But like starting a new job, you had to learn how things were done, the same way you had to get to know a person. If only, if only things didn't happen the way they always seemed to happen.

As quickly as she had felt their joy, icy fear twisted around her heart. Ann spun around convinced someone stood in back watching her. Scott had left her alone while he went to assist with a problem they had in starting the parade. Later, she saw him talking with the blonde from the beach. She shifted uneasily casting nervous glances up and down the street noticing no one unusual. The fear reminded her of the condemned dance hall.

Ann turned her attention to the parade. The music blasted Yankee Doodle Dandy from trumpets and tubas and drums. Clowns showing off skipped to and fro, in and out and tossed candy pieces into anticipating crowds. Painted floats, flowered and decorated, rolled at a snail's pace behind the majorettes and color guard.

"Sorry about leaving you alone so long, Annie."

"So you prefer blondes and I know when I've been stood up. But don't worry, my feelings are still in tow and I promise I won't hunt you down and kill you anytime soon."

"Ouch." Scott clutched at his chest. "Nothing like stabbing a guy in the heart. Glad I'm not your enemy."

"Did you invite *her* to the barbecue?"

"How'd you know that?"

"Oh, please, Scott. You're as obvious as a sixteen year old getting her first kiss."

"That bad, huh?"

"Yes. That bad."

He laughed, answering, "Yeah, I invited her, but if I didn't know better, I'd think I detected some jealousy."

"You're nuttier than a fruitcake, Scott."

"And I suppose you think it's nutty the way Chase eyed you this morning. In fact, me thinks you've got yourself a new admirer."

Scott *had* noticed and Ann spoke with an edge in her voice. "There you go again, exposing all that shit you're full of."

Scott wrapped Ann in chokehold giving her a noogie.

"Scott!"

"Say uncle."

Ann slugged Scott in the gut, grabbed him and flipped him on his butt. "Uncle my ass," she crabbed. "Don't mess with me. I learned at very young age how to take care of myself."

"Geez, Annie."

Ann lifted her knee out of Scott's gut and extended her hand to help him up. "Consider yourself warned."

"Damn, woman, you wanna play on my offense?"

"And risk breaking a fingernail, I don't think so."

"You tried that move on Chase, yet?"

Ann flashed Scott a defiant look.

"Maybe you should." Scott held his hands up to stop her rebuttal and said, "Come on, the ending's coming up and we can head back to the resort."

***

Max began the pig roast around two in the afternoon. Food had been spread endlessly on checkered covered tables, set up inside the cabin. The feast ranged from various breads and rolls to every kind of salad, including potato, beans, various macaroni and lettuce, beans with dogs, brats and burgers, ice-covered cakes and fruit-filled pies with cookies and bars, chips and dip among veggies, bread and butter pickles and olives. Ann had never seen such an abundance of food and believed the entire state of Minnesota could gorge oneself for a week if necessary.

Carrying through into the afternoon, kids competed in more games, constructed sandcastles and moats near the shore, played volleyball and football, went swimming and boating and stuffed their bellies until they couldn't eat anymore. Ann met Scott's cousin Karen and her husband Pete and their son Jake and watched younger boys waiting awestruck for Scott to autograph their football cards. The only somber thought she'd had all day was why Max had been avoiding her. A lump lodged in Ann's throat. She'd spotted him several times with a look on his face—concealed sadness and grief mixed with depression and heartache—it splintered her heart into pieces. His faded, gray eyes were a million miles away in some other lifetime. His muscles quivered and shook when Chase approached tapping him on the shoulder. They spoke only for a moment and Max and his long face loped away.

Ann had been stealing looks at Chase the entire afternoon. He and Jim Beam had become the best of friends. The more looks she stole, the more she comprehended. Chase was a symbol, a token secret preoccupied by trained doubts, guarded and continuously alert to his surroundings. His dark eyes were shark-like, cold and indifferent—distancing him from feeling emotions. His drooping lids, with brows always drawing in, indicated a sadness. Even his shortened dark hair suggested less fun, despite his intelligence and complexity. Ann knew Chase was more dangerous than the criminals he sought. Though not excitable, Ann had no doubts Chase desired excitement the way he regularly invited a challenge.

The dancing and music began early and Ann only watched the couples. She smiled several times when Max perked up as he swung Angela in and out of his arms, around and around in circles.

"Walk with me, Annie," he whispered into her hair.

His husky voice and simple words had seduced her. Ann swung around and stared at Chase wordlessly. If she hadn't witnessed his bourbon spree, she'd never have known he'd been drinking. The stubble was gone from his jaw and he smelled clean and fresh of soap.

"The fireworks are just about to start and I know a secluded spot not far from here."

It wasn't really begging, it was unmistakable pleading Ann saw in his eyes. Chase had taken her elbow guiding her south away from the crowds.

"What do you think?"

She thought, he was very disturbing to her in every way. His hand still held her elbow causing her heart to thump erratically. "About what?"

He laughed sincerely amused. He was expecting, almost hoping she'd ask her questions. He wasn't sure what he'd do if they ever stopped. "The way Masquerade celebrates."

"I think astounding best describes it."

"Astounding?"

"Most of these people have never met. A tornado and a national holiday brought them together. It's simply astounding."

They'd neared Angela's house and Ann turned to look at the first round of fireworks exploding over Crypt Lake.

"Ann, we got a problem. Wait here."

"What is . . ." before she could finish, Chase had removed a gun from under his shirt and was shrinking away in silence toward the house.

Ann swallowed dryly, frozen to the spot. Her eyes darted insanely, picking objects out of the dark. Startled by another round of fireworks, the sky lit up and Ann saw Chase entering the open French door of Angela's house. The continuous passage of their existence felt non-existent as she stood there incapable of running even if she had ordered her feet and legs to move. When it seemed like Chase would never return, Ann couldn't decide. Should she follow him or go for help.

Chase ultimately stepped outside and Ann exhaled the air trapped inside her lungs by her own doing. He'd re-holstered his weapon under his shirt making his way back to her.

"I've called the police."

Fireworks exploded and before Ann could speak, the monster figure approached Chase from behind. "Chase!"

With the speed of a squirrel, Chase drew his forty-five, turned and aimed. "Damn it, Jack!"

"Yer lady's down," Jack chortled.

His adrenaline had pumped spastically when Ann screamed his name. Chase jerked around muttering more profanities seeing Ann had fainted. He re-holstered his weapon a second time and when Ann didn't respond immediately to his rousing, he lifted and carried her up the deck stairs placing her on the lounge.

Several minutes later, Ann opened her eyes at the same time a police car arrived. She sat up feeling dazed and heard the conversation.

"Chase, what've you got?"

"Entry through the front door. Think I interrupted them and looks like they bailed out a back window. Caz, this is my partner, Jack Trevor. Jack, this is Chief Casimir. The semi-conscious lady here is Ann Longworth."

Chief Casmir, a portly man in his fifties wearing glasses beneath receding gray hair seemed pleasant.

Chief Casimir acknowledged, "Miss Longworth."

Ann gawked at Jack's stolid and physically unmoving body. This behemoth thing with the black-eyed stare was Chase's partner? Jack had nodded to her before following the Chief inside.

Chase moved closer to Ann. "You okay?"

She nodded and stood. "Chase, my laptop and files are upstairs. Did anything happen to them."

"I dunno, it's pretty ugly in there, wait out here until we finish inside." Chase lighted a cigarette for her before he went back into his mother's house.

"At least your mother wasn't in there at the time."

With disbelieving thoughts Chase learned one more thing regarding Ann Longworth. She worried more about others than she did about herself. He couldn't believe she hadn't whimpered a word relative to her fainting.

Ann sat down catching the grand finale of the fireworks and smoked the cigarette.

An adolescent green-eyed officer, young enough to be in high school arrived and nodded at Ann.

"They're inside, go on in."

Some time later, all four men exited the house. Ann's intuition kicked in considering Chief Casimir. She'd been questioning his name ever since a flashlight had displayed the spelling on his badge.

"Is there something else, Miss Longworth?"

"No. It's just your name is very intriguing." Ann's vision had more than adjusted to the dark and she saw a purple tinge in his eyes communicate his interest.

"Why's that?"

"Casimir is Old Slavic Kazatimiru meaning one who commands peace?"

Caz nodded, surprised with Ann's knowledge.

"I find it interesting your heritage means leader at peace with himself and the world. The correlation between your name and your job are extraordinary."

Casimir blinked, extremely impressed with the bright little lady, and pretty, too, he had noticed. "I've never met anyone who can even pronounce my name, let alone know its origin. That's why the guys over at the station just call me Caz."

By this time, word obviously had spread, though Ann had no idea how. Max had driven Angela home and Scott wasn't far behind them. The greetings between Caz and the others were short as tension rose.

Much later, Ann lay wide-awake in the antique bed. It was to hot to sleep, not that she could have anyway. Chase had scared off whoever committed this crime and they never made it upstairs. A window on the back side of the house had been broken from the inside indicating the suspect bailed out that way. With Max giving orders, Chase and Scott boarded up the window until it could be replaced. She'd overheard Chase and Jack talking to Chief Casimir and between them someone would be watching the house throughout the night.

Ann couldn't shut her mind down and stop the questions.

Who would want to break into Angela's house? What where they looking for? Was any of this related to her case? It seemed nothing was missing, but things had certainly been damaged or destroyed. It appeared the perp was looking for something. It had to be her files, since she'd already stirred things up with interviews.

CHAPTER NINE

After major cleanup from the break-in to Angela's house and the tornado, the electricity had finally been restored to Masquerade. Christie went undercover on Monday after the Fourth in the accounting department as Susan Bradford's secretary. Since she had a background in accounting, the setup actually worked in their favor. Christie would be able to observe Susan Bradford daily. Ann stayed at the house inspecting and comparing the Agency's records with bank statements.

At three in the afternoon, on the third day, Ann's eyes were bugging out of her head. She'd stared at pages of printed black and white columns and numbers until it all became a maze of puzzles. She stood up, stretched her arms over her head then poured herself a cup of fresh coffee.

Ann leaned against the counter sipping and meditating. She'd been through the first twelve months of payroll and was plugging forward at a snail's pace. Flawlessly, every credit and debit matched perfectly. Stubbornly, Ann would push ahead until she could prove Susan Bradford was the one behind the fraud. She was also obstinate enough to prove Chase wrong in his accusations of her. Her uncertainty lied in the fact she couldn't find a blasted ounce of proof implicating Susan. Worse, in most fraudulent cases of this nature, the suspect usually left a trail of large purchases. Maybe a smoke screen, but Susan lived just above poverty level. She'd even bounced a check or two, perhaps to give the appearance of innocence, Ann guessed. The two exceptions, her wardrobe and her trip to Mexico, prompted checking into. Ann discovered Susan had spent more than three grand in one week. Someone barely able to make ends meet didn't throw away three thousand dollars on a whim. But without proof, Susan would say she'd been saving for a long time.

The bank's hundred pages of returned checks had proven a waste of time since the checks matched the Agency's records.

Ann even contacted the Department of Economic Services and discovered the orphanage didn't receive the entire funding in one lump sum. The State had passed the funding onto the County who issued allotments twice a year, in April and October. Both the state and federal funding were calculated by percentages. Broken down, the allotted funding was one point five million dollars every six months. Adding up the figures, the Agency should have excess money left over on December thirty-first each year.

Since the orphanage had opened just shy of two years ago, six million dollars had been earmarked. The most recent allotment wasn't recorded and Ann assumed it was an oversight with the audit and Mandi being reported missing. Then, Angela brought the records home. Ann was more than half way through all of the books and the figure on the bottom line made the Agency appear bankrupt.

She rubbed her temple and popped a couple of aspirin swallowing the pills with lukewarm coffee. Ann brooded over the numbers. She was missing a vital point about the numbers? It was almost like they were too perfect, but that wasn't it. Refilling her mug, Ann couldn't quite grasp what it was she felt sure was obvious and clear. As she stared at the mess, Ann muttered out loud, "There's no such thing as a perfect number, unless the price is right."

She remembered something Angela said and like a bolt of lightening, it hit her. Excited with her train of thought, Ann hurriedly flipped through the pages. She found the payroll that began in January of last year, the month the Agency opened. At a glance, everything looked normal. Ann flipped the pages to December of last year and saw it. She looked at January's record of the current year, then December again. Ann shuffled through papers and found January's payroll for the current year. She picked up the cancelled checks, comparing several. There they were, the *perfect* numbers. She compared last December with this January's payroll against the signed checks. "Gotcha! Clever, Bradford, but you've made one big mistake. Huge! I can't wait to find out what you're doing with all this money."

Hastily, Ann flipped to April and March of this year. Mandi disappeared sometime in May and paychecks had been issued in Mandi's name through June. Ann reasoned, unless paperwork showed Mandi's termination, or death as the case may be, her payroll check still had to be cut. But why was a check still being issued after Angela filed a missing person report?

Ann dialed Angela's number at work. "Angela, can you bring home copies of the last three payroll periods and the last increment of State and Federal allocation?

"Sure. What did you find?"

Ann rubbed at her temple again since the aspirin hadn't started their magic. "I'll show you when you get here. I want guarantees before I say anything."

"I'll be home in a few minutes."

Ann couldn't believe it was this simple. She flipped back to December and counted the employees listed. There were one hundred fifty employees. As of January fifteenth this year there were one hundred fifty-five. Angela had told her she had one hundred and fifty employees working for the Agency. Could Angela have been mistaken? Ann thought not, since the five extra employees were all being paid identical, hefty salaries.

Ann heard Angela come in the front door and met her half way. "You got 'em?"

"Right here. What did you find?"

"Give me about ten minutes and then I'll show you."

"Ann?"

Ann started reading the papers as she returned to her paper mess in the kitchen. Pleased with herself she said, "I think I've figured this out." Ann soon afterward asked Angela, "What did you want?"

"How come you didn't tell me Chase suspected you of being involved in Mandi's murder?"

Ann stopped and faced Angela. "I didn't know he suspected me of that."

"What does he suspect you of then, if not murder."

Ann took a deep breath and exhaled. "Angela, it's a long story. I didn't have anything to do with Mandi's murder or anything else Chase might believe and I promise I'll explain everything. Right now, I need to show you how I think Susan is embezzling."

Ann lifted the accounting book off the table and showed December to Angela letting her look over the page. Ann then handed January to Angela.

"I'm afraid I have no idea what you're trying to point out to me."

Ann also pointed out where Mandi was still receiving a substantial paycheck even after the police report and her death had been reported in May.

"Oh, my word! This has to be an oversight."

"Oversight my ass. From the one who claimed there are no mistakes after the fact, I don't think so."

Ann handed December and January's records to Angela again, and said, "Look at them together for a minute."

Gasping, Angela said, "Ann, this is unbelievable! I've never met five of these people. These five names right here are not employees in the Agency and they all seem to have been working at the Agency for six months without my knowledge."

Pleased with herself, Ann smiled. "I know," but something still gnawed at Ann. She just didn't know what.

"Oh, my God!" Angela clucked, "look at these salaries."

Ann calculated a few numbers hastily and the totals as of May first appeared astronomical. Susan, by her own admission, had to be the one who entered the five names onto the payroll and most likely the one cashing the checks as well. Ann saw something else and realized if she could see it, any expert would easily verify the signature on Susan's cancelled checks matched the five employee's cancelled checks. Ann stared at the five names. She wrote them down on a blank sheet of paper, twice even. She wrote them in reverse order as they were entered and saw it instantly. To the unknowing eye it wasn't obvious, but to her it screamed guilt loudly. It became painfully clear why Chase suspected her.

"Angela, when the County issues the one point five million in funding, who's responsible for depositing the money? Who actually receives the check?"

"It's done by direct deposit and it's just under a million, not a million and a half."

Dumbfounded, Ann looked up at Angela. "Angela, I spoke with Economic Services who said the funding is one million, five hundred thousand dollars issued every six months."

"Oh dear," she squawked, "we've never received that much!"

Angela's face contorted into horror and disappointment convinced she had evil employees working for her. Ann swore her heart stopped, recalling Angela's words the day they met and she'd said *someone big had to be involved.* At this moment, Ann felt as crushed and deceived as Angela did and Ann hated all of them.

She hated Madison, who she couldn't make contact with. She hated Geoffrey for dying so she couldn't have him prosecuted. She hated Chase for thinking she had anything to do with this corruption. Daniel, she squared her jaw, Ann never did like him. And as long as she was hating them all, she added her father to the list just for abandoning her. Ann was positive Madison was someone big and bringing her down didn't seem quite adequate enough.

Ann didn't look up when Christie came flying into the house. She was writing the names down since she'd figured things out.

"Angela, Susan Bradford went home sick right after you left."

"Really?"

"Come 'ere, look at this." Ann showed the list of names to Angela she'd written. The first, Maddie Kareb was next to the name Madison Baker. Donald Cargia was next to Daniel Garcia.

The last name, Jeffery Loyde was next to Geoffrey Doyle. Ann hadn't figured out if Beth Anderson and Bailey Jones were real people or not. The more Ann stared at the names, the more she had to concede Chase had been right. As much as she'd subconsciously wanted to believe Geoffrey's innocence, she couldn't anymore. Her dead fiancé was a deceitful, conniving bastard while he was alive. Since Madison Baker qualified as 'someone big' Ann needed to discover how she had gained access to change the amounts of the issued checks. By process of elimination, Madison *had* to be the one with gaining entrance to alter those direct deposits. *But how?* Furthermore, how did they all know each other? A quick calculation showed the loss skyrocketing toward millions and Ann felt her heart sink deeper.

"Ann, what's wrong?"

Ann faltered and finally told Angela the name of her fiancée was Geoffrey Doyle.

Ann had a job to do and said, "Ladies, we've got our work cut out for us. Angela, I need you to pull the files and get me the applications for all five of these employees including Mandi and Susan. I want to check social security numbers. Christie, I'm gonna put you to work."

"What do you need?"

"I'd like you to go back to the beginning, find all of these names and come up with the subtotals and grand totals from their paychecks. Pull every cancelled check and combine them with copies of the record totals. Compare all the names to the authentic list of employees all the way back to the beginning. I'm going back to the Cities. I'll be back in a day or two."

Angela's head shot up. Those piercing blue eyes held a distant, determined gaze.

"Ann, you can't!"

Her voice rang with command. "Oh, can't I? Well, you just watch me!"

"Ann, I'm begging you not to return to the Cities. You have no idea what will happen. Please, let Chase handle this."

She stiffened recalling Chase's challenge. "Angela, I have to do this." She faced Christie, and said, "I also need you to go through the records and come up with the total dollar figures of Federal, State, FICA, pensions and medical paid out on these five employees since they were first issued paychecks. Also check any potential claims against workers comp. In time, each agency will have to be notified of any and all existing discrepancies."

"Ann, please, let me call Chase and he can at least go with you. I couldn't live with myself if anything were to happen to you."

Ann looked at Angela. Blatant terror infiltrated her large, blue eyes and they were glazing over. "I'm going home first and I'll call you when I get there. After that, I'm going to the office and I'll call you when I get there, too"

"At least let me call Scott and he can go with you."

"No!" Ann ignored the way Angela threw her hands up in defeat. She ran upstairs to her bedroom, muttering the words, "This is between me and that bitch."

Thirty minutes later, Ann was in her Trans Am heading out of Masquerade. Biting down on her bottom lip seemed to stop some of the rage bubbling over. Ann lit up a cigarette and inhaled so hard she choked. Her anger buckled sharply. No wonder Madison had screamed at her about this case. Ann spoke out loud just to relieve her pent-up emotions. "Baker, you knew I'd discover everything. What you never banked on, is that the AG would assign this mess to the two of us." She squashed her cigarette in the car's ashtray and muttered to herself, "Doyle if you weren't already dead, I'd kill you myself."

Ann arrived two hours later at her apartment in St. Paul. She took a deep breath and exhaled before exiting her car. She'd been going round robin beating herself up for being a stupid fool in love and thought, never again.

She forced herself to settle down after almost ripping the door off her mailbox. Mail spewed from the box onto the floor inside the foyer's entrance. Flipping through the bills and advertising as she walked upstairs, one envelope from a bank and addressed to both her and Geoffrey, stopped her dead in her tracks. Unaware of any account with this bank, Ann ripped open the envelope and read the letter.

> *It has recently come to our attention that you and Ms. Longworth have a safety deposit box with our bank. At this time, we must inform you that the monthly payment has not been maintained for the past three months. We have in the past deducted the monthly fee from Mr. Doyle's checking account. However, at this time the account's funds are significantly below the required monthly fee. In order to continue the safety deposit box service, we will require that you pay the past due fee of $225 in order to maintain the safety deposit box and that you make additional arrangements with us. If you wish to close out this account, please contact us at the letterhead address.*

Ann stopped reading and blew out the words. "Like hell I will." Unlocking her apartment door, she entered and slammed it shut. The hot apartment smelled stale, musty, old. It stunk of corruption. All but the bank's letter was tossed on the kitchen counter.

She knew absolutely nothing about any safety deposit box and never signed papers for it. Now that she thought about it, she'd probably have to pay the overdue fee in order to get inside the box. What could Geoffrey possibly have hidden in there? Ann realized nothing would surprise her where Geoffrey was concerned. Where had he put the key? She glanced at the wall clock. There wasn't enough time to get downtown to the bank today. Ann called Angela as she promised.

She tossed the letter on the counter along with the rest of her mail. Upon looking inside the refrigerator, an unopened, gallon bottle of bargain wine sat alone on the top shelf. Ann picked up the phone and ordered a pizza drinking the wine and thinking the wine worth more than Geoffrey's cheap ass.

By the time the pizza arrived, Ann had digested half of the red syrup and was feeling no pain. She stood to answer the door and lost her sense of equilibrium. Pickled into giddiness she opened the door and handed the delivery kid cash telling him to keep the change. He stopped her from shutting the door.

"Um, lady, you still owe me ten bucks, this is only a five."

She hiccupped, "Oh! Jus' a min'it."

Ann returned and said, "ow's this?"

"I don't have change for a fifty, lady?"

Ann swayed pulling more bills from her wallet. She watched the delivery boy stoop to pick up her falling money.

"You only owe me ten. I'll take these two fives. Here's the rest of your money."

"Wait," she'd scrunched the bills in her hand looking for a ten. When she found it, Ann grinned. "Here's your tenner, keep the change."

Who was he to argue with a drunk? If she wanted to throw her money away he'd take it. He took the extra ten and left.

Ann sat in a happy stupor in the middle of her living room floor drinking more wine than eating pizza. Through bloodshot eyes, she saw the cardboard box of Geoffrey's she'd found earlier. "You ass jack," she hiccupped. "I's a damn good thing . . . you're . . . dead 'ready."

Since she'd misplaced her drinking cup, Ann grabbed the neck of the bottle and guzzled the remnants of wine. She spoke loudly to anyone she thought might be within earshot, "I'm 'runker than a brewer's fart." Backward she fell, sprawled out on the floor anesthetized with cheap alcohol.

***

Ann woke up and didn't dare move considering it felt like someone had nailed her head to the floor. The ceiling spun and she thought, for sure, she'd been hit with a bag of lead. Blinding sunlight shot sharp pain into her aching eyes. She rolled over to cover them and whiffed cold pizza. Instantly, Ann jumped to her feet holding a hand to her mouth. She ran to the kitchen sink, since it was closest, and regurgitated wine and pizza. *This was worse than the morning with Chase.*

After cleaning out the sink, Ann navigated an unsteady line toward the bathroom. Using both hands, she held her head and moaned. Stepping inside the shower stall, she turned on the cold water letting it gush over her throbbing head. Sometime later, Ann stripped away her drenched clothing and finished bathing.

After chewing down three, extra strength Excedrin she thought would surely help, red rivers in her eyes stared back at her from the bathroom mirror. Irritated with Geoffrey for leaving an empty Visine bottle in the cabinet, Ann hurled the bottle and heard it hit a wall. She thereupon stumbled back to the kitchen to scrounge up some coffee. The *box* sitting in the middle of the floor next to the pizza blared, 'you're guilty'. What Ann had discovered inside the cardboard box last night, had been the start of her commune with the spirits.

An hour after galvanizing herself with a full pot of coffee and nicotine, Ann brushed her teeth twice and still felt like a Russian army had trampled through her entire body sometime during the night. Skipping breakfast, she placed the contents of Geoffrey's box of goodies in her trunk and drove downtown St. Paul to her office. Marching directly into Madison's office, she couldn't demand without disturbing the ungodly hangover playing bongos on her head, so she delicately asked to know Madison's where-abouts.

"Ms. Longworth, you and the entire world want to know her whereabouts. Chief Deputy Edwards, the FBI, you, myself included, all want to know what happened to Madison. I don't know."

Her voice lowered even softer. "When was the last time you saw or talked to Madison?"

"The week you left for Masquerade."

Moisture welled in the secretary's eyes. "Why are you crying?"

"Chief Deputy Edwards is livid. He's removed all of her files from her office and said she's fired." Choking on her own sobs, Tanya wailed, "I'm gonna be out of a job."

Ann hadn't taken into account the predicament Madison had created for others. This poor kid was frantic believing she was gonna lose her job merely by association. "Tanya, the State isn't going to fire you. They'll move you into another department or let you sit it out until . . ." Ann had to be careful what she said and finished, "everything is resolved." She handed Tanya a tissue and asked, "Do you know if the Chief Deputy is in today?"

She shook her head in unison with her uncontrollable sobs. Her words stuttered out, "He's out of town."

"Would you mind if I went through Madison's office?"

She blew her nose shaking her head once more.

"Tanya, don't worry any more about your job. I can and will certainly vouch for your work." Ann stepped toward Madison's office and said, "I'll only be a few minutes."

Ann didn't have a clue what she was looking for but walked in any way. Everything looked the same. Madison's mahogany desk was centered in front of the large window with a panoramic view of the Mississippi River. Two green and gold, tapestry chairs were placed in front of the desk. A two-seater sofa with matching mahogany tables were placed to the right. Ann sat down in the large, leather chair behind the desk and began opening drawers. She found nothing out of the ordinary.

Flipping backward through Madison's desk calendar, nothing had been written on the monogrammed sheets. She continued flipping the pages until she came to the first week in May. Written in Madison's script were the words *Danny G, 1:30.* Madison had an appointment with Daniel Garcia? About what? Going back even further, Ann saw another name with a notation to call. Ann ripped both pages out of the calendar.

She breathed, "Oh my God!" For whatever unconscious reason, Ann's second language from college came back to her. Still holding the pages from the calendar in her hand, Ann looked at the date. The second note she saw had been written in April. She stood up, the shock consuming her with more uncertainty than ever. The words whispered off her lips. "I can't believe this."

Ann slid back into Madison's chair as her already queasy stomach played racquetball inside. She swiveled the chair around slowly in order to face Madison's computer. Tiny, white stars flickered in front of her hung-over eyes and slowly she turned on the computer. During the wait, Ann made a silent vow she'd never touch alcohol, ever again, not never. The computer bleeped. Ann hissed, "We'll just see who the fool is, now," as she plugged in Madison's password. "That bitch never should have trusted me."

Opening, reading and closing several of Madison's files, Ann had no idea what she was looking for. "Anything that doesn't look right," she'd answered in a whisper. The computer screen became a blur as Ann's vision competed with her hangover.

She rubbed her eyes and continued scrolling through files and documents. Then she saw the file. She clicked the mouse and opened the document reading the words Department of Economic Services.

Scrolling through, dates and figures were revealed. After several minutes of reading, Ann was able to confirm Madison was entering into the account on the same day a direct deposit was made to the orphanage. Unknown how, but Madison had discovered the password to access the account. She would plug in the changes directly depositing nine hundred thousand dollars for the orphanage into their bank account and the remaining six hundred thousand was being deposited into an account in San Luis Potosi, Mexico. Madison had been doing this for eighteen months, since the orphanage had opened. Ann checked the printer for paper and printed off two copies of the document. Out of curiosity, Ann looked at the first printed page and sure enough Susan was right. Dates and times were printed in the bottom right corner.

Ann now had the proof linking Susan Bradford to the embezzling. Though not recorded on tape, Susan admitted she went to Mexico on vacation. When Ann checked into Susan's vacation expenses, she'd learned her destination had been San Luis Potosi, Mexico. Why, Mexico? And what was Madison's connection to

Susan besides *Danny*? Ann looked at the calendar pages. How did each of them know the other?

Ten minutes later, two complete sets of the report sat in the printer's tray. Ann scooped them up, folded and stuffed them into her purse. She logged off and left Madison's office.

Ann stopped in front of Tanya's vacant desk. She assumed Tanya must have gone to the ladies room to fix her makeup.

She walked to the elevator and pushed the button, hating the idea it looked like she was guilty as sin. Standing there waiting, Ann realized the bank was one block away and decided walking might release her swelling rage.

In all her wildest dreams, she couldn't fathom why Geoffrey had obtained a safety deposit box. Especially since discovering his box of goodies had been in *her* apartment. The thought danced through her mind. How long had that box been hidden there. She never thought of it until now, but what if she couldn't gain access to the safety deposit box. At the last second before leaving this morning, she remembered to grab Geoffrey's keys out of the envelope returned from the coroner's office. One of them had to fit.

Along the way, Ann gazed out at the river from Kellogg Boulevard.

Entering the bank with letter in hand, her gait carried her toward the nearest teller. She was directed to another woman who read the letter as Ann wrote out a check to pay the fee after muttering an apology and explaining Geoffrey's death. She removed her driver's license to identify herself. The woman handed her a card to verify her signature and Ann signed the card. She then followed the woman who led her toward a wall covered with various size boxes located in a back room. Ann found it odd the signatures had matched and wondered how Geoffrey had accomplished it? After nervously fidgeting, Ann located the correct key and inserted it into the box's lock. The woman opened the door and pulled out the box, placing it on the table and left the room.

Her fingers trembled nervously as Ann lifted the gray, metal cover and opened the box. An enormous, yellow envelope crushed to fit had been placed inside. Tugging the squished envelope out, several ID's and social security cards lay in the bottom of the metal box. Ann picked one up and, of course, it read Jeffrey Loyde. Why would she be surprised to see the picture in the right hand corner was Geoffrey? Upon picking up another ID, Ann read her own name with Madison's picture laminated inside the plastic. A third showed Madison's photo with the name of Maddie Kareb. She fumed momentarily and then reeled in her anger.

Picking up the heavy envelope and opening the clasped end, Ann looked inside. "You son-of-a-bitch, what have you gotten me into?"

An unknown amount of twenty-dollar bills were packed and bound and undoubtedly would match the counterfeit plates she'd located in *her* apartment inside the cardboard box.

Ann re-closed the envelope. Not waiting another minute, she stuffed the envelope and the ID's into her briefcase, along with the printed accounts and calendar pages she removed from her purse. She stood, left the room with the box open on the table and closed out the account on her way out of the bank.

Weeding through the crowded streets of downtown St. Paul, Ann stomped her way toward the river. It seemed to be the only way to relieve her wrath. The heavy, warm air was packed in between the skyscrapers and stifling. She was definitely working up a sweat. Upon reaching Warner Road just below Kellogg Boulevard, Ann retrieved the ring from her purse. With a hefty toss, the five-thousand dollar diamond engagement ring sailed into the Mississippi River.

CHAPTER TEN

The digital on her dashboard read ten thirty when Ann steered her car into Angela's driveway. The light over the kitchen sink was on and had remained on at night since the break-in. She quietly unlocked the front door, entered and slipped off her pumps. Her hangover seemed to worsen throughout the entire day and she'd smoked more cigarettes and consumed more liquids today than she ever thought humanly possible. Ann went to the kitchen for a can of Pepsi.

The last person she expected to see this late was Chase. He leaned against the counter wearing only a pair of jeans. His muscular arms and chest were bare except for accumulations of slivered hair sliding down his rippled stomach into his jeans. She stood in the threshold and slid a hand through her mass of waves. Life had already been drained from her hollow body and Ann didn't believe she could tolerate another confrontation with Chase. The day's events didn't help her self-induced headache and Ann hadn't rationalized what to do with any of her discoveries today. Nervously, she glanced down at her briefcase and back up at Chase. His dark eyes cast a languorous gaze over her in an impudent manner. Edged with a neurotic fear, Ann asked, "Why are you here?"

As much as he detested the color red, he had to admit it belonged to her. It praised her careless, dark hair and the seductive strand always falling across her forehead. Her fidgeting contradicted her forthright nature. "Here we go again with the twenty questions. The last time I checked this was my house also. I should be asking you if you found anything or anyone. Like, your boss, Madison Baker."

Emotionally drained and holding incriminating evidence in

her hand, Ann was too exhausted from last night's stupid stunt to argue and said, "Then you already know she's disappeared." The assumption Angela had called and told Chase she'd gone back to St. Paul didn't surprise Ann. "According to her secretary, Madison left the week I arrived here and she hasn't been heard from since."

He already knew Baker's whereabouts and was testing her. Chase carefully thought about what else Ann had done for an entire day and a half in St. Paul.

Without thinking, Ann set her briefcase and purse on the floor and retrieved a desperately needed Pepsi. She turned meeting Chase's gaze and moistened her dry lips. "Why did you tell your mother you suspect me of murdering Mandi?"

Her bloodshot eyes had been darting back and forth nervously, but now her independent spirit glared back at him. "I didn't."

"Then why does she think I did?"

"Does it matter what my mother thinks? *I know* you didn't kill Mandi Marriano."

Ann inched her way toward the table and sat down. "And that's supposed to make me feel all better, I suppose."

She was jittery and restless. Her trembling fingers squeezed the Pepsi can leaving indentations in the side. Before she had turned away from him, Chase noticed her bottom lip had started quivering. He knew she was concealing something, but he felt an urgent need to kiss away her nervous trembling. "If my mother had her way, I'd be tarred and feather for even the thought of suspecting you," and finished by saying, "of doing *any* thing crooked."

Tormented with blustering anger, Ann rose. "I need a cigarette," and she went outside through the kitchen door.

Her mind's on some other planet and he was determined to find out why. Chase grabbed a can of pop out of the frig for himself, picked her purse up off the floor and followed Ann onto the deck. "You'll need this for your cigarettes."

What she needed was more time to think and sort out her latest discovery. She'd placed her Pepsi on the table and began twisting her hands. Should she tell him . . . how much should she tell him . . . should she just keep it to herself?

When she didn't look at him, Chase set her purse down. He reached out swinging Ann around to face him. He had to see her eyes. Her wide-eyed innocence was merely a smoke screen. She was as scared as she was bewildered. "What's wrong with you?"

His extraordinary brown eyes blazed and glowed as he gripped her shoulders. Rising panic mixed with a familiar excitement he made happen inside of her. Ann shifted uneasily. She felt like she had only one chance left. One chance to prove her innocence to him.

"What happened in St. Paul, today?"

"You won't believe me."

"Try me."

Ann licked her dry lips again. Her stomach had balled itself into a bunch. "You were right. Everything's in my briefcase."

Chase let go of her and lighted up one of his cigarettes, handing it to her. He stepped inside and returned, giving Ann the briefcase.

"Chase, I've figured out how Susan Bradford has been stealing the money."

He didn't respond, but sat down with the pop he'd retrieved and opened his second pack of cigarettes today. He pulled one out lighting it for himself.

"They're all in this together somehow. Madison, Daniel, Susan and yes, Geoffrey. I went to the Cities to talk to Madison and stopped at my apartment first. I'd received a letter from a bank telling me Geoffrey and I owed three months of back fee on a safety deposit box we had jointly." With a pleading look, Ann said, "I swear I didn't know anything about it."

So far she hadn't told him anything he didn't already know. Except, maybe that she knew nothing of the box.

"Last night at the apartment," Ann hesitated thinking she couldn't call it hers anymore, "I tore the place apart going through everything of Geoffrey's looking for a key to get into the box. What

I actually found," and she massaged her temples, "caused this worthless hangover."

He rolled his tongue inside his cheek to keep himself from grinning. Then he watched her open the briefcase on the table. She was so feeble and delicately fragile he couldn't look at what she was doing, but studied her. He'd never seen her bite her bottom lip before tonight and favored the thrill it gave him.

"Chase, you have to believe me. I didn't know anything about these." Ann removed the counterfeit plates from her briefcase dropping them on the table.

His pop can slipped from his hand spilling on his bare feet. He bolted forward in his chair when he saw the plates and instantly scanned the area around them. She'd already pulled an envelope and several ID's out. "Ann, put it all back, now!"

Ann gaped at him in stunned silence and did as he said.

He couldn't touch any of it before it was dusted for prints. "Ann, have you talked to anyone about these?"

"No. I know the Secret Service, or Treasury, someone has to be notified, but I was afraid to contact them because you've suspected me from the beginning."

"What's in the envelope?"

"I don't know how many, but twenty dollar bills that I'm guessing match the plates."

"You found all this in the safety deposit box?"

"No. Geoffrey had the plates hidden in the apartment inside a cardboard box. The money in the envelope, which I'll bet *is* counterfeit, was in the safety deposit box with the ID's. These ID's match the false names on the Agency's payroll of which I discovered five names have been added and Susan Bradford has been cashing their checks. The signatures on the back of all the cashed checks matched her handwriting. I just don't know where the money is and it's well into the millions so far. I'm also guessing since Susan went to Mexico, she has some connection down there. With whom, I don't know. I also don't know how she knows Garcia and Baker."

His mind raced. If Doyle had left the plates in their apartment, *the thought of her sharing an apartment with anyone really bugged him and he wasn't sure why*, it meant Garcia or Baker would come looking for the plates. They were stealing money from the Agency, counterfeiting, murder, and Bastide was involved some way. He'd had no idea how big this case was until this moment. He looked up at Ann and the dread that flowed in his veins surprised him. Taking a deep breath, Chase stood up, thinking the money at the murder scene had been the real stuff. What Ann found, probably was fake. "Ann, you didn't close out the account on the safety deposit box, did you?"

"Yes, after paying two hundred and twenty-five dollars to see what was inside, I couldn't afford to keep it, let alone I don't need it."

His brown eyes had darkened trying to hide it, but she saw his alarm. "Dammit, I never even thought about it at the time. They're gonna come looking for the money, aren't they?"

Whether caused from his need to do away with his inhibition or the desperation he saw in her eyes, Chase didn't know. He pulled Ann close wrapping her in his arms. He pressed his lips against hers and before long gently covered her mouth.

Ann was shocked by her eager response. Her blood surged from her fingertips to her toes and satisfying the potent aching in her limbs indicated more doom for her.

She tasted sweet. Sweeter than he ever believed possible. Raising his mouth from hers, Chase gazed into Ann's smoke-blue eyes and saw virtue and integrity. "Yes, Annie, they're gonna come looking for the money and the plates."

Without looking away, Ann backed out of his grasp because she needed too. His kiss had left her more doubtful. "Do you believe me? Believe that I had nothing to do with any of this?"

"Yes," lightly laughing, Chase told her, "you've convinced me." *At the moment, he wasn't sure why he'd changed his mind, but he had.* A small amount of the strain in her face had dissipated when he'd answered her. Until now, he'd never gripped the significance she'd placed on his words.

"Chase, what do I do with all of this?"

"You don't do anything. It's evidence and I'll contact the Secret Service." He picked up both her briefcase and purse, took them inside the house and returned.

His assured manner soothed her, releasing some of her pent-up hostility. Just then, the smoldering flame she saw in his eyes thrilled her and it was becoming too easy to get lost in his gaze. Ann nervously fidgeted.

Chase skimmed Ann's arm lightly and tugged her closer. He'd been aching for sometime with his longing and she had instantly set his blood on fire. His unsettled urges were swelling. Chase lifted her chin with his finger tilting Ann's head and feathered her bottom lip with his thumb.

Her whole being seemed to be filled with waiting. Ann could feel the sexual magnetism that made him so self-confident and slid her arms around his waist..

Chase bore a gaze into her with a silent expectation. His mouth came down nibbling and tasting, seducing her until her lips parted and met his.

Her mouth ignited with fire as he teased and lightly touched her like a warm breeze. Ann quivered as he proceeded to caress her mouth. He showered her jaw, that erratic pulsing hollow at the base of her neck and murmured his warm breath into her hair. Totally entranced with his skilled touch, Ann felt like a breathless girl of eighteen until he nibbled her ear. "Ahh!"

Drawing her in nice and tight, Chase attended to her mouth with a thirsting quench. The uncivilized response she provided became eager and frantic like challenge and fear all rolled into one. The more she gave, the more he needed to satisfy his own naked appetite.

His lips had snared hers more querulous, more crucial. Her desire climbed and her needs turned into spasms as he smothered and drew her into his hungry web. Her thoughts spun, her emotions whirled and skidded and her knees buckled.

He held snugly to her and Ann became conscious of his bare torso pressed in contact with her breasts. He'd locked his hands behind her back and his mustache lightly touched her skin sending tremulous shivers through her body. Softly, his breathing fanned her face.

"Come on, let's go for a walk down by the water."

"In my suit?"

"Why not? Just take your jacket and shoes off and we'll walk in the water."

"But, I'll have to take my nylons off, too?"

Chase flashed her a wicked grin. "Oh, Annie, never say that to a man you've just kissed. Especially when he dangerously wants to assist you."

Hot waves swept through her belly and flushed their way into her face. His throaty laugh taunted wickedly and his grin declared victory.

Chase slid Ann's jacket off her shoulders kissing her with his eyes and then his mouth.

Wearing a sleeveless blouse, his heated fingers grazed a line along her skin leaving shivers on her arms. He'd prodded her intimately skimming his hands along her back. With showering as tender as a summer rain, he planted another tantalizing morsel in the hollow of her neck and Ann weakened into dandelion fluff. A low groan filtered out from nowhere when Chase lightly nipped her ear lobe once again.

"Would you like help, Annie, removing those hose?"

He'd whispered the words into her ear jolting her down to her core. She dragged her fingers through the hair on his chest toying with his bare, hard muscles. Ann had no impulse to withdraw from his embrace and pressed her mouth to his.

Chase parted her lips a second time joining their tongues in persistent frolic.

"Chase . . ." Ann moaned against his mouth as waves rolled in her blood more rapid than the tornado had struck last Friday.

Chase tugged the blouse out of her skirt and slid his hand

inside feeling the heat of her silky skin. He wanted more and relished in the creamy soft contours of her neck.

He'd traced her nipple with his thumb and Ann's insides mushroomed and she pulled away. "Chase, no."

He let go immediately as his blood stopped cold.

Ann went inside the house momentarily.

He stood there in anticipation, wondering what she was doing and if he was getting himself in over his head.

Ann stepped outside and said, "Let's go for that walk."

He noted her bare feet and legs and his own heated urges heightened a second time as he flashed her a smile. Anxiously, Chase went inside the house returned moments later locking the door behind him before he extended his hand to Ann.

She took the hand he offered and smiled.

Chase guided Ann in the dark, down the stairs. Strolling out of the yard towards the water, they walked along the shoreline letting the water slap at their ankles in the warm night air. She hadn't been this quiet since he'd met her. He felt a dull ache sear his chest the way her hand clung to his. It was her undying strength touching him somewhere deep inside and he believed she was out of his reach. She was different from anyone he'd ever met. Some how he knew even if the ache in his chest were satisfied, the intensity of his woeful mourning wouldn't fade easily. How could it when he didn't even know what he was longing for? She felt like electricity riveting through his body arousing and confusing him into a startling state of being.

Ann looked up at the midnight sky filled with brilliant stars and the thumb nail moon daintily reflecting itself off the water. The vastness of space portrayed her life. Her feelings hobnobbed between desire and despair. Desire for what she wanted and desperately needed and despair because it had never been further from her grasp. She felt an utter loss of hope and a sense of defeat. Hopelessness she'd never find her father and defeated by false love. Ann tried to think of a happier moment in her life when she glanced up at Chase and his endearing smile sent her pulse racing. He told her he believed her and her heart pitter-pattered an extra beat because she had convinced him. She felt her lips flutter and Ann beamed with gratification.

The momentary silence between them had changed his opinion of her. Chase couldn't remember the last time he felt satisfied with anything. Since he'd walked into Ann's life, a kind of peace he'd never known had taken control of him. After a background check, he thought he knew everything about Ann and recognized he knew nothing. He also grasped for the first time, a life filled with Cindy would have been a serious error in his judgement. Chase looked at Ann. "What are you thinking about?"

"The screwed up mess I've made of my life."

Chase stopped walking, but didn't let go of her hand as he stared at her.

She'd been swung around by his abrupt halt and stared into his eyes.

"Ann, you can't seriously believe that you're responsible for what others made a conscious choice to do?"

"Chase, I'm trained and educated and should have been able to read the situation. Instead, I allowed my emotional needs to blind me by the blatantly obvious."

He read the disappointment of failure in her eyes and it wrenched on his insides. He let go of her hand and turned to face the body of water. "I see it too often. Victims who pay the price because they had no knowledge someone they trusted had chosen a life of crime and worse, used them for personal gain." He faced her and said, "You can't take responsibility for their decisions, Annie."

Ann saw years of pain and suffering in his eyes and something inside of her wanted to heal the wounds of his broken idealism. She'd begun to understand the distance he kept between himself and others. "True, but I am responsible for allowing my personal needs to blind me. It's the same thing in my book and it all boils down to selfish greed. I wanted and needed to belong to someone so much I chose to ignore everything going on right in front of me."

Chase couldn't clarify the ache chewing up the inside of his stomach. She'd damn near described the last five years of his life. He'd been too wrapped up in a personal loss, it almost caused another serious mistake. He believed Ann and certainly wanted to trust her with his heart. There wasn't any room left for more pain. His heart overruled his mind and he stepped toward her pulling Ann into his arms. With a crushing urgency, his mouth swooped down to capture hers.

Eager vibrations whisked through her veins. Reckless abandon escalated and swelled and Ann had been possessed by her own fiery passion. The previous statements she spoke became lost within the power of his mouth devouring hers.

She was drawing out his uncivilized side. He tasted, savored and relished her scent, her flesh, driving himself wild. As his appetite increased, she answered and responded to his exigency forcing him over the edge of senselessness. With a wanting he didn't understand, he manipulated and stroked Ann's curves, then roamed more intimately over her breasts. Her nipples were taut beneath her silky, *red* blouse and he subconsciously thought he was starting to welcome the color. He strayed over her back and hips and imprisoned her firm bottom. In a fervid groan, "Annie," slipped from his lips.

Her senses radiated with pleasure as his warmed breath whispered her name into her flesh. The heat from his roving hands burned through her clothes and Ann's insides were firing up. He played and teased the tip of her nipple driving her into demented delusions. She'd lost control by the time he unbuttoned her blouse and slid his hand inside the lace of her bra. Her head careened backward, letting his mouth tempt and entice her unveiled flesh.

Chase unzipped her skirt letting it fall and expertly undid her bra. Stepping back, his gaze dropped from her eyes to her shoulders to her bare breasts. In the dark, he saw the silhouette of her full-bosomed and willowy figure, and swallowed eagerly.

Frozen in place, Ann's skin flamed to life as his gaze seduced her. Her heart spurted and scampered frantically inside her chest when he pulled her into an intimate embrace. Her skin tingled concurrently as her flesh met with his bare chest and jeans. He tenderly manipulated and explored the lines in her back, her waist and her hips smothering her skin in a sea of passionate kisses. Ann reached and unbuttoned his jeans sliding them down his hips and swelling manhood.

Chase stepped out of his jeans and lifted Ann carrying her into the water. He couldn't get enough of his troubled orphan and paved her skin with his mouth to the crevice between her hardened tips. His mouth located and met with a firm nipple he nibbled between his teeth. The sound she uttered was robust and called out to him.

Her desire rose like the hottest fire, skin touching skin, flesh stirring flesh and hands stroking and caressing each other. Ann arched her body as his tender, moist kisses dawdled, loitered and delayed until her veins throbbed into oblivion. Another gasp escaped when he nipped the swell of her mounds, first one then the other.

Chase journeyed deeper into the water until the level became waist high. He let Ann glide along his torso and the thrill of his own chills clashed with the warm water, cracking his insides. Discarding her panties and then his underwear, his hand coasted teasingly down her belly.

Untamed excitement bee-lined through her. His darkened eyes enslaved her and involuntary tremors seared each caressing stroke within her sacred domain. Ann cried out rising skyward into orbital proportions.

Chase drank in every inch of bare flesh greedily and dragged Ann close in his arms. Her legs snaked rapidly around his hips and her arms circled his neck. Deep within him a guttural moan sounded as they merged into one.

His mouth turned stormy, seeking and demanding. The hint of his hardened manhood seared her senses, and then her. Ann's mind reeled into an unknown world as they excited and drained each other in the warm fluid. Entangled in new awakenings her despair transposed into deepened commitment she had no doubt she'd given up.

Chase became lost in the yearning he had to fill. He took and he clung to the entry he made into her and she intruded on his darkness, spreading light into his world. His lust for her had been drowned and he experienced a replenishing of his lost soul. She'd dived into and penetrated the depths of his sea of seclusion.

As their madness advanced in ravenous waves, they fell into the depth of the water swirling around. Chase hung on tightly as Ann clung desperately and he stood up carrying her onto the beach where he laid her in the sand.

She never dreamed his body and hands could spread such warmth, be so tame, or cause her passion to be so unshackled. Her limbs quivered as his teasing assault to her senses continued. Instinctively, she arched forward as he nipped and tasted. Her selfish need overrode every turbulent incident between them. The dormant sexuality of her body had been jolted into a new awakening. Ann had never appealed for so much in her life and pleaded to him for more.

Chase sensed Ann's excitement and skimmed her flesh to the shroud and core of her existence. What began as wantonness had turned into longing, a craving and appetite he'd forgotten existed within his life. He couldn't stop from delving into her deepest moiety as he heard her wild cries. She liquefied against him and he gorged and hunted in a hoggish manner until his tastes had appeased and satisfied both. Chase felt a groan catapult from a place deep inside of him. And his moan mustered out sending him on a caper to a high he'd never live without. He knew he'd render and provide it all for her, and only for her.

She shattered, crying out for freedom and growing to ignitable dimensions. He had penetrated the layers of distrust piercing through her camouflage. She was in his power, his command and charge. Ann rose to meet him as he plunged deeper and deeper propelling her to greatness, her outcry became a yearning to belong to him.

When Chase lowered himself upon her, Ann's breath came rapidly. As flesh stroked flesh, man met woman under the naked twilight sky on the sandy beach. Desire ripped through her body and she ruptured in a downpour with a welcome she couldn't disguise. Their unity turned pure and explosive. Her trembling limbs clung, rising with the mold they created in the birth of each other. Lust and devotion flooded through her joining their confusion into togetherness. Her breath came ragged at first, then in surrendering moans and Ann realized a great deal more had consumed them both, more than any sexual desires. He had unlocked her heart and soul.

***

Making sure Annie was locked inside the house, Chase had filled a large paper sack with the evidence and returned to the cabin. He had uneasy feelings leaving three women alone in his mother's house, but he needed to talk to Trev. He also didn't feel great about what had just happened and not because Ann hadn't satisfied him either. She'd more than satisfied him. More than he had ever prepared himself for. And that's exactly what bothered him. The same way she always seemed to confuse him.

His past and present clashed with each other angering him all over again and he stormed into the cabin where he and Jack had set up temporary house. Slamming the door with a huff, Chase froze when *sleeping beauty* aimed the gun barrel of his forty-five directly at him.

Jack eased off and replaced the gun into his holster. Lazily he closed his eyes, muttering, "Good way to gets yer head blown off."

Chase snarled under his breath and dropped the grocery bag of evidence on top of his chest.

"What's this?"

"Open, but don't touch."

Jack grumbled, "Just tells me."

Chase impatiently explained what Ann had told him and when he finished, Jack was still lying on the couch with his eyes closed.

"So's you still think she's involved?"

"No, but I think she's in danger. She closed out the safety deposit box her and Doyle had together. And you know they'll come looking for her wanting the money and the plates."

"So assign someone to her apartment. When they try to break in, we arrest 'em."

"It's not that simple. Doyle's dead, but obviously Baker and Garcia know about the safety deposit box since the money and ID's were inside. They'll come after Ann when they find out she's closed the account and taken everything."

"And that's if Baker comes back to the States."

Chase stared at Trev just lying there without a care in the world. *How could he be so calm about this?* All of a sudden, like a bee had stung him, Chase watched Jack sit upright on the couch placing the bag on the floor.

"Chase-man, we gots us another problem."

"What?"

"If Doyle had the plates here, that means their shop's somewhere here in Minnie'ota and we don't know where they've set up."

"That ain't all, Trev. Tell me why a drug cartel like Bastide is getting himself involved in counterfeiting, and this far north? I wanna know real bad how they all know each other and why was that girl taken from Minnesota and murdered in New York."

CHAPTER ELEVEN

Ann awoke with a roaring in her ears, drenched in her own sweat and tangled in bed sheets. The nightmares continued. She was trapped inside and Chase was stalking her for a crime she didn't commit. This dream had been the first with a face.

Tumbling out of bed, her body felt depleted and she headed for the shower. She hadn't purposely left out the rest of what she uncovered yesterday, she just didn't remember to tell Chase everything. Speculating, it might not be a bad idea to have a few aces in her corner. Everything about Chase Franklin perplexed her and added to her doubts. As she rubbed a hand through her hair, sand from the beach was still engrained in her roots. They'd gone for a swim after making love in the sand. She wasn't sure what to make of the tender, exciting way he had made love to her a third time. Last night, he had benevolently devoted himself to her in a way she'd never known before. A way she couldn't describe and Ann recalled what Scott had told her—he'd never lie or cheat because he respected women. What Ann felt last night exceeded respect by leaps and bounds. She'd almost felt like a fragile piece of expensive porcelain someone might cherish and hold dear above all else.

The strange euphoria she felt, quickly changed to a vibrant anger thronging in Ann's blood when she thought of the man she had committed two years of her life with. Geoffrey was a double-dealing crook and had mastered ways to entangle her in his guilty crime. In her mind, she'd already tried and convicted Geoffrey Doyle.

Ann stepped out of the shower and dried herself off. She was going to burn some ass if it was the last thing she did on earth.

Thinking about it, she had worked ten years with Madison Baker and never saw through her. *Maybe she didn't want to see the evil.*

Ann shut her hairdryer off and stared in the mirror. The words whispered off her lips. "How did Madison and Geoffrey meet? And, you're a damn fool if you think otherwise," she announced to the mirror's reflection. Ann flipped the dryer back on and finished her hair.

Through the rest of her morning routine, Ann rehearsed what she would tell Chief Deputy Edwards. She debated whether or not to inform him of anything until she had every fact and piece of paper neatly compiled proving her own innocence. Ann groaned knowing she should have waited for him yesterday, but reasoned with herself he was out of town and she couldn't wait. In fact, she never even thought to ask when he would return. The teeth-cutting headache from her hangover had made everything irrational.

Incredible as it might have sounded to a friend listening, if she had a friend, Ann realized her and Chase's little escapade on the beach last night had dissolved the throbbing pain in her head. Dressed casually now, but comfortable for a special day, Ann went downstairs to the kitchen. Somehow she had to put last night behind her.

Angela shrieked, Ann jumped, and Angela clucked, "Good Lord, child, you scared the dickens out of me! When did you get back?"

"Last night."

"Did you find out anything?"

Ruminating through the chain of events, including their love on the beach, Ann masked inner turmoil with trained and artful poise. "Plenty," she muttered

A moment passed when Angela chided, "Well, are you going to tell me or let me try and guess, like my son does? And please, don't shock me like he did two nights ago."

Ann's ears perked up. "Shock you?"

"Yes. Just when I'm starting to accept what's happened in my home, he walks in and lays more bad news on me."

"What kind of bad news?"

"I guess I'm over the worst of it after I cried myself into hysteria the past two nights. My son came home the first time to tell me he's being transferred out of the country permanently."

Ann's insides coiled just before her blood went cold, her heart jumped to her throat. Quickly she turned away from Angela to hide how she'd been caught off guard by the news. Her heart was going to burst and she was filling with mistrust. *He used her and he wasn't any better than Geoffrey.* Ann mustered up the energy to ask, "Really?"

"Yes, really. So what did you find out?"

Ann needed a minute to regroup. Apparently, she wasn't the only one keeping secrets. She turned to face Angela while holding her coffee cup, took a deep breath and said, "Angela, this is bigger than we ever would have guessed."

"What on earth are you talking about?"

Ann shifted as she sat down and looked at the decorative ducks on a roll of paper towels extended from the wall. She refused to divulge the details and too quietly said, "I figured out why and how the Agency is receiving less than the allotted amounts we talked about the other day."

"You did? Tell me how?"

Ann looked at Angela. "Can you arrange another interview for me with Susan Bradford on Monday morning?"

"Yes, of course, I can. She's behind all of this, isn't she?"

Ann sipped her coffee while holding the cup between both hands to conceal the tremor in her fingers. Her mind still on last night fought with Angela's news a few moments ago. "She's the connection to the Agency, but you were right. Someone else very big is definitely involved."

"Who?"

Whether Ann wanted to admit it or not, she was positive now the break-in to Angela's house had been because of her. They'd already assumed she had the money and the plates and came looking for them. "Angela, I can't tell you everything. I will say this much, Chase is aware. Last night when I arrived back here, I told him what I had discovered."

In her clucking voice, Angela said, "You don't trust me!"

Ann set her coffee cup on the table. "That's not it at all. Angela, I'm the missing link in a crime I had no knowledge of. Your safety is at stake and frankly," her voice cracked, "I don't wanna deal with what Chase will do to me if anything happens to you. I should never have agreed to stay here."

"Nonsense! I invited you. You're being ridiculous."

Besides, right this instant, Ann was engrossed in fury with the way Chase had used her. She knew he'd played on her emotions in order to get her to divulge the facts on *her* case. As if she'd lost all her self-control and needed to take her vengeance out on someone, Ann shouted the words with brutal force. "Ridiculous? Angela, Mandi's dead, your house has been broken into because of me and I guarantee you, these people won't stop until they've got what they want!" She heard the tone of her voice increase. "In fact, I'm debating whether or not to take Christie off the case and send her back to the Cities just to get her away from here."

"Ann, you can't possibly be serious!"

"I'm dead serious!"

"This is absurd!"

"Angela, it's being cautious!"

"Well, what you do with Christie is up to you." Her eyes pierced, "But no one, and I mean no one, will run me out of my home!"

"What's going on, I heard my name with a lot of yelling?"

Neither woman budged and stared with icy glares at each other.

Ann took a deep breath and said, "Christie, you're going back to the Cities today. I don't need your help anymore. Report back to Chief Deputy Edwards."

"Ann, why? What've I done wrong?"

"Nothing," with a sideways glance, she added, "I don't need your assistance." Ann's heart shriveled up and died seeing the flabbergasted look paint itself across Christie's face.

"I have something for you, regardless."

"What's that?"

"Susan Bradford received a phone call from a man yesterday. She closed her door before taking the call and I decided to listen in."

"Christie!"

"Wait, she didn't know. In any event, the guy never said his name, but Bradford kept referring to him as Daniel. I remember that being one of the fake names, no one of the real names, no wait the real name replacing the fake name of Donald on the payroll. Whoever this guy was, he made sure he didn't say much on the phone. Basically, he was checking in with Bradford. When she asked him, 'why he did it', he laughed and said 'you're the one who caught the bitch red handed'."

Ann choked on her coffee and slammed the mug on the kitchen table, liquid splattered out. "Damn it, Christie! You've just put yourself in grave danger. You're going back to the Cities immediately."

The petite blonde, clad in a green, terrycloth robe sat down without the slightest drawback from Ann's outburst. Ann watched a smile part her salmon-colored lips.

"There's more."

Ann seared Christie with a piercing glaze when she reached into the pocket and waved a miniature cassette tape in front of both women.

"I recorded the conversation."

Ann's muscles tightened and her stomach knotted to the size of a baseball. The rookie's eagerness showed determination. "I need to hear it."

Christie displayed her miniature recorder stating, "No problem."

The conversation lasted all of two minutes and other than Ann recognized Daniel Garcia's voice, she felt an impossibility to prove it. They also would have a difficult time verifying who said 'why'd you do it' which Ann knew meant why did you kill Mandi.

The answer, 'you're the one who caught the bitch red handed' indicated Susan Bradford told Daniel Garcia about something Mandi Marriano knew. Therefore, Ann presumed Daniel killed Mandi. The question of the hour, Ann thought, is what did Mandi find or learn to cause her death?

"Ann, I also finished the paperwork you asked me to work on."

"Everything?" Pleading filled Christie's eyes, eagerness Ann had a hard time ignoring.

"Yes."

Ann examined Christie's child-like enthusiasm for a moment. "What'd you find out?"

"A total of five hundred thousand dollars has been paid out since January on the five salaries of the fake employees. Susan Bradford has been living on a paltry amount since she began working there. Mandi on the other hand was issued checks with a substantial raise just before Angela filed the missing police report."

"Bradford's been a bit busy. Did Mandi actually disappear before or after being given the raise?"

"Before. I've tied all the paperwork together and made individual reports of taxes and other withdrawals. Please, let me stay and finish this case with you."

"I said no!"

"Ann, why can't she stay and help?"

Ann's patience went into overtime and maintaining every ounce of diplomacy she answered. "Christie is new and neither of us has experience handling a criminal's reactions to our findings in any case let alone this one. We're paper pushers, that's it!"

"I think you're being unfair to Christie."

"Ann, I think you're being unfair to me as well. How else am I supposed to learn if not through experience."

Ann heaved out a frustrated breath. Her boss was involved and at the moment, Ann didn't know if any others within the AG's office could become implicated. Her hands were basically tied. "There's only one way I'm going to let you stay, Christie."

Both women asked in unison, "What's that?"

"Christie, under no circumstances can you go back to the

Agency unless you go with Angela. The second condition is, neither of you can let the other one out of your sight. And the third, Angela, you call Max and get a cabin for the two of you. You're not staying here at the house another minute."

Angela clucked stubbornly, "This is preposterous!"

"You both agree otherwise Christie is going back to St. Paul." Ann looked directly at Angela, "And I'll call Chase right this second and have him figure out a way to keep you in protective custody. After Mandi's murder, the break-in and what I told Chase last night, he won't think twice about saving your butt."

"That means—"

"Damn it, Angela, I know what it means!" Ann watched the two women exchange looks with each other. This second, she wasn't sure whom she was madder at and the list definitely took on epidemic growth.

"You're more stubborn than my son ever thought of being."

"I'll take that as a compliment. And I could care less what you think of me. My concern lies with your safety and not your thoughts of my personality, Angela. Now, call Max and use that magical charm of yours that you're so well known for. Quietly get a cabin for the two of you."

"Can't," she said haughtily, "he's booked through the end of July."

"Then you only have one choice left. Christie, go and pack. You're outta here. I'm calling Chase to have him figure out what to do with you, Angela."

"Ann wait," Angela pleaded, "we'll stick to each other like glue. Won't we Christie?"

Eagerly, Christie bobbed her head up and down.

Ann studied both of them not liking it at all she was going to give in to their impulsive actions. "Fine. I've got some things to take care of. I'll see you both later."

"Ann, what do you want me to do with the tape?"

"Give it to me." Ann snatched the tape and dropped it into

her briefcase. "So help me, if either one of you loses sight of the other I'll have both your hides in a sling."

In unison they both said, "We won't leave the house."

Ann left in her car headed for anywhere but near the water or Devils Point. Today she needed time to be alone which meant no Angela, Chase, Scott, Christie or anyone.

She parked her Trans Am on Bayport Road in downtown Masquerade and walked towards the little shop she saw the day of the parade. Closed that day, she'd peeked inside the window of the place called Ships N Things. The sign on the door said they would open at ten.

Ann walked along the street reflecting on the last several months. She never saw the criminal psychology behind Geoffrey. It snuck up on her and smacked her in the face. Thinking about it, Geoffrey always did play battle of wits against the experts. His motivation had been desirous of proving a theory, but more consequential to Geoffrey was the financial gain.

Madison, the perfect white-collar criminal, had power and influence in a position of trust and always saw herself as being above others. Ann should have suspected something when Madison frequently complained of tenure and salaries. Justified action and rational behavior Madison would call it.

Of all three, Ann had always been suspicious of Daniel. She was of the opinion he came from a culture of violence and had been coached into it by peers or a mentor. Somewhere he'd learned to value power, and punishment didn't deter him from the act.

Ann's cell phone rang and she hoped it was a response to the call she made last night. "Okay, thanks. I don't have access to a fax. FedEx it to the address I gave you." She knew after hanging up Geoffrey's airline was almost two million dollars in debt to the IRS. Seven months ago a million dollars of that debt was paid off and came from San Luis Potosi, Mexico.

What she hadn't figured out, was Geoffrey's connection to Mexico. The background check she'd requested on him would take until Monday. He'd told her he had no family. An only child, his parents died in a car accident when he was eight. Another stupid mistake she made due to her selfish greed and false love. Ann assumed the state became his guardian. The entire scenario was more proof of her gluttonous need to use Geoffrey in locating her father. He'd been supportive of her compulsion and even flew to other places when she discovered new leads. All in all every single lead had proved futile. Ann wondered more than ever why Geoffrey had been excessive with his devotion to her.

Glancing at her watch it was almost ten and Ann turned around walking back toward Ships N Things. Today was her thirtieth birthday and maybe she'd just buy the blown glass ship if the price weren't too outrageous.

Bells jangled on the door as Ann stepped inside. The quaint shop contained artwork of ships, bottled ships, plates, books, pillows, candles with ships and tons of replica boats and sailboats. The isles went on with every imaginable trinket displaying it all. Ann looked at, picked up and held the fragile blown glass replicas and couldn't decide between two until her eye caught the painting.

She'd never seen anything like it. It was simply a dark stormy day. The colors mingled and merged into magnificence, Ann thought. The sea beneath the raging sky matched with a somberness hiding overhead. Incoming waves actually moved. Luminous white scumbled at the foot of the jagged wall crashing against rocks beneath the dark and dreadful-looking cliff. It was a moody, atmospheric seascape.

Oh, how she wanted this painting. The price exceeded more than two months worth of what she allowed herself to spend on frivolous things. She reasoned it's her birthday, her thirtieth birthday, she deserved it, she knew exactly where she'd put it—in her new apartment. She could charge it, but it would take five months to pay it off. Maybe if she paid half cash and charged the rest it wouldn't hurt so badly on her checkbook. But then she'd written out that check to get into the safety deposit box and was a little short of funds.

Ann left the shop agreeing to think about it. The painting reminded her of Chase and she'd instantly fallen in love with the turbulent seascape. *Fallen in love*, why had she picked those exact words? Especially when she would never lead herself into false love a second time.

As Ann walked toward her car, she'd been running away from the thoughts in her mind. The ones that burned with the memory of his kisses and touch. It was foolish ecstasy she felt when he held her and made love to her in the sand last night under a sky shattering with stars. They'd been totally drunk with each other's power. Her thoughts were idiotic yet Ann couldn't stop thinking about the tender way he had held her last night. She realized now the painting was symbolic. Chase was a life preserver in her stormy sea of life. No, she decided, she didn't need the reminder or another round of painful memories. Chase had used her for personal satisfaction and that's all there was to the indiscretion. Besides, he was leaving the country.

"Long time no see, Ann."

When she heard his voice, Ann swung around so quickly her knee snapped. "Daniel!" He'd changed some, longer hair, facial growth, hollow cheeks and Ann noticed, as he moved closer, an acrid odor about him. His fleering grin mocked her.

"We've been looking for you."

"Why's that and who's 'we'?" Ann could feel the pain as her knee began to swell.

"You know very well why I'm here."

"Do I Daniel," she spoke with bitter resentment. "Do I really know why you're here?"

"Ah, pet, you can't fool me."

Her voice turned thick with insinuation, "Look who's fooling who." She heard him hiss and carefully watched his eyes seethe over with rage.

"Where are they, Ann," and he leaned forward, "I'm warning you."

With a critical once-over, Ann hissed, "Warn me? Let me warn you. I'm gonna bring you all down!"

He'd throttled forward so fast Ann couldn't move in time before Daniel's hand grabbed her throat and squeezed.

"Don't you ever threaten me, bitch."

Though the air was being trapped in her lungs, Ann thrust a knee upward with brute force hitting Daniel in jewel town. Immediately, his grip loosened. She grabbed him at the shoulders, set her foot in place and dropped him to the ground thrusting her soar knee into his chest. She hammered out her own threat. "Don't you *ever* touch me again!"

"Ustedes perrado!"

Daniel's vein pulsed in his temple and Ann ignored the fact he'd called her a bitch for the second time. Today she absolutely owned the right to be a bitch. "And tell Godefredo, he's going down with both you and Baker."

Her day had reached a high when Daniel's beady little eyes bulged right out of the sockets.

"Miss Longworth, everything okay, here?"

Ann removed her knee from Daniel's chest and stood up. She already felt increased swelling and knew the thrust she gave Daniel in his crotch wasn't the smartest of moves she'd ever made. "Chief Casimir, how nice to see you again. Yes, everything is fine."

"This man giving you any trouble?"

Ann suppressed a disgusting laugh when she peered at Daniel lying on the ground. "Not anymore, he isn't." Daniel cautiously picked himself up, sniveling with rage.

"This ain't over."

"Miss Longworth—"

"Chief, please just call me Ann," she said while watching Daniel scamper away considering the injury she'd just rendered him.

"Who was that? I was cruising the area and saw him go for your throat."

Then he probably saw what she did to Daniel, too. "Someone from my past."

Caz had already heard from Scott how Ann could take care of

herself. He didn't believe it of such a pretty little thing until he
saw it for himself. "Looked like an angry someone from your past."

She'd kept one eye on Daniel as he attempted to rush toward
a car and finally drove away from the area. "Not to worry, Chief."
Ann turned and faced Chief Casimir. There was a sparkle replacing
the purple tint in his eyes. Sweat rolled off his balding head and
trickled down his forehead from the reigning heat and humidity.
"Do you have any new leads on the break-in to Angela's house?"

"Nothing yet," he said pulling a white handkerchief out and
wiping his face.

"But you'll let us know, won't you?"

"Of course. Ann, just be careful. Chase has filled me in about
your role and these people are serious. I'll be seeing you around."

He'd left her standing with her mouth open. Chase was one
FBI man who went against everything they stood for. He'd been
talking to everyone, and accusing her. Ann realized now the chances
Chase Franklin believed her last night had all been fabricated so he
could get what he wanted.

CHAPTER TWELVE

Chase was so damn mad he could've spit tacks. He'd run into Caz who told him everything, all the way from that little weasel choking her, to Ann flipping Garcia on his ass. And it all happened while he was inside Ships N Things. He slugged his fist into the cabin's timbered wall and only his heart felt the torment.

Chase fell to the couch and lighted up a cigarette. He sat there staring nowhere and remembering. Last night with her had been too easy, so simple, and so extraordinary. Why did it feel all-out complex and obscure? Because, he thought, those old hopes taunted him worse than any fear. She'd cheated and deceived him into assuming he was inadequate, unworthy of her love. The brutal ache in his heart stopped him cold. Ann hadn't caused it. Cindy did and maybe his mother, as well.

His mingled thoughts were interrupted when Jack entered the cabin. This time it was Mickey D's as Jack called McDonalds. Yesterday, it was White Nasties and Chase swore White Castle was *thee* worst hamburger joint in the country. What next? Trev was gonna blow up from all the junk food he inhaled. When he did, lard would pour like rain from the damn sky. Chase ground the words out between his teeth. "Garcia's in town."

"How's you know that?"

Chase watched Jack suck in the wad of grease as juice slurped out of the corners of his mouth. The only time his black eyes glazed over was when he ate, which seemed to be all the time. "Caz saw him over on Bayport Road giving due consideration to Ann. I told you he'd come looking for her."

"Never doubted it for a minute."

Imitating Jack's words, Chase sneered, "Never doubted it for a minute."

"You's smi'en with her."

"No I'm not, you burger-inhaling moron! What's Garcia gonna do when he figures out she doesn't have the plates or the money?"

"Secret's Service boyz will be here tonight. Revenue boyz said they'll stands back until he's in custody. They's already staking their claim on Garcia."

"Don't forget DFA. In fact, why don't we invite the President and just have one big brawl over who gets the dirty bastard."

"Gots to find the party house first."

Chase glared at his partner fully aware they were going to go head to head. An abnormal shortage of patience possessed him and he'd been on edge ever since last night. "You heard anymore about Baker?

Chase watched Jack crush his sack, toss it over his shoulder into a waiting garbage can, guzzle his pop and belch. "Geezus, Jack!

"Larry called. I's cleared it with the boss and I'm going to Mexico. Seems they's gots some movement down there with Baker and Bastide."

"When you leavin'?"

"T'nights."

"You find out where Garcia was born or came from?"

"Accordin' to his birth certificate, New York, but his mama was from Mexico. It weren't til he joined the Air Force that's when he met Doyle. They's discharged together and moved here to start the airline bizness."

"Why here? Why Minnesota?"

"Dunno."

"I'll stay on Garcia and Bradford. There's something about Bradford I don't trust. I've got Caz running checks on her. Caz also said Garcia speaks Spanish with an accent."

Jack looked up. "You's loves sending me on wild goose chases, don't you."

"Since you're going to San Luis, figured you can do some digging. Besides you wouldn't be chasing if you thought it was bullshit."

"You tell yer mother about's the transfer, yet?"

"Yeah, I told her."

"How'd she take it?"

"As well as could be expected."

"Chase-man, you's gots to talk to her before we go over. It's not her fault your dad died. You can't keep letting it eat you alive inside. You's can't keep this distance between you. Yer all each of you's has."

His own eyes glazed over and Chase just stared past Jack.

"Chase-man, I've told you before our mother's might not always like us, but they'll always love us."

Chase went to the fridge for a beer. He stared at the cans like he had a choice. Michelob or Michelob. Finally, grabbing one, he popped the top and lit a cigarette. Jack just didn't understand, Chase had decided a long time ago. The man came from a family of seven kids with a mother who doted on every one of them like flies on shit. The man's phone bill had to be thousands the way he called each of them every month. Chase couldn't imagine what the phone bills would look like from overseas. "I'll talk to her," he muttered.

"So's what'd the dame in red want the other day."

Chase collapsed onto the couch having second thoughts about last night. "Who?"

Jack grinned and said, "Cindy."

"Same as always."

"You's told her to take a flying leap, didn't you?"

Chase guzzled his beer, nodded and watched Jack consume the second burger and fries.

"Good thing." He stood and belched again. "Cuz I's still thinks your smi'en with the little rag muffin. I's outta here."

"It is not smi'in, you idiot! It's smit-ten!" He threw his empty beer can at Jack as the door closed, and yelled, "I am not!"

He was not smitten with her. She'd only cause more trouble for him and he was going to Japan, damn it. He *was* going. The transfer papers came from John a couple of days ago.

He strapped on his forty-five and headed to the house. He had to see her, to tell her what a damn fool she'd been for confronting Garcia. Didn't she know better? After he'd told her.

***

Ann returned to Angela's house. Upon stepping inside she flinched and recoiled with horror. The pool of blood inside the foyer was ghastly and Christie lay in the middle of it. Angela was on the floor at the base of the staircase.

Peering about wild-eyed everything had been destroyed. Ann checked for pulses and Angela was unconscious but breathing. She ran to the kitchen to dial nine-one-one.

"Damn it, Christie" Ann yelled, "you're not gonna die on me!"

She'd grabbed towels from the kitchen and returned staring at Christie's heaving chest. Momentarily, Ann was stunned as foamy blood and air sprayed from her chest with each expiration. She knelt and packed the red-soaked hole. The ultimate clock was ticking and the towels were instantly saturated with the vital fluid of life.

Ann heard the wail of sirens, but didn't know what else to do. She'd warned them, she'd ordered, she'd even become angry and yelled, but they wouldn't listen to her. All she could do was keep pressure on the wound, what else? She didn't know.

She glanced up at Angela's feeble body lying limp at the bottom of the stairs.

The paramedics arrived and Ann heard one say, "We need another rig, code three."

She watched one paramedic briefly check Angela and return to help his partner who'd already placed an oxygen mask on Christie's face.

"No breathing sounds, Charlie. Christ! She's got a sucking

chest wound. Pneumothorax. What happened here, lady?" All they could do was pack and go.

Ann didn't speak as two more paramedics entered the house followed by the police. She watched Charlie pack and ready Christie to transport.

Dazed, Ann followed the paramedics, "I'm going with," and Ann climbed into the back of the ambulance. She held Christie's hand listening to the screaming siren over her head while she stared at the oxygen mask covering Christie's small features. Her blond hair had been stained with red blood. The other paramedic, she didn't hear his name, induced life-saving drugs into an IV port he'd hooked to Christie's left arm. He pumped up a blood pressure cuff on her other arm with his right hand while feeling for her pulse with his left.

Ann's muscles flinched when she heard him yell, "Step it up, BP eighty by palp. Got her on full oxygen and I'm losing her!"

She watched him remove equipment with the words, 'Life Pack 12' from a compartment. He applied gadgets to Christie's chest and yelled, "Systolic sixty, defibbing. Back away, Lady."

Ann moved. What did that mean? Moments later the siren stopped. Panic percolated in Ann's blood. *Isn't that what they did when someone died, stopped the siren? Or, was that just on TV? No, Christie can't be dead!*

The rig slammed to a screeching halt and Ann slid off the seat. The back door swung open and the driver grabbed the back of the gurney pulling as ER staff rushed out of the emergency room doors. Wheeling the gurney, the pneumatic doors flew open.

Ann jumped out of the diesel ambulance following and heard one of the ER staff say, "STAB room one, stat," and Christie was swept away.

The sign above the double doors where they wheeled Christie, read *Stabilization Room*. All Ann could do now was wait.

Not five minutes had passed when the pneumatic doors at the ER entrance swung open again. Ann watched with numbed horror as EMS brought in Angela, and Chase followed. His brows were drawn together and Ann observed his flaring nostrils. She heard the curses cut through his strangled breath as he stormed through the ER entrance toward her.

Chase marched over, grabbed Ann by the wrist and dragged her outside of the emergency room.

His dark eyes flashed with warning. "Chase! What are you doing?"

"You deceptive little liar!"

He'd ground the words out between his teeth. The cold, exactness of his tone was earth-shattering. "Chase . . ." His blackened eyes glaring down at her told her he was more powerful than she was.

"I knew you were keeping something from me. But, do you tell me? No you continue to lie to me! I have to learn from my dying mother that you're withholding information in a federal case! Allow me to make it crystal clear, you've committed a felony! And you've got exactly ten seconds to tell me where that tape is or you're under arrest!"

Ann's patience with Chase had finally been tried. "No! You self-centered, manipulating jackass! You want that tape? You can just get yourself a fricking search warrant. You can't arrest me because I haven't done anything wrong!"

He let go of her wrist like she was on fire and he'd been burned. She'd crossed her arms securely in front of her and met his glare.

"You don't know where the tape is?"

Ann hesitated slightly. "I didn't say that."

Too late, he thought. The first thing they teach at the academy is the slightest hesitation means they're lying. And she was lying through those pretty little lips of hers. He had other ways of getting around this. "Did you listen to the tape."

"Yes."

He whipped out a pair of cuffs from behind his back and shackled them to Ann's wrists. "You heard the tape, that's withholding evidence in a federal case."

"Chase! Christie is dying in there and I'm not leaving this

hospital!"

"So's my mother and you're under arrest."

"You can't arrest me!"

"Bet me!" he growled. "You don't have any choice in the matter!"

Ann gasped then choked on all of his words. His danger-coated eyes warned her again. "All right!" she screamed, "all right, I'll tell you where the tape is."

He stopped and waited.

"It's in my briefcase in the trunk of my car.

"The keys?"

Though cuffed, Ann dug around in her purse and handed her keys to him after removing them.

Chase roughly removed the handcuffs then swiped her keys away from her. "Anything else you're keeping a secret from the FBI?"

Ann met the nasty flicker in his eyes with her own evil stare. "No, Agent Franklin, I think you've personally taken advantage of everyone and everything. You've made it perfectly clear what your real motives are."

Chase backed away from her. She intentionally tried to hurt him and it had worked. She'd thrust her words at him like shoving a knife into his gut, then twisted it for extra measure. Positive she wasn't telling him everything, he announced, "I warned you once. So help me God, if my mother dies or I find out you're keeping anything else from me, it will be a cold day in hell before you say daylight again."

As soon as he stopped talking, his heaving chest subsided. The color in his eyes had become void, unoccupied, gray and lifeless. Ann realized she had emptied his eyes of any life and drained him of all emotion. It was the same look she saw the first day she met him. "Chase, I'm sorry."

"I don't give a tinkers damn anymore what you are." He turned on his heel and stomped back inside the ER.

CHAPTER THIRTEEN

Laid back in a chair inside the ER waiting room with his head against the wall, his arms and ankles were crossed and his eyes were closed. Chase didn't have to look. He could feel Annie's presence sitting on the other side of the room. The only picture he saw in his mind was Mandi Marriano and twenty-seven stab wounds. When he walked in on the pool of blood inside the foyer of his mother's house, he went bizerk. He really believed it was Ann's blood. His mother was lying there unconscious and he was worried . . . no scared is what he remembered feeling. So scared his hands shook and his mouth went dry. He'd never been so scared in his entire life. He felt his brow drip with wetness and his heart, he thought for sure, had gone into cardiac arrest.

When EMS brought his mother to life they told him . . . told him it was Christie, *not Ann*, and Ann had gone to the hospital in the ambulance with Christie. His brain flooded over with a mixture of relief and guilt. Enroute to the hospital is when everything changed to madness. Chase knew terror had caused it. He was actually frightened by the belief Ann had been taken from him. His mother told him they'd just learned of the tape this morning. Why had he taken out his panic on her? Would Annie *ever* forgive him?

Red lines streaked her fingers from dry blood. The coloring blended with the wrenching she was doing to them. How could Chase just sit there sleeping when Angela and Christie were dying? Ann never felt this alone in her entire life as she felt just now. She'd never forget the hurt flashing in his eyes because he believed she lied to him. She did lie to him and he doesn't even know the worst of it.

Her guilt would haunt her forever. She looked down and

Christie's blood had dried on her hands and shirt. If she hadn't given in, both Christie and Angela would still be full of life. If she had only insisted Christie go home. If she had only stayed home this morning it would have been her, not Christie and Angela lying in the STAB room surrendering their lives. At the same moment she saw the doctor come out of *that* room, Scott ran into the ER.

Ann gaped at the doctor's eyes. They were expressionless and she knew.

"Annie!"

She heard Scott, but she couldn't make her muscles move. The doctor walked toward her. God, what was that smell? It was mixed with rubbing alcohol and permeated the air. A phone rang at the nurse's station and Ann heard a woman laugh. The blue on the doctor's chest had flecks of Christie's blood and she could smell death on him as he approached.

"Ms. Longworth?"

Somehow she managed to stand and felt Scott holding her arm. Her eyes transfixed with dread.

"I'm sorry."

Ann swallowed hard biting down on her bottom lip. Deep sobs racked inside of her and tears blinded her eyes. She choked, then screamed, "Nooooo!" Then, Ann broke down crying as her body wracked with convulsions of grief and squeezed on her heart. It was the first time in her life she'd ever shed tears.

"Annie . . ." Scott grabbed her before she collapsed. He held her in his arms rocking her as her hands clung tightly to his shirt. She sobbed uncontrollably into his chest.

Chase had opened his eyes when he heard the doctor, then Scott enter the waiting room. The words struck him like an explosive device being detonated, but not as hard as seeing Annie's misery. Spasms of grief and guilt clawed at his insides when he heard her cry 'it's all my fault'. All he could do was silently thank God she hadn't been there when it happened.

A second doctor appeared to tell him his mother was resting

comfortably. She had a concussion and they'd be keeping her at least twenty-four hours to do a cat-scan and for observation. There was a small laceration to the scalp.

"Can I see her?"

"Just as soon as we get her upstairs."

He saw Scott wave him over, but Chase hesitated. He felt an utter loss of hope and futility. There was no solution to the defeat consuming him. All Chase could do was try to think of happier times spent with his father and he failed at that, too. There was no end to the emotion of what had occurred and he knew Ann wasn't to blame for the burden of his guilt, nor was she responsible for the loss of life.

***

Clearly the dark, penetrating look in his eyes said he wasn't going to take any crap. "Chase, its Sunday, let's go fishing."

Chase reluctantly gave in to Scotty and they packed sandwiches, beer, fishing gear and were underway in the twenty-five-footer. The outboard motor hummed as Scotty steered the runabout to the middle of Crypt Lake, shut the motor off and dropped anchor.

The hooks baited and lines cast in the water, Chase sat back and propped his feet on the starboard side. The sun glared off the brightwork and gulls screeched overhead happily diving into the water to catch their lunch. *The gulls didn't know another murder had gone down.* To block the sun, Chase put on his navy blue, baseball cap with the white FBI emblem. Normally, he never advertised his place of employment, but it was the only cap he could find. Out here it didn't matter anyway, he and Scotty were alone.

Scott handed him a beer and they clanked the bottle tops together, toasting with a silent nod. Scott knew the meaning of this excursion.

Remnants of Chase's past were inundating his mind. He really missed days like today with his dad. They'd come out here in the middle of nowhere, with no people, no sounds except water slapping the side of the boat and the gulls screeching. It was here his dad taught him how to bait a hook, not to cheat on a woman, or lie to his mother, gave him his first taste of beer, told him never have regrets, and be the best he could. They talked about his grades, baseball and football, the Twins and the Vikings, had arguments and made bets. He'd listened to preaching and praising in a boat similar to this one. He'd learned how to budget, and how to spend, to hate shopping with women, and his ABC's. He grinned remembering his first kiss, hell, he mused his dad even told him about sex that time. Those talks had shaped his life. Unfortunately, his dad never taught him how to mend or deal with a shattered heart. This one wasn't because of Cindy. It really was his own fault and Ann was at the center of his pain.

Yesterday afternoon took him by surprise. The anger she had induced in him led to his outburst. It began out of . . . shit, he didn't even know anymore. All he knew right now was he couldn't forget the way Ann had responded to him the night before last. The feeling he had—they both needed each other—was playing havoc with his mind. Then when Caz told him about Garcia and he walked in and saw the blood, his insides shriveled up and died instantly. Once again, she caught him off guard and the little spitfire's irresistible challenges drove him to do all of what he did. He'd discovered somewhere between the sandy beach and the emergency room he was in love with her. He wanted her more than anything he'd ever longed for. What he needed, was for her to forgive him.

He was still livid with her since he'd talked to Caz. His seek and destroy tactics at the hospital were a result of his terror. Once again, she seriously lacerated him with her words. The more he thought about it, the more he knew she was right. He *was* a self-centered, manipulating jackass. He'd been confused since she pranced into his life. Within a few weeks, she'd completely jumbled everything into massive disarray of order. He couldn't be falling in

love with her, he just couldn't. He was being transferred out of the
country. He glanced at Scott.

"Feelin' better?"

He shrugged his shoulders. "Scotty, there's somethin' I need
to know."

"W'as that."

"Has Max ever mentioned having another sister besides your
mom?"

"This *is* interesting."

Scott's eyes were hidden under his Foster Grant sunglasses as
he re-cast his line. "What's interesting?"

"First Ann, then Max, now you. Sure wish one of you would
tell me what the hell it is you all know."

"In the process of my investigation—"

Scott removed his sunglasses veering sharply to gape at Chase.
"You don't honestly believe Ann's criminally involved in your case?"

He shook his head. "I learned Ann's mother was Letitia Phelps.
Her obituary said preceded in death by sister, Annaleigh Rose
Phelps."

Scott sat upright from the bolted chair in the runabout.

"What's confusing, is Letitia's death was six years after you and
I were born. She wasn't married, but only your mom is listed as a
survivor in the obituary."

"Fish ain't bitin', lets go ask Uncle Max. I wanna know more
about this right now."

They reeled in the lines, raised the anchor and headed back to
the docks at Devil's Point. They found Max in a cabin and
confronted him.

"Oh, God, I knew it, the day I heard her. I just knew it."

Chase asked, "Knew what, Max?"

"Letty *is* my sister. She was twenty-six, almost twenty-seven
when she ran away from here."

Chase watched Max's gray eyes pale considerably like he was
going back thirty years. The lines in his face became long and
drawn out. "Max, what happened?"

"It was summer. Letitia was working here at the resort when that . . . that s-o-b showed up. Letty was bewitched with him, taken with his smooth and charming way. I didn't trust him. I knew he was no good for my baby sister. He was a leach, mooching off of everyone. He drank too much and bragged about not working, even said 'why not take advantage of something if it's standing right in front of you'. I happened in on them," Max stopped and slid a hand through his thick, gray hair. "One of the cabins she'd been cleaning . . . she and I . . . we had a big argument that night. Quarreled and bickered for a long time. I kicked him out of the resort, but he just got a room over at the Lazy Inn. When I did that, it only pushed Letty further away from me."

"Did Mom know what had happened?"

Max glanced at Scott. "Yes, your mother knew. She understood, but told me it wasn't any of my business what Letty did. Said Letty was gonna do what she wanted to anyway. God, how Letty loved and worshipped your mother. They were like two peas in a pod whispering all the time, you know talkin' about girly things. Your mom did everything with Letty. Scott, you didn't know it, but I'm the one who broke your mom's heart. I made Letty run away and neither of us ever saw our sister after that."

Max stood up and walked towards a window. Chase wondered if Max knew Letty had died.

"I'd forgotten his name, but something about Ann triggered stuff. Think it was the eyes, first. They're identical to your mother's, Scott. But that day I heard her yell at Chase, 'call me Ann', was when I knew. It was the voice. She has her mother's voice. I used to tease your Aunt Letitia and she'd yell at me the same way. Anyway, during our quarrel that night, some things were said between us."

Chase had seen the similarity in Ann's eyes as well. He continued watching as Max's shoulders drooped where he stood in front of the cabin window. Somehow Max looked as if he'd aged another ten years upon hearing the information.

"I said words I've never had a chance to apologize for. The next

day, Letty ran away from home—with *him*. Haven't seen her since."
Max turned and looked at Scott and Chase. "You boys were too
young to remember and six years later I lost my other sister. I don't
believe your mom ever forgave me for making Letty runaway, but
neither of us knew Letty was pregnant."

"Uncle Max, Mom was never angry with you."

"She got over it some, but deep down I know it hurt her. She
loved Letty as much as Letty loved her. Scotty, don't misunder-
stand, I love you as if you were my own. But in some ways the only
way I could earn your mother's forgiveness for what I'd done was
to make sure you turned out the fine young man you are."

Chase had been silent and said, "Max, I'm really sorry."

"It's not your fault, Chase. In some ways I couldn't believe, no
I didn't want to believe Letty was pregnant. Do you know what
happened to Letty, where he . . ."

Max couldn't finish and it tore Chase apart. "You sure you
wanna hear this, Max?" His head drooped simultaneously with his
shoulders and slowly he bobbed his head up and down.

"It's not pleasant."

"I have to know. Maybe I can close that chapter of my life."

Chase exhaled knowing it would hurt Max more. "You're right.
Harlan Longworth was a drunk. Staggered into the street one day
in Topeka, Kansas and was hit by car." He waited momentarily.
"That was a couple of years after Ann had been born. Her mother,"
pausing, he said, "Letty, died from complications during Ann's
birth on July 10, 1960. She named her daughter Annarose Leigh
Longworth."

Max choked and turned away. "What happened to Ann after
that?"

He'd never tell Max Ann had had a difficult time in six foster
homes. "She was placed in foster care after her birth. Her father
bailed from the relationship before she was born."

Almost wishing he hadn't started this, Chase had to continue.
"Max, Ann's done an extremely fine job taking care of herself. She
worked two jobs putting herself through college, has a Master's in

criminology and Bachelor's in accounting and graduated with honors. She's worked for the State for ten years and has received outstanding achievement awards. She's turned out to be a remarkable human being." Chase almost thought he was trying to convince himself of what an exceptional person Ann Longworth had become under the circumstances.

"She never got what everyone needs . . . deserves. The most important thing in a young person's life is parents and a family. She never had anyone to love her and it's all my fault. Where is she? I have to talk to her."

"At the hospital with my mother."

Max left, skulking out of the cabin like a kicked dog.

CHAPTER FOURTEEN

Ann opened her eyes and moved with slow and deliberate actions from the painful kink in her neck. Sleeping only parts of the night in a hospital chair, she waited and watched Angela. Now late Sunday afternoon, she had been dozing on and off and never left the hospital. The doctor came in once and told her Angela would be fine after ample rest.

The *other doctor* had allowed her to see Christie afterward and she couldn't remove the image of Christie's lifeless body from her mind. Scott had gone with her and stayed by her side until they let her into Angela's room. Someone had helped her wash up. Chief Casimir came and took her statement at some point and told her he would notify Christie's relatives and the State. She'd been sitting here ever since and only knew day had turned into night and daylight had returned.

She'd tried to rest on and off but the difficulty sleeping came from the reoccurring nightmares. Chase wasn't running after her to arrest her. *He was running away from her.* The dream was distorted, so real, probably because of the last thing he said to her as he walked away yesterday. The unforgiving look in his brown eyes told her she'd screwed up badly. At this moment, Ann couldn't determine if her achy head and exhausted body were from lack of sleep, a result of what happened to Christie, or the way she'd lied to Chase.

Pulling her knees up to her chest and hugging them, Ann's life continued to be shattered disappointments and painful memories. His name hung on the edges of her mind and she would try to remember the feeling of satisfaction Chase had left with her, instead of the hurtful way they'd left each other. The uncompromising damage was done with poisonous words tossed carelessly in the heat of the moment. With her mind made up, every piece of paper in her investigation would be turned over to Chase through Angela and she would return to the Cities.

Ann stood up and walked over to the bed. Angela slept and Ann took her hand, squeezing it, hoping and praying Angela would open her eyes.

The hospital room door opened and she saw white out of the corner of her eye. Assuming it was another nurse, Ann didn't bother to look up.

"Ann."

Turning, she saw his blue eyes. Ann let out a scream and the next thing she knew she'd been hit in the head with a blunt instrument. She felt herself falling and everything in the room spun with vibrant color. The pain in her head was sharp and throbbed harder as she met the hard floor with a thump. She attempted to raise herself, but the room continued spinning. Prior to her eyes closing, she saw a second person standing over her. Panic flowed through her veins as she fought to keep her eyes open. She couldn't make out the second human form. Her eyes wouldn't open and the voices sounded cold, and far away. Her efforts to scream were futile as a cloth was shoved into her mouth trapping the air inside her lungs.

The savagely, muffled voices echoed in her ears. She felt her dead weight rising and heard his gruff voice swear. Seconds later, body heat made contact with her exposed skin before she was dropped onto soft cushions and covered. Feeling movement, and what felt like forever, she was later lifted a second time and dropped into something hard. Horror swam through her as she attempted to defy death. The nightmare had come to life and *they* had finally caught her. She believed there was no one who knew the secret she had kept, or anyone who cared.

Ann struggled to open her lids as a humming sound drummed in her head. The noise became louder and sounded like rear-end wheels of a vehicle. Her hands were bound behind her back in the cramped space and prevented her from moving any part of her body. Her heart rate increased rapidly, her throat maintained a repetitive throb and pain pulverized the back of her head. A moist substance trickled down the back of her neck. Stark and vivid fear consumed her as the humming increased in volume. Her mind spun rapidly on a merry-go-round and the last thing she remembered was sucking in her last strangled breath.

***

Max opened the hospital room door slowly, unsure of what he would say to Ann. A female nurse was attempting to hold Angela down in bed. She was swinging her arms and yelling she *had* to talk to Chase and the police.

Max scurried over to assist the nurse. "Angie, calm down. What's wrong?"

She blinked and stared at him. Her voice rose frantically in agitation. "Max, call Chase and the police. Ann's been kidnapped!"

Unconsciously, his pupils widened. "What? What're you talking about?"

"Max just call Chase, please," Angela started to cry and begged him, "please, Max, call them."

Another nurse had entered the room and gave Angela a shot. Within minutes she was sleeping peacefully, undisturbed.

***

Garcia swung the inside door open of his temporary dwelling and stepped inside. The muggy summer heat had grown unbearable. Without circulation of air or any type of cooling system, Garcia's anger elevated. He longed for an air-conditioned room with a clean bed instead of the soil-stained mattress lying on the floor at the back of the camper-type trailer. Years ago a flattop metal grill and oven had sat in the same spot evident by the gigantic three-pronged outlet and overhead air vent. There were no walls to separate the rooms. Old metal cupboards with doors removed, lined the external wall. An aluminum tub-size sink still remained, but lacked running water and Garcia hissed out offensive language in Spanish. He didn't even have drinking water.

Garcia ambled through the wood and stone tunnel where the temperature seemed several degrees cooler. He opened the second door leading into the attached structure. Stepping inside the enormous room, tile cracked and missing fragments, covered the floor. A stage sat at the far end opposite the tunnel door and wouldn't serve their needs.

It had been nothing but a fluke when Godefredo found this location. And at the very most, Baker had been pleased with Godefredo upon his discovery. The condemned building constructed of wood planks, logs and stone sat on the water's edge north away from the activity at the resorts. The property proved extremely convenient for flying the shipment out with a seaplane.

Upon his own arrival in Masquerade, Garcia had watched the place making sure no one went near it, or used it. He'd also been keeping an eye on Ann since her arrival, following her wherever she went. He'd almost shit his pants the day he saw Ann walking along the shoreline toward the building. If it hadn't been for the storm, she may have proceeded further. In the end, he actually couldn't believe the tornado that day hadn't destroyed the place.

He and Susan quickly started preparation to progress with counterfeiting of hundred dollar bills. *At least they still possessed those plates.* Hundred's would be harder to pass than twenty's, but he refused to be blamed for the stupid mistake? Hell no, he wouldn't take responsibility.

After Saturday morning, Garcia had notified Godefredo immediately, telling him Longworth was onto them and threatening. Godefredo returned to St. Paul from San Luis Potosi and blew up learning the safety deposit box had been closed. In fact, he decided the time had come to heat things up a bit. Garcia argued it might cause trouble they didn't need and could only imagine how Godefredo planned to follow through.

With malicious thoughts, Garcia smirked, confident their lucrative business would pay off. They were all going to turn a tidy little profit this time. The law would never find any of them here in this forsaken humidity.

His pending dilemma sprouted additional rage. Baker nagged him daily to find where Ann had hidden the cash and the twenty-dollar plates they knew she'd taken from the safety deposit box. Baker's reckless course of action always denounced him. No doubt *those* plates posed problems if in the wrong hands, but it wasn't his fault. Yes indeed he knew the funny money they'd stashed inside the box at the bank worth something and Ann had it and the ID's. She'd gotten lucky figuring out the whole shebang and his scare tactics, like his threats, hadn't work. He'd broken into the old lady's house on the Fourth, the first time, out of restlessness. He didn't have enough time to steal anything, let alone look for their possessions because of the interruption by the bitch's son.

Yesterday when they broke into the house, he and Susan never expected that blonde from the temp agency, or the old lady to be there. He'd only left Ann a short time earlier with the *copper* and debated whether she had been foolish enough to inform the locals. He and Susan were arguing about it when the old lady appeared. At the moment the chaos began, the blonde emerged. Both he and Susan understood for the first time Ann had planted the blonde as an undercover investigator and they were being set up.

Panicky with finding *both* women in the home at the time, Garcia slugged the old broad with the butt end of his gun, knocking her to the floor. He remembered Susan's wicked laugh, only because it reminded him of Madison. In that split second, his rage escalated and he pulled out his knife stabbing the blonde in the chest. He'd heard the old lady had survived and he should have stabbed her instead.

They tore the house apart looking for the counterfeit money Ann had stolen from them. Time had been on their side this time, but they found nothing.

Daniel sucked in a deep breath through his teeth and walked through the room inspecting the machines. Soon this operation would be ready for the gray market and he saw nothing wrong with their opportunity to make a fast buck. After all, they really hadn't purchased anything without paying for it. And it was irrelevant how they came by the funds.

The more he thought about the missing currency Ann had, the more his blood boiled. It was *their* money she took and had been set aside to cover expenses and pay the help he flew up here from Mexico. They were foreigners and the three of them agreed the Mexican's wouldn't know the difference between real and funny stuff.

The vein in his neck pulsed and swelled up dangerously like a growth of cancer. Baker and her constant bitching provoked a majority of his petulant behavior. When she called, he'd felt her wicked, cat-like eyes boring a hole into him as though she were standing right in front of him. Instead, she screamed bloody curses at him through the fucking phone. She'd threatened one to many times about locating the fucking paper from the safety deposit box and one day he might just have to give her carving lessons also. He didn't care whether she was the *biggie* and had done the pencil whipping. Falsifying records in white-collar crime was part of the job.

Besides, he'd made the arrangements to fly the *accordion management* they needed from Mexico to Minnesota so they could begin the printing. They still had the paper Madison withheld from the orphanage and frankly he didn't understand the uproar and why everyone had a wild hair up their ass.

One thing did remain clear. Baker wasn't at the top though she'd made a point of excluding him from any discussion of the ongoing dealings. Garcia knew she controlled everything from day one up to a point, even Godefredo, and he didn't know why. He also didn't know how Baker had been capable of changing figures through government bureaucracy. He didn't know if the fake money was being used to replace the stolen—he didn't even know how the plates were being made. He only handled transportation and bloodshed and now printing. He was the dirty mark so they could remain good and pure. And if not for a reasonable payoff, Garcia would tell them both to go fuck themselves.

His thoughts veered to Susan Bradford. The day she walked into her own office and saw her secretary standing over the desk holding the hundred thousand dollars and the plates in her hands became d-day and all hell broke loose. Bradford was as barbarian as Baker. She went nuts, a lot like Godefredo did occasionally and she clubbed the girl in the head with a stapler is what he thought she told him. Like he's their solution to everything, she called and *ordered* him to get on the horn to Baker. The girl wasn't dead when they arrived in New York on one of his Cessna's and they kept her tied up in that apartment for a long time.

Garcia didn't mind the gore, but customarily he never did it in front of anyone. No witnesses, no conviction remained his philosophy. Since the day Marriano threatened to expose them, they were each starting to get sloppy in their work and trying to blame the other for the mistakes. Aside from Baker mandating that girl's fate, the stupid bitch wanted to watch the ugliness.

Garcia saw something in Baker's eyes that day. Those witch eyes lit up like lightening during a storm. She yanked the knife out of his hand after he'd already done the job and took on a demon's obsession. When they heard the wailing sirens, both fled. Later, Baker screamed and blamed him because the money Marriano had discovered had been left behind in a rush to vacate the building.

Garcia walked around the room. He only had a couple more things to resolve before the printers were ready. He'd stashed the immigrants in the abandoned house and would move them here to do the work tonight.

Garcia heard the door of the trailer open followed by Godefredo's bellowing voice.

"Garcia, get your ass out of bed!"

Daniel walked back into the trailer and saw him standing in the room with Baker. "What the hell's she doing here?"

"Come on, we've got work to do," he ordered.

Garcia looked at Baker not knowing if he hated her feline eyes more or less than he despised her. "What's going on?"

"Never mind that. I've got a surprise in the trunk. We need to move her now!"

"Her?"

Flashing his familiar grin, he said, "Yes, her."

Garcia followed Godefredo and Madison out the door. They drove south to an old run down house approximately a mile off the highway.

Upon exiting the car, Godefredo opened the trunk.

Assuming she was just unconscious, Garcia stared at Ann's crumpled body inside.

"Get her out of there and move her into the basement."

CHAPTER FIFTEEN

After his and Scott's chat with Max earlier, Chase had received the call he'd been waiting for. Since this was the first moment he'd had to relax, he sat in a recliner inside the cabin thoroughly pleased with the break in his case. Following the second break-in to his mother's house and listening with Caz to the tape Chase had confiscated from Ann, he set out to hunt down Garcia and Bradford. The Chief's patrolmen had spotted Garcia after being instructed not to approach or apprehend, just contact him immediately, which they did.

They observed Garcia at the Kozy Kafé and when Chase arrived, he stayed back waiting and watching. Garcia led him to the old, run down dance hall. Once Garcia entered the trailer, Chase snuck around the outside. All windows were boarded over, but he found a hole located on the east side facing the lake where a wooden deck had originally been attached to the building. He did a quick look-see inside and spied the printing machines set up and ready to run. He also observed more boxes of ink and parchment paper, but saw no one else inside.

Since he couldn't do anything without a search warrant, Chase returned to the cabin. All in all, the excitement of this discovery couldn't eliminate the fact a second murder had gone down. Chase inhaled deeply on his Lucky Strike and took a gulp from a beer. Part of the job was the death notification with relatives of the deceased. Every cop hated it and Caz took this one for him.

The phone ringing was a welcomed distraction from his thoughts of death and he answered hearing Trev's voice.

"Jack, we did it, I found the home base. It was right under our noses the whole time, a condemned dance hall."

"Great. My works almost done and you ain't gonna believe whats I learned."

"Tell me."

"Can't talk now, I'll see ya sometime tomorra night."

"I called John and filled 'em in. He said get the Chief to assist with a search warrant for the dance hall and he'd be notifying and sending more agents."

"Works for me, later."

Chase no more than disconnected when someone pounded on the cabin door.

He opened the door and felt his heart skip a beat seeing the same look on Scott's face he remembered from when they were twelve. "Is Max okay? I'm sorry about the way everything came out earlier today."

Scott shuffled his feet nervously stepping through the threshold. "Chase, it's not Max."

"My mom . . ." he swallowed hard, "what happened?"

"Max called me from the hospital."

Chase felt his old acquaintance with death resurface within his veins. It contained a smell you never forgot.

"Chase, not your mom. It's Ann. She's been kidnapped. They've been trying to call you." Scott watched Chase's face pale to a ghostly white. "They told me to come over and get you. Com'on, I'll drive you to the hospital."

Chase snatched up the shoulder holster containing his forty-five and grabbed his jacket. The speechless ride to the hospital seemed to take a million years. He pulled his weapon and checked it to keep his mind occupied recalling how nine millimeters were standard issued for the Bureau. Both he and Jack had tested and qualified to carry a forty-five. Chilled bleakness engulfed him— why had he thought about that—Chase distinctly recalled the graphic details of Mandi's murder. Quickly his erratic pulse became impossible to control inside his body, fully aware his own stupidity had caused the circumstances.

Scott glanced across the truck's cab. Chase's bloodless face displayed the look of an enraged killer. His raven eyes had filled with icy contempt. Grief overtook the ashen stain and his broad shoulders heaved with his irregular breathing.

Scott slowed the Bronco nearing the hospital entrance and Chase bailed before the truck stopped, bolting through the hospital doors.

Moments later, he stopped suddenly in the threshold of his mother's room before propelling toward the side of her bed. Chief Casimir, another officer, Max, a nurse and a doctor were all in the room. An antibacterial smell filled the hallways.

He felt his muscles tighten seeing her eyes enameled over from medication. Chase approached and took his mother's hand asking, "Mom, are you okay?"

Angela gripped her son's hand. "They took her, Chase. They've got Ann. *You* have to find her, please, don't let them do to her what they did to Christie and Mandi."

He watched his mother's eyes brim over with tears and he leaned over giving her a peck on the forehead. Huskiness lingered in his voice as he spoke in an undertone, "I promise, I'll find her."

The doctor then barked out orders removing everyone from the room.

Chase turned away from his mother to conceal the rage structuring inside his gut. Caz was murmuring something to the doctor and the doctor nodded. Chase left the hospital room and waited for Caz in the hall. The only time he ever remembered being this angry was the morning he walked into his and Cindy's bedroom. What he felt then didn't even rate a close second to what he felt bubbling in his blood today.

Chief Casimir exited the room and approached Chase. "Let's go down the hall."

Scott had arrived and waited with Max and the officer in front of Angela's door.

As they walked down the hall, Chase said, "Caz, what the hell happened?"

"Max called and told me Angela was hysterical and screaming

gibberish someone had kidnapped Ann. When I got here, the doctor had given Angela a sedative. She just came around a few moments ago. I told the doctor we're gonna need a statement from Angela and he asked me to give him a few moments to check her over. Then he'd let us both in there."

Chase didn't speak. He'd always pushed hard to nab his suspect. This time he would attack unmercifully, more than he'd ever done in his entire career. He didn't give a damn who he dragged down along the way.

"We honestly don't know anything, yet. But, we did find drops of blood on the floor that were already smeared by Max and the medical staff. We can have it analyzed but I think it's obvious who it belongs to. Did my men come through for you?"

"Yeah, they did. We need to get a statement immediately from my mother, Chief. I'm positive Daniel Garcia is behind this. Then I'm gonna need a search warrant."

"I agree Garcia's behind it—"

The police officer came up behind them and said, "Chief, the doc said you can go in now."

Back in Angela's room, Chase went to his mother's bedside. "Mom, we need to find out what you know. Caz is going to ask you a few questions."

Angela acknowledged, then said, "Chase, don't leave me."

He saw the pleading in his mother's eyes and believed her reference pertained to the immediate situation. "I'll be right here."

"Angela, tell me what happened and just take your time."

She inhaled deeply. "Yesterday morning, Christie told us she had taped a phone conversation she believed had been between this guy Daniel and my employee Susan Bradford. Ann became very upset with both of us and insisted Christie go back to the Cities and not work on the case." Angela looked at her son. "She said she had been put in the middle of a crime she had no knowledge of, but told me she had talked to you."

"Yes, we talked when she returned Friday night."

"Well, Christie and I sorta ganged up on her when Ann threatened to send her back to the Cities. She was going to have you put me in protective custody. Anyway, she conceded after a lot of yelling and arguing and made us promise we wouldn't be left alone. Then she took the tape putting it in her briefcase and I watched her leave putting everything in the trunk of her car."

"Mom, what do you mean *everything*?"

"When she opened the briefcase, I saw piles of paperwork inside. I just assumed it was everything she had put together from her investigation in St. Paul since she'd left the other paperwork at the house. She seemed so pre-occupied with other things and I know she didn't say it, but she was worried after listening to the tape."

Caz, asked, "Why, Angela?"

"It was obvious from the tape Mandi had learned something and that's what caused her death. I know it has something to do with Susan Bradford, but Ann wouldn't tell me anything. What I can't seem to quite fathom is if she told you everything. Chase, something was really bothering her. She seemed distracted. She knew more, but wasn't divulging it."

Chase shifted his feet, recalling Friday night on the beach.

"Angela, did Christie tell you which day that phone call had been made?"

"That was Thursday, the day Ann went back to St. Paul. After Ann left the two of us yesterday morning is when Christie also informed me of something she'd forgotten to tell Ann. Friday afternoon she'd gone back to the office to finish up some work on the investigation. She walked in and heard Susan on the phone say 'Garcia, just because I caught her red handed holding the money and the plates, didn't mean you were supposed to listen to Baker and kill her'."

Chase experienced relief knowing his mother's mind was sharp as it had ever been. But when he glanced at Caz, they exchanged a knowing look with each other. *His mother's life was in danger.*

"Angela, how could Christie forget to mention this part of what she had learned?"

"Christie didn't want to go back to St. Paul. I think the argument Ann and I were having sort of distracted her. She ran out of the house trying to flag Ann down, but it was too late. Maybe if we had done what Ann wanted, Christie wouldn't . . ."

"Angela, what happened next?"

"The two of us spent the day talking about what we knew. I heard someone on the deck and went to the front door to check it out and that's when that guy bust his way in through the door. I started to turn and run but he hit me from behind."

"Can you describe the man, Angela?"

"He was Hispanic, longer brown hair and that's about all I remember."

"Angela, do you remember anything else at the house?"

"No."

Chase had been carefully observing his mother while he paced. She amazed him with the way she was handling Christie's murder. It had to be the painkillers and sedatives they had given her. "And, this is the same man who kidnapped Ann, Mom?"

Angela shifted her gaze to her son. "Oh, heavens, no!"

Chase stopped pacing and the two men shared another look with each other.

"This man was white and six feet tall with yellowish-brown hair, sorta the color of wheat. Oh, and his eyes were bright blue. I remember that."

Chase stared in disbelief totally confused at what his mother told them. Maybe her vision had been affected during the attack at the house. "Are you sure? I mean, are you absolutely sure about the man's description."

"Yes, I'm positive of what I saw once I opened my eyes. I can't be sure, but I think I heard him say her name before that."

Chase inhaled, slid a hand through his short hair. Taking the back of his neck, he stared at the ceiling for a brief moment. Yesterday outside the emergency room Ann's eyes told him she hadn't divulged everything she knew. What else had she learned? Who the Sam hell was the guy his mother described? He'd never forgive himself for screwing this one up.

"Angela, was this man alone?"

"Um, no, but I don't know who else came in. I closed my eyes out of fear for my own life and now I may never forgive myself for doing that."

"Angela, you get some rest now."

"Caz?"

"Yes."

"I think whoever hit me was looking for the accounts from the orphanage."

"Why do you say that?"

"Ann figured out they'd already stolen over three million dollars between falsifying the payroll records and the misappropriation."

Chase challenged his mother's words with a direct look. "What misappropriation? I thought the money was being taken by way of salaries and cash withdrawals?"

"Yes, that's true as well. Ann did discover the names of her boss, her dead fiancé and this other guy, Daniel were on the Agency's payroll. She tried to cover up her anger and disappointment about her fiancée, but I knew she was upset. To disguise their real names, they had rearranged the letters creating a new name. Ann asked Christie to calculate payroll numbers and come up with totals paid out right before she left for the Cities. Christie did, and the payroll figure was in excess of five hundred thousand dollars. This paperwork is still at the house, or at least it was before everything happened. With Christie's numbers, well over hundreds of thousand dollars had been written on the account for cash marked as pay outs to non-profit agencies."

Caz said, "Go on."

"Less than a million out of the three plus million missing. Ann didn't tell me when she returned what she had learned, but before she went back to St. Paul I told her the orphanage received less than a million unlike the million and a half she learned we were supposed to be getting. At that point, I'm not sure she even knew herself how it was being done, and that's when she decided to go back to St. Paul."

"Is there anything else?"

She shook her head. "No."

"Angela, get some rest now."

The door to Angela's room opened and both men over reacted. The man entering the room froze, seeing a forty-five aimed at him.

Angela shrieked, "Chase, I know him."

Chase concealed his weapon and the man moved slowly around him and Caz.

"Angela, I just heard. Are you okay?"

"Edward, I'm sorry about this. Please, sit down. You already know Chief Casimir. I don't know if you remember my son, Chase. This is Edward Adams. He's on the Board for the orphanage."

Caz acknowledged, "Ed."

"Chief, the rest of the Board and I are in an uproar over this . . . mess. With money stolen from the orphanage, kidnapping, break-in's and now a second murder, we're all concerned a killer's loose out there and people are scared. Who was the poor woman?"

"Ed, there's no need for the town folks to worry."

"No need to worry!"

"That's what I said. I'll be issuing a public statement as soon as possible."

"That's not good enough! We need to protect our town as well as the tourists."

Chase had heard enough from the older gentleman. "Mr. Adams, I assure you we're handling this."

"And just who the hell *are* you to interfere? I was speaking with the Chief."

Chase loved this part of the job. "Special Agent Franklin. And this *mess* you're referring to is a federal matter. Disclosure of *any kind* won't happen."

Edward Adams shrunk backwards.

"Chief, we're done here," and Caz and Chase left the room.

"You know Ed is right."

"How the hell do they find out so damn fast, Caz?"

"Small town. Who do you think this other guy is your mother described?"

Chase shifted and looked both ways in the hall. Max and Scott stood near the coffee machine. "No clue. Trev will be back tomorrow night and said he had new info. Give me a lift to the cabin."

They left the hospital and Chase informed Caz where the home base was and asked Caz for assistance with a search warrant.

When they reached the cabin, Chase jumped out and Caz asked, "What're you gonna do now?"

"They don't know me Chief, I'm going for a walk."

"What for?"

"Gonna snoop around a bit."

Chase, lemme get one of my men to go with you. It won't take long for him to change out of his uniform."

"We've wasted too much time already. I'm goin' up there, alone!"

"You're so damn bullheaded!"

Shrugging, Chase said, "I've got a cell phone, if I need anything I'll call."

CHAPTER SIXTEEN

Early Monday, barely past dawn, he sat in the lounge chair on the deck in front of his mother's house. A slender slice of the early morning sun inched its way over the lake's horizon. Heavy dew hung low just above the glass-like water. He hadn't slept.

Scott suspected this is where he'd find Chase. The look in his eyes was no longer death defying. The once menacing glare and secret expression were gone and all that remained were horror and fear. No, in fact, Scott thought to himself, his broad shoulders were hanging like the dew over the lake. His square, prominent jaw and high cheekbones sagged against his paled skin. A few more gray hairs had spread along the temples of his jet-black hair and Scott actually wished he could find a woman to love the way he knew Chase was in love with Ann.

Handing him a cup of freshly brewed coffee from the thermos he brought with him, Scott asked, "You been out here all night?"

With a slight twinge evident in the back and forth movement of his head, his words came out throaty, raspy. "I looked all night. I couldn't find her, Scott."

Scott sat down in a chair along side the lounge and poured himself a cup of coffee. If for no further conversation, he knew his friend would accept his company. It was a silent pact they had between them since his own parent's death. They watched the sun inch upward as they'd done so many times as young boys.

When the fireball had risen entirely above the waterline, Chase muttered, "I don't know where else to look for her."

Scott emptied his coffee cup. "Chase, there's something I have to tell you. I don't remember much about my parents being killed. Maybe because I didn't see the accident happen, maybe because I didn't want to acknowledge the most important thing in my life had been snuffed out and I'd been cheated. I do remember how your parents and Uncle Max took me under their wing and helped me through my grief. But what I will never forget above my own loss, is the grave adversity you suffered."

Chase looked at Scott. "Me? I wasn't the one who'd lost my parents."

"No, you weren't. But ever since that day I've never forgotten that it was you and you alone who watched my parents being blown to smithereens. Everyone was to busy fussing over me and worried what would happen to poor Scotty Welston an only child who'd lost his parents, that no one bothered to think about the fact there was another twelve year old boy who had witnessed the horror. Another young boy whose life had been drastically altered the same day and it's always bothered me nobody cared enough to see *your* pain. I saw it then and I see it now. And it will forever be a constant factor in my life."

"Constant factor for what?"

"Survival. For doing the best that I can and being the best at what I do. You stood by me through the worst times of my life and never once threw it back in my face. Chase, through all my angry outbursts, you never gave up on me. I know there's not a damn thing I can do to help you find Ann, but don't you dare think of giving up now."

Chase wondered how he could express gratitude to Scott for his unforeseen insights. Through the years he'd thought about Scott several times and how they'd lost touch with each other, but this morning Scott proved to him geography had no boundaries on the meaning of their friendship. Unexpectedly, the promise he'd made to his mother became reachable. "Thanks, Scott, I won't. I need to talk to my mother."

They stood together and Scott said, "Chase, I know you'll find Ann."

***

Angela looked at her son when he entered the hospital room. An intimate understanding for her son's emotions, thoughts and motives fulfilled her with heart-breaking compassion. Angela understood what had driven him all of his life. She saw the hidden fear some live with daily. She saw the protection he gave his country without condemnation. She saw the downfall, the failures and ruins that came from losing what one battles with all one's might to keep. Angela understood everything about her son for the first time in her life.

Chase sat down in a recliner and muttered, "I've looked everywhere for her. And we still don't know who her abductor is."

There was nothing she could say to dissolve his suffering and grief. But, Duke could. Yes, her precious Duke would know exactly what to say to her only child. "Honey, do you remember when you and Dad would go off together in the boat?"

The air in his lungs heaved out slowly. "Yeah."

"Close your eyes, and think about Dad. What would he say to you right now if he were still alive? What kind of advice would he give you."

She watched him from her hospital bed, wearing the small check-printed, hospital garb they'd provided for her. His humble jaw was painted over with black stubble.

Several minutes passed when he opened his eyes searching his mother's face for the answers.

A weak smile overtook his features. Duke's gentle, kind and loving eyes stared back at her. The time had arrived for her to make amends and say what she knew he needed to hear. "Chase, I love you more than anyone else in the world. I loved your father more. He was the best thing ever to happen along in my life, you were the second. He was my first love, my only love, and you are a part of him. I know how much you loved your father and I know how much you miss him."

"I do miss him and I know I haven't been here for you since

his, well, it's just that . . ."

Angela's heart burst wide open. "It's just what?"

"I just never understood . . ."

"What, my jealousy?"

He gaped at her.

"How could you understand?" *And now she knew both her men had loved her as much as she loved them.* "Honey, I know you miss Dad. He loved you so much. You were the light of his life and his inspiration for living in the end. He was so proud of you the day you became a Special Agent." Angela paused, "He was just as proud of you as I am."

Her words had stunned him. "You're proud of me? But—"

"I've never been more proud of anyone than I am of you in this dire moment. I'm afraid I owe the second best thing in my life a huge apology."

He scrunched his eyebrows together as a lump hardened in his throat. He could barely speak, "For what?"

"Chase Edward Franklin, you have definitely tried my patience over the years." She sighed releasing some of her pent-up exasperation. "It's, also, not easy for a mother to admit to her child when she's made a mistake." Angela stared off at some distant memory and said, "You were born so late in our lives." She looked back and hesitated speaking just to contemplate the confused look in his eyes. "I was spoiled rotten with the attention your father gave me prior to your arrival into our lives. We both wanted more children, but it wasn't possible. When you came along, his attention turned from me to you. I didn't know how to deal with the transition. I was envious of the attention he gave to you. Oh, in the end I knew better, but by then it was too late for me to correct, or for you to understand."

Chase blinked for the second time on this early morning. The back of the recliner caught his falling head. He finally grasped the missing part of his past. All his dismay, perturbation, anxiety and trepidation were gone. She wasn't disappointed with who or what he had done with his life. His choice to disregard her for detesting him, omitting her from his life, feeling the contempt toward her lack of love for him, were rigid mistakes *he'd* made.

All of a sudden, like his father had tapped him on the shoulder and told him what he had to do, he flew out of the recliner. "Mom, I love you." He approached the bed and hugged her. "I really do love you, but I have to go. I'll be back, I promise." *Spitfire or not, he wasn't going to lose her.* He practically ran to the door.

"Chase."

"Yeah?"

Recognizing *that look* in her son's eyes, the one she saw in Duke's eyes oh so long ago, Angela forgot what she was going to say and said with surprise in her voice, "You *really* are in love with her!"

He gave her a weak smile and nodded his head.

"You'll find her, I know you will."

***

Chase met Chief Casimir at the station with the rest of the contents from Ann's briefcase. He'd found the computer printouts from DECS where Madison Baker had been making withdrawals of the orphanage's money. The puzzlement came from the two pages she'd ripped out of Baker's monogrammed calendar. He understood the one page with the name *Danny* and had smiled to himself thinking his little orphan knew the significance of being able to tie Bradford, Baker and Garcia together. The taped statement where Susan referred to Danny and this calendar page did exactly that. It was the other page confusing him and if Ann felt it was evidence, he had to keep digging to figure out what the hell *Godefredo* meant. He only knew one person who spoke Spanish, which is what he believed, was the origin of Godefredo.

One patrolman interrupted and told the Chief he had a call. Caz picked up the phone exchanging minimal words with the caller and hung up flashing an alligator grin at Chase.

"What's that look for?"

"Last night after you told me where they were setting up I started thinking they're gonna need power to run printing machines, right?"

"Yeah."

"Well, that was the electric company. I had them check records for the old hall. Madison Baker requested the power be turned back on."

Chase didn't look up from reading the printout he had retrieved from Ann's briefcase.

"Chase, that's not all they told me."

Deep into reading the printout, he muttered, "What else?"

"Power's been pumped back into the old man's house too."

He shot upright from the hunched over position he'd held over the table. Pacing around the miniature office, Chase said, "Caz, I gotta go out there. It's less than a mile from the dance hall."

"I don't think so." Caz removed his glasses. "Listen to me, Chase. The property is posted and it's owned by one of the old man's relatives, who's God only knows where. You go in there without a search warrant and your case goes up in smoke."

"Not, if Ann is inside."

"Chase, for chrissake you're not thinking. What happens if you slam-bang your way in there find evidence, but not Ann? You can't take the evidence without a warrant and by the time we come back with one, they'll have cleared out and taken it with them, and you know it."

He'd stopped pacing and attached his hands firmly on his hips. "Fine. How long 'til we have both warrants?"

"Be a couple hours to get both typed and signed by a judge. I want you to do them. You know what you're looking for. I'll get my guys together, how many you figure we're gonna need to do both places."

"How many can you afford."

"I'll call the Sheriff, get some of his deputies and a few troopers to assist."

"By that time Jack 'ill be back from Mexico and hopefully whatever he discovered will tell us who this third guy is."

"Chase, tell me what you know about this Bastide character down in Mexico."

"You know about him?"

"Now why would that surprise you?"

"Doesn't really. I'm just having trouble with how he and his reputation would have made it this far north."

"So what's his story?" Caz asked.

"He's got his own little Mexican Mafia in San Luis Potosi, Mexico. The DEA has been trying to snare his ass, without help from the Federale's for as many years as he's been smuggling drugs across the border. Jesus, Caz, maybe that's the connection."

"What's the connection?"

"We had no idea he was involved in counterfeiting until this case jumped up and bit us in the ass. Bastide has always smuggled his drugs into the US. He's probably smuggling the counterfeit plates in as well."

"Doyle Airlines, I bet."

"Afraid I wouldn't make that bet with you right now. Jack's there now putting it all together. And with any luck he'll be able to fill in the missing parts for us. He's got the system beat, Chief. The Federale's don't care about the drug smuggling and we know it's not their money he's stealing or counterfeiting." He glanced at the paperwork on the table. "Ann stumbled into this purely by accident and has been used along the way. We had no idea Bastide was behind it, until Baker and Doyle's prints surfaced on real money at Marriano's murder scene in New York and led us to Mexico."

Caz leaned back in his cloth-covered chair and let out a low whistle. "How much you figure is the loss from the orphanage?"

He glanced at the paperwork on the table. "So far, my mother was right. It's in excess of three million. This time that son-of-a-bitching Bastide is goin down."

"You'd really like to get your hands on this guy, wouldn't you." Caz stood up from the chair behind the desk.

"Goes without saying."

"Well, Special Agent Franklin, there just might be a way." Caz strutted around his desk yanking and re-adjusting his gun belt.

Chase weighed the man's purple eyes seeing an unfamiliar glimmer. Within a split second flashbacks tainted his mind. Officer Casimir, as he was called years ago before his promotion to Chief, had been the beginning of his own interest in the law. In his younger days, it was indisputable that Caz loved his work and his job. He attacked it with vigorous knowledge and understanding. Chase had been impressed with the control, the being right, being able to find justice in an already cruel world filled with hatred.

Caz and a situation Chase had no control over, are what mounted his interest at the age of twelve. Scott called it. He'd been the only witness to the drunkenness of some out-of-towners vacationing here in Masquerade. Three men had rented a speed-boat from Devil's Point and he watched them walk into the bar, come back out some time later staggering and babbling like idiots. To this day, Chase still didn't understand why the guy rented a boat to them. Maybe Scotty's parents would still be alive. Chase heard and saw the explosion a few minutes later after they raced away from the dock. He'd always been grateful Scott hadn't been with him that day.

Returning to the present, Chase looked at Caz. "Don't toy with me."

Like they were in the same time warp, the Chief shook his head slightly and said, "I'd never do that, Chase."

"What have you got?"

"I checked on Susan Bradford for you. She doesn't exist."

"What do you mean she doesn't exist?"

"I ran her name through NCIC and routine warrants."

"And?"

"She doesn't exist, no driver's license, no past, nothing comes back on the name Susan Bradford. Got me to thinkin' while I was running a criminal history and nothing came up there either. I ran a check on the social security number she used at the orphanage.

Notta. I went and asked your mother if I could check out Bradford's office. Had the County lab boys go over and take latents from her office."

Chase could only imagine what Caz was going to tell him.

"Prints came back a few hours ago. Her name is Caccila Bastide, twenty-eight years old, not thirty-six as she states here on one of Ann's tapes. She was born in San Luis Potosi and I've had my boys watching her and informing me of everything she does."

"She's Bastide's daughter? Who's her mother?" Chase was quickly learning a valuable lesson and hoped it wasn't too late to save the one he *truly* loved. He'd been so wrapped up in assuming Ann's guilt he'd slipped at the most important things in a case. The tiny details and things that mattered, pinning cases together giving them probable cause for their arrests.

"Her mother's name wasn't known. I figure thou, if we get the word to him that we have her in custody—"

"We don't have her in custody, Caz."

He strutted back behind his desk picking up the mike from the two-way radio on the counter and made contact with one of his squads.

Chase listened to their babbling something about meeting for lunch. "What the hell was that all about?"

"I've had a code worked out with a couple of my men I put in unmarked cars last night. Depending on the time of the day, I ask them about meeting to eat. If they've got Bradford in sight, they respond with how long it will be before we can meet. If they don't, they tell me they're on a traffic stop."

"Let's go pick her up and I'll make the phone call to Bastide myself. Then we can get those search warrants."

"Think I'm gonna contact SERT to assist us instead."

"SERT?"

"Sheriff's Emergency Response Team, same as SWAT. Our county boys are trained for high risk situations."

"Highly trained?"

Caz grinned. "With.308 rifles, nine millimeter submachine

guns, Def-Tec diversion, flash devices, Avons, take your pick."

"How many?"

"They cover the county, thirty-one officers, four paramedics and three volunteers. Will that do?"

"Better than I expected, thanks Chief."

Forty-five minutes later, Caccila Alba Bastide, alias Susan Alba Bradford was locked up nice and tight in county jail and Chase was working on the two search warrants.

***

Trev returned to Masquerade in a rental car Monday afternoon instead of that evening after flying into Minneapolis from San Luis Potosi. The Secret Service weren't far behind Trev and he and Chase waited for them inside the cabin.

"We got good, and we got bad news," Chase told him.

"Gimme the bad news."

He told Jack what happened at his mother's house and felt the muscle twitch slightly in his shoulder before he finished with, "Ann was kidnapped late yesterday from my mother's hospital room."

Jack looked into his partner's eyes. He wasn't an unfeeling man, just gave everyone the appearance he was. What he saw in Chase's eyes, made him think of everyone they'd ever lost. "Your mom see who done it?"

"She's got a good description and it wasn't Garcia. Garcia obviously found someone else to replace Doyle"

"What's the good news?"

"The day Ann went back to her office, she printed off documentation from Baker's computer on how a majority of the money was being embezzled. John contacted someone in the Cities office and they went in and secured Baker's computer. They'll advise us when George figures out how she accessed the State and County files."

"We got the proof?"

"We got it all. Ann also found monogrammed pages from Baker's office with Garcia's name. It looks like Baker had a meeting with Garcia on this one here. For some reason, Ann also ripped out another page with the name *Godefredo* written on it."

Trev's large mouth had split into a thin smile. "What?"

"Damn, she did our work for us, Chase-man. And here I thought I was the one to break this case wide open."

"Maybe she did, but we still don't know who took her and what Godefredo means. It had to be something she figured out would tie this all together. I've got another call into John since he's fluent in Spanish."

"You got anything else?"

"Yeah, according to my mother, Ann's partner overheard Susan Bradford implicate Garcia in Marriano's murder. Chief has a patrolman over at the hospital keeping an eye on my mother since she's the only living witness."

"What else you got, Chase?

He told Trev about Bradford's real identity and the plan he and the Chief executed to pay Bradford's motel bill. Chase also informed Trev about the electrical being hooked up and the decision made regarding SERT. "What'd you find out?"

Jack swallowed a mouthful of food and slugged it down with a glass of milk. "Bastide sure's been a busy boy."

Assuming Jack was referring to Bastide's illicit business Chase pointedly glared at Jack. He already knew the man was a busy boy and untouchable because he never left Mexico or his castle enclosed within a ten by three-foot thickness made of solid brick. It was pure exhaustion and anxiety that caused his sarcasm. "You think! Dammit, tell me something I don't know."

Between bites, Jack said, "I found our missing link to all of them. Baker is Bastide's cupcake on the side."

"Lovers! How long?"

"Thirty-four years, never married. And Bastide lent Doyle a mil to start his airline bizness seven years ago."

Jack never gave exact answers and he watched him finish eating. When Jack swallowed his last bite, his grin had broadened and Chase said, "Okay, I'll bite. Why would Baker's lover give Doyle a million smackers?"

"Because partner," Jack finished off a second glass of milk.

Through ten years of partnering with the same man, Chase had learned how to wait for Jack.

"Baker was Doyle's mother and Bastide was Doyle's father."

Astonished, "You're shittin' me!" Chase blurted."

Jack said, "Nope," as he wiped off his mouth.

"I'll be damned, Bradford and Doyle were brother and sister."

"Exactly. Looks like we did it again, partner. I also learned the counterfeit plates are made in Columbia, South America and are flown to Bastide under radar in single engine planes."

"Doyle Airlines."

Jack nodded. "Them plates are smuggled into Mexico and then the US. Grinning, he added, "You're hunch was right, Chase-man. Garcia is Spanish ul right, born in San Luis Potosi."

"What about the Air Force, his birth certificate?"

"Lied, wasn't born in New York. Mother was Spanish, too, but couldn't find the father. She made her way to New York right after Garcia's birth. Pro'bly lied, cuz he wasn't legal. Garcia has lived in 'n out of different states and Mexico."

"And he changed his birth certificate the same way they invented the ID's Ann found in the safety deposit box."

The phone rang and Chase grabbed it. He listened for about a minute and the words exploded from his mouth again. "No shit?" and he ended the call.

"That John?"

"Dammit, where the hell is it!" Chase shoved files and papers around searching for the background report on Ann. After finding the report under a stack, Chase scanned the pages quickly and found what he was looking for. He'd overlooked another fact and read Ann's second language was Spanish. She already knew what he'd just learned of the missing piece to their case and she'd kept it

CONCEALED JUDGEMENT   193

from him at the hospital on Saturday. Chase shoveled his emotions to the back burner.

"Trev, John just told me Godefredo is Spanish for Geoffrey. Which means according to this calendar page with Baker's initials on it, Baker had a conversation with her own son, Godefredo, alias Geoffrey Doyle a month after his death."

"Unless Baker's a psychic."

Chase dug through more paperwork and found a photo of Geoffrey Doyle. "Any bets my mom will ID *this* bastard as Ann's abductor?"

"Chase, you realize Bastide will probably tell Doyle to get his sister out of lock up instead of coming himself."

"Then I guess we'll have to put Doyle in lock up, as well. I'm gonna get Bastide out of his castle if it's the last fucking thing on earth I ever do. And Trev, who in the hell do you suppose they buried in place of Doyle?"

Jack ripped out a revolting belch. "Damn, Chase. I didn't even think of that." He punched himself in the chest and burped again. "I'll call the Minneapolis Bureau and get a Federal warrant for exhumation."

"Right now I gotta date with a judge."

"I'll wait for the Secret Service and we'll meet you at the station and start briefing the troops so we's ready."

Chase checked his weapon and took his jacket with him.

"You think Bastide 'ill come looking for his daughter?"

"One can only hope. I made damn sure he learned we were holding her on murder charges. If he doesn't come, we'll just have to come up with another plan, won't we."

"You think Bradford really killed the girl?"

"I know from this tape she's the one who informed Garcia that Mandi Marriano found out she was stealing."

"Mighty thin but I'll take it."

"My middle name is thin. I'll meet you at the station." Chase hurried out the cabin, knowing when Bastide came to get his precious daughter out of jail he'd bring his own army with him. Right

now he and Caz had to get the search warrants signed by a judge
Caz had called. He took Doyle's photo and would have his mother
ID the picture.

CHAPTER SEVENTEEN

Dismally trapped, Ann sluggishly adjusted her vision to the murky darkness. The ominous silence spelled gloom. Numbness had set in throughout her limbs, but not enough to overlook the moldy moisture she laid in, or the stabbing pains pulsating through the middle of her back and head. A gag covering her mouth prevented her from swallowing. Her throat felt parched and seared. Almost wishing the gag covered her nose, Ann could then ignore the insipid odor hanging like death in the air. A nylon rope binding her wrists behind her back, burned into her flesh and someone had pounced on her skull unmercifully. Her nightmares had come to life and Ann believed herself to already be dead. She'd been sent to hell for lying to Chase.

With her cheek pressed flat against the damp, cement floor Ann was forced to look straight ahead. Her eyes roamed, searching, examining and exploring her surroundings. The vast space around her spun while tiny speckles of light danced in front of her eyes. She blinked and re-focused. Droplets of sweat slid down her forehead while the flesh of her cheeks burned with fever. Queasiness depleted her strength and without further warning her stomach contracted fiercely. Her conscious mind faded rapidly on the dry choke, her eyes rolled back, and slipping into blackness, she began descending. Plunging head first into blackness, a familiar depth of emptiness surpassed the speed with which she fell. It became a race against time, time before she crashed. The urgency swelled inside of her like a sponge soaking up water. She had to rectify her mistake. Ann had to tell him, tell Chase everything. She had to see him one last time before he slipped from her life forever.

The destruction that shattered her thoughts was an excruciating whack to the side of her stomach. Choking on the gag and barely able to see, the man's face had been shrouded by darkness. Straining to raise the lids of her eyes, Ann glimpsed light illuminating through a passageway. Feeling another thrusting blow to her side, her lids squeezed shut almost mechanically. Languidly, Ann opened her eyes a second time and peered upward through blurred vision upon hearing Geoffrey. His voice had changed to bitter sarcasm, yet remained so familiar and clear in her mind. A towering figure concealed him.

"Well pet, I see you're finally awake."

The heavy accent couldn't disguise Daniel's voice. A flicker of fear raced through her. Daniel's body hunched over hers and with a mighty tug to her head, Garcia removed the gag. Gasping sounds expunged from her mouth. She gulped on short breaths of stale air letting it penetrate her lungs. At least she was still alive.

"Where's the money and the plates?"

His words became lost in her mind—her throat burned with dry rawness. Over and again the race against time, an unknown urgency seemed to be the only fleeting thought in her mind. One, lone word slithered from her parched mouth, "Why?"

Bellowing, "Ta Perrado," Garcia spat and paced in front of Ann. "Perrado, you know why."

Intense pain tap-danced through Ann's entire body. She could hear Daniel's nostrils snorting. Then, his rough hands seized her by the shoulders yanking her body off the floor and shaking her violently.

"Perrado! I slice your throat too!"

"Garcia, back off!"

Garcia dropped her and Ann hit the cement floor with a thud. Pain exploded everywhere, but not before the icy chills slithered up and down her back. She hated Geoffrey with a passion and this really had to be one of her nightmares. She would wake up and mechanically search the bedroom finding no one. The room whirled once more and at sonic speed. Ann swallowed hard and closed her eyes to stop the spinning and wake herself up. Slowly opening her eyes, his voice echoed in the background and Ann had to see him before she'd actually be capable of believing he was still alive. If Geoffrey wasn't really there, she'd know this was just a *painfully* bad dream. Her sixth sense had never been wrong and right now her intuition told her this was real and not another nightmare.

Daniel squatted down and stroked the side of her cheek with a calloused finger. Ann flinched and jerked away. The impulsive action drove tormenting pain non-stop into every bone in her body. Garcia snapped her into an upright position.

"Maybe you an' Danny boy cud has some fun. No? Eh, wutch you tink bout dat, pet?"

Ann lifted her head staring at Daniel as the stench of his breath emitted a foul smell. She attempted to spit in his face but only blew out dry air.

Instantly, a forceful hand met her cheek knocking Ann on her right side to the concrete floor. Garcia yanked her upward and she clearly saw the five-inch blade he'd brandished.

"Ta perrado, you gots t'ree secon's to tell me where da money and plates is or I slice your preeeti neck!"

Her eyes met with Garcia's wicked stare. At the same moment, a woman's screeching voice in the background pierced the air.

"Just kill her and get it over with!"

"Your anger is overwhelming right now, but not yet."

When Ann heard *his* voice the second time, she had to see him for herself, but Garcia had moved again, blocking her view. With the sound of footsteps nearing, Ann listened to the well-known hiss of Madison's voice and knew this wasn't a dream.

"You pull that blade again without using it and I'll have you castrated with the damn thing. And you know I'm capable of doing it."

Garcia swung around. "I've had enough of you, bitch!"

"Knock it off! Both of you!"

The verbal eruption between the three of them didn't stop Ann from remembering what got her into this mess. Stupidity should really be her last name, she thought. Why hadn't she told Chase everything? Now, he would never know, or find her. Dismally, she knew her pending death loomed.

"Godefredo, my hijo, just get it over with and kill her!"

"Damn it, Mother, we aren't going to kill her here!"

"Why not?"

"They have one of ours, we have one of their's." Geoffrey bellowed impatiently, "Garcia, put her in a chair. I want to talk to her."

Did Ann hear that right? Hijo was Spanish for son. Ann's already frazzled mind couldn't absorb the shock of hearing Madison Baker was Geoffrey's mother. Doomed from the very beginning, Ann felt her loneliness take on a brand new meaning. There was sadness in the way she had never belonged to a family, never belonged to a lover as she once thought. She already knew she never loved Geoffrey. Instantly, she figured out why. She came into the world unwanted and she would leave the same way.

Garcia did as he was told and picked Ann up off the floor placing her in a chair in front of Doyle.

Ann shifted her gaze and saw *him.* Until this second, her subconscious mind still argued with her conscious mind that he really was dead. As she eyed him, he stood slender, rather than tall, like she had remembered. He had grown a light colored beard and it jutted his jaw forward adding plumpness to his already round face. She didn't remember his wavy hair being wheat colored. It had always been more brown than yellow. His once cloudless, blue eyes were self-righteous and affected. His smile wasn't the way she had remembered it either. His lips twisted cynically and were coated with sourness.

She swallowed with difficulty feeling the burning sensation slither all the way down until it hit rock bottom in the pit of her hatred. *How could she have loved someone she hated this much?* The two emotions merged into a festered wound that went beyond description. In a heartless and frigid voice, Ann asked, "That bitch is your mother?"

"Ah, my little Anna Banana, subtlety was never your strong suit. You should have heeded Mother's advice. Perhaps, if you had been less persistent and more subtle, you wouldn't be sitting here facing your untimely demise."

Ann inhaled deeply before applying a condemnatory smile. "Geoffrey, or should I call you Godefredo?"

"Either."

"Snake is more appropriate," Ann snarled, "your exaggerated demeanor is saturated with mounds of deception." Her throat burned as the words blew off her tongue, but she continued anyway. "Tell me why you involved me in your felonious ways?"

"An available woman, why not? Mother always accused me of not being able to ignore my needs."

Unshaken, Ann glared sharply at Geoffrey. After temporary silence, she asked, "Why would you propose to me if you had no intention of following through?"

"Anna Banana—"

"Stop calling me that, you son-of-a-bitch!" Immediately, Ann recalled the day she yelled at Chase for calling her Orphan Annie. If she'd only known Chase's gesture had set off her subconscious mind regarding Geoffrey's pet name, things might not seem as bleak right now.

A smile ruffled his mouth. "You see what I mean, Mother. How can you not help yourself to fall for her."

"Just kill her and get it over with!"

Ann watched Geoffrey's armed grin fill with an air of wicked pomposity. The same grin she recognized had trapped her into believing she could love him.

"Not yet, Mother."

As if she couldn't take any more of either one of them, Ann shrieked over both of them. "Answer me, you bastard, you owe me at least that much!"

Doyle eyed her with graveness. "Always with the questions! I admit, however foolish it may have been, I did fall for you. But your constant interrogation drove me insane.

"Is that what did it?" Ann wheezed.

"When it became clear you couldn't be trusted because you wouldn't turn your scrupulous and moralistic practice into my way of thinking, I had no other choice."

"No other choice? For God's sake! You could've told me your intention wasn't marriage and dumped me the old fashion way."

"I had to concoct a believable plot to escape you. I knew if I didn't die, take myself out of the picture, you wouldn't give up. You never give up, Anna Banana. Eventually, I knew you'd figure out what was really going on."

"So you feign death to escape being committed."

He eyeballed her, knowing her meaning was twofold.

Meeting his stare, Ann asked, "Who was the poor soul in the car?"

"A homeless drunk."

The words whispered off her lips. "You're criminally insane."

"I suppose that's an ethical way of looking at it."

"Why did you have to murder that poor woman from the orphanage?"

Shrugging, he said, "Since, you're demise is nearing, I'll tell you. She was the first to discover our scheme. Susan caught her and her snooping caused her death. Mandi had discovered the plates and the cash advance in Susan's office. The plates, I remind you, you now have. And I didn't kill her, that was all my Mother and Garcia's doing."

"Oh, there's a comfort, " she sneered. How long had the cash advances been going on Ann wondered. "Tell me this. When did you hide the plates in *my* apartment?"

"I had extra keys made since I knew mine would come back to you from the morgue. When Mother called and told me you were handling this investigation and had come here to Masquerade, I went back to *our apartment* and hid them."

Ann didn't respond.

"Anna Banana, we were making small withdrawals from the orphanage, but it just wasn't enough. There's never enough when greed runs interference. And I'm sure you're familiar with greed. The last extraction was a little larger than what had been our norm and that's what Susan's secretary discovered."

"Small? Madison . . ." stopping and rephrasing, Ann said, "your mother was changing the deposits in her computer, Susan faked the names on the payroll, and you were making withdrawals from the orphanage besides. I wouldn't call three million small."

"I see Mother was right again. She said it wouldn't take you long to figure everything out. Mother has had you pegged from the beginning."

"From the beginning?"

"Ann, did you really believe it was just a coincidence the first time I met you? Mother had it planned from day one to implicate you in the scheme of our plan. Think about it and what better way than through the affections of your heart. The orphanage opened nineteen months ago. We already knew what the Legislature was doing and well, we needed to have a scapegoat just in case. On the day we met, Mother is the one who told me where to find you."

Ann recalled how she literally bumped into Geoffrey at the Mall of America and dropped her packages. He'd helped her pick them up, checked to make sure she wasn't hurt and then invited her for coffee. The incident had occurred nine months before he asked her to marry him. The three of them had been masterminding long before it even passed legislation.

"Now, since I've answered your questions, you tell me, when did you figure out I was still alive?"

A painful smile curved her lips. "Your mother is an idiot, Geoffrey." Ann heard Madison's breathing quicken and she continued. "I never would have figured it out if she hadn't written a note on her calendar to call *Godefredo* after your death. I'm sure she forgot Spanish is my second language. Having her computer password just made it easier for me to find the withdrawals from D-E-C-S." She sent him a torrid glare. "How the hell did you forge my signature on the safety deposit box?"

His smile turned grim as he cast a glare at his mother for her foolish mistakes. He knew Ann spoke Spanish, it was one of the first things that attracted him. He growled and turned back to face Ann. "You should never have discovered the safety deposit box!"

"Just another flaw in your escapade. But then I'm sure you deluded yourself into thinking the bank wouldn't send a letter regarding the monthly fee you forgot to cover in your checking account after your death. I imagine it was difficult for a dead man to make deposits."

"An oversight!"

"Oversights are incriminating. Like leaving your little box of goodies in the apartment. I'm sure you assumed you'd get them out before I returned."

He pondered everything she'd told him thus far. "As thorough as I know you are, I'm sure you obviously made copies of the reports you found in Mother's computer. Where are they?"

"You must really think I'm stupid." Ann heard Madison shuffling behind Geoffrey.

"On the contrary, I know you're not and therein has been our problem."

"Tell me which one of you broke into Angela Franklin's house and brutally murdered my partner."

"Garcia."

"Godefredo, she's been hanging around that bitch's son, the FBI agent."

Flinching from his solid stance, Geoffrey swung around to face his mother. "What the hell are you talking about?"

"Angela Franklin's son is FBI. I thought you knew that," Madison sneered. "You expect me to do everything!"

Smearing his face in the oversights, Ann jeered, "Didn't Garcia tell you? I thought for sure with all the snooping he's been doing, he'd have figured out the FBI has been here for some time now."

Ann received a great deal of pleasure from watching Geoffrey's nostrils flare while his eyes overflowed with rage.

"Well, Mother, looks like you're gonna get your wish sooner

than I planned."

"How come you and your mother don't have the same name?"

"Same reason you don't, I'd assume."

Blood drained from her already pale face. She'd forgotten the last phone call he made to her. She hadn't really forgotten, she'd assumed his phone call that night was part of their plan for his bogus death. "Since you're going to kill me anyway, you owe me at least that much."

His laugh overflowed mirthfully. "Same old Ann, still searching. A never-ending quest to find out who you are, where you came from." He laughed again. "I can see the pending questions in your eyes, the wanting to know, the frustration of not knowing where you came from. Its called greed, Ann and it's intoxicating to the point of pure obsession. Isn't it?"

"Godefredo, just kill her. We've got work to do?"

"Not yet. Garcia, let her think on it awhile."

Without warning and caught off guard by the undeniable truth of Geoffrey's words, Ann felt the blow to her head. There she went, falling again, into that disheartening blackness. This time the fall wasn't as far when she landed with a thud but not before she heard Geoffrey's words, *he's gonna come looking for his sister.*

What she heard him say had siphoned the life out of her body and sickened her to death. Ann plunged deeper, never wanting to return.

CHAPTER EIGHTEEN

The Sheriff's Emergency Response Team maintained a semi-re-laxed position dressed in full gear while cramming into the con-fined briefing room at the Masquerade police station. Police offic-ers were united with Secret Service and FBI agents. Special Agent Trevor dominated and commanded their attention explaining Bastide's notorious counterfeiting operations. Agent Trevor's in-structions had grave effects. Each officer's mentality could be le-thal to say the least and one by one they remained cautiously mindful of avoiding thoughts of ultimate endings. Their level of concentration remained intact but their eyes zeroed in on the enor-mous man wearing a baseball cap backwards. As they carefully listened, some were captivated with the navy blue jacket over a ballistic vest. Whatever held their vision, none permitted their minds to dwell.

The Comm Center, otherwise known as the communication van, would operate from the station's parking lot. The obvious strategy with the use of flashbangs, a device creating a burst of light when the Team forced entry, always provided the element of surprise. Both teams would simultaneously hit the old dance hall and the abandoned house. The radio squawked.

They'd been notified, six potentially dangerous and most likely illegal aliens from Mexico, Doyle, Garcia, and a redhead were armed heavily and observed leaving the house and going inside the dance hall. Ann Longworth wasn't with them.

With a new plan, SERT would hit the old dance hall first, since the Chief's undercover men reported the movement from the house to the condemned structure. Agent Franklin arrived with both signed search warrants. He wore an FBI cap, navy blue jacket exhibiting the large white, FBI emblem over a ballistic vest, t-shirt and jeans. The SERT Sergeant handed him a bone vibration headset, which he put in place. Each Team member wore one to communicate with each other, freeing their hands for the potential use of weaponry.

As Caz had promised, Chase observed several SERT members carried Remington.308 rifles outfitted with night vision scopes while others were armed with 9 mm submachine guns. The Team included two of the four police paramedics, highly educated in tactical paramedic courses, FBI SWAT School, and Chemical Munitions training. The Team Sergeant advised FBI Agents, ballistic shields used for entry were available in the equipment van along with any other gear they deemed necessary.

They would hit the dance hall in forty-five minutes and synchronized their watches. Agent Trevor would be in charge at the dance hall following forced entry and securing the location. Remaining officers would advance to the old house executing the second warrant with Agent Franklin in command. Communication and the order to force entry into the dance hall would be executed from the Comm Van at exactly twenty forty-five hours. The van's Com-operator would give the command with Chief Casimir and Secret Service Agents as backup. Radio transmissions and further movement from the Chief's undercover men keeping surveillance on the abandoned house would be communicated. It was now twenty fifteen hours.

Chase swallowed hard, straining to maintain his FBI composure and keep his raw emotion in check. *They'd most likely done away with her already.* Thought provoking, he refused to dwell on the idea. His career with the FBI made these situations a way of life. He knew the only significant difference this time was his deep devotion to the hostage.

Twenty minutes later the uniformed team members slithered into positions surrounding the dance hall. Ten prowled silently with the moves of a jaguar cat into their positions surrounding the abandoned structure. With only two man-door entries, Agents

Franklin and Trevor each led seven officers. They waited, as the power of their adrenaline became their driving force. Each man knew the thrill of danger surging through their veins could lead at any moment to the agony of death. Agent Trevor's team would use flashbangs on the west side and enter while Agent Franklin's Team would enter the trailer on the south side blocking escape. The east, Crypt Lake's shoreline, had coverage from SERT members trained in water maneuvers as well as the north end of the structure.

Through the headsets each officer heard the pre agreed upon code if Bastide were sighted. "The rooster's left his nest. One minute to entry."

The next order through their bone vibration headsets came. "Four, three, two, go, go, go!"

In one split second a barrage of bright light and gun sounding blasts detonated into the night from the flashbangs. Both Teams forced the doors, weapons drawn and aimed, yelling, "FBI!"

Chase heard rapid succession of automatic gunfire erupting inside the dance hall. Five additional uniforms followed his Team inside and he knew five extra were with Trev.

Agent Franklin had the undying pleasure of coming face to face with Doyle and Garcia. "FBI! Drop the guns!"

Both did and after a pat-search and cuffing, the Team bulldozed their way into the tunnel met by a redheaded female. "FBI!" Chase yelled again. "Madison Baker?"

"Go to hell!"

"You're under arrest for conspiracy and embezzlement." Chase never blinked keeping his weapon aimed. "Cuff her and read 'em their rights."

A deputy came from behind Chase and did so, coercing Baker into the trailer with Doyle and Garcia.

Upon entering the dance hall, Chase observed three downed men. Agent Trevor's Team had weapons aimed as additional agents cuffed the others following a direction from the SERT Sergeant.

Active machines printing counterfeit money had drowned out

normal conversation. The sergeant shut down the machinery once all suspects were in face down position on the floor and secured in cuffs subsequent to a weapon's pat search.

Chase challenged Angle de la Bastide's with a sharp piercing glare into his Hispanic brown eyes as five men kept high caliber weapons pointed at Bastide. "Angle de la Bastide, you're under arrest for counterfeiting US monies. You have the right to remain silent. Anything you can and do say may be used against you in a federal court of law. You have the right to an attorney. If you cannot afford one, one will be chosen for you. Do you understand these rights as I have explained them to you."

Bastide spit in Agent Franklin's face without further response.

"Angle de la Bastide, do you understand your rights?"

"Si. And you are either a very bold man or you are crazy."

The exactness of Chase's voice forbade any question. "Both!" And he shifted, looking around the room. Where the hell was Jack? Half the FBI and all of DEA had waited years to feel the adrenaline rush of Bastide's long awaited arrest. Another deputy cuffed Bastide and placed him on the floor near the other prisoners.

Agent Franklin, announced, "Secure," and heard the words through his headset, "Officer down!" Out of the corner of his eye, Chase saw one of the trained paramedics kneeled down with a man lying in a pool of blood. The man was Trev. The siren in the background grew louder, then stopped, masticating his bones. Over his headset came the words from Caz, "The hospital's on alert."

"Caz, its Trev." His commanding voice went void of emotion. "I've *got* to execute the second warrant."

"Chase, I'm on my way to the hospital right now."

Rushing to Jack, Chase saw three, dead on the floor were Bastide's militia. SERT officers left them where they had fallen. Trev's eyes were halfway open and his eyeballs had rotated. Chase gripped Jack's hand. "Hang in there, Trev. We got Bastide." He felt Jack's grip tighten.

When medics wheeled Jack out, his heart hammered hard and

his stomach twisted into knots. Chase looked at Bastide. Miranda warning was being read to eight of Bastide's militia and eight illegal, Hispanic aliens. He approached the drug cartel and in a voice no one heard, Chase told Bastide, "If my partner dies, you'll never make it to trial. I'll come back and kill you, you bastard."

Squad cars arrived in front of the hall, along with a police van for transport and booking. The suspects would be housed in the County jail until extradition could be arranged. Bastide, Doyle, Baker and Garcia were transported separately to keep them from talking.

Agent Franklin put Agent Stonebrook in charge of the scene and evidence. Five men stayed along with the Sergeant while Chase and the others executed the second search warrant at the vacant house with the same precision used during the first execution.

Whether from the anger of a downed comrade, or their rising adrenaline, the remaining SERT members blitzed the house with amplified enthusiasm. Special Agent Franklin and three deputies rescued Ann after finding her lying on the cement floor in the basement. Her hands were bound behind her back and Chase's heart pumped erratically inside his chest. Agent Franklin shouted upon checking, "She's alive!"

A SERT officer aired through his headset, "House is secure, we need another ambulance, code three."

Chase handed his weapon to an officer standing beside him and kneeled down removing the nylon rope from Ann's wrists. He carefully lifted Ann into his arms as broken words sputtered off her lips.

"Geof . . . alive, Geoffrey, alive."

Cradling Ann tenderly, Chase whispered in her ear, "You're safe. We know," and carried her upstairs. His heart stopped palpitating and returned to normal for the first time in forty-eight hours. He knew he was in this for life, devoted to her.

Once Ann had been transported to the hospital, Chase returned inside the house. Nothing further had been discovered inside and all returned to the dance hall for inventory of property and evidence.

Chase knew it was going to be an all-nighter. The large machines had to be moved and marked for inventory, maintaining the chain of evidence. Charges of murder, counterfeiting, embezzlement conspiracy, and kidnapping were just a few to be sorted through. They only had thirty-six hours in which to federally charge everyone. The paperwork would make a trail from here back to New York.

At twenty-three hundred hours, Chase hadn't removed his headset when Caz' voice infiltrated the airwaves. Chief Casimir spoke personally to Special Agent Franklin. Special Agent Trevor had died in surgery ten minutes ago. A silence and utter stillness besieged the dance hall as SERT officers stopped everything, their heads dropped.

"Fuck!" And the lone curse blared throughout the dormant room. His chest tightened and his brain froze somewhere. A second time in Chase's life, his knees weakened and beads of sweat formed across his brow. As in his father's death, Trev and their bickering and arguing *brother's* do, laughing and joking best friends share, support and tolerance between partners of every moment the two agents had spent together flashed and whirled through Chase's mind. His partner of ten years was gone.

For three days the FBI and police worked with DEA, the Secret Service and the IRS filing reports and statements. Numerous charges were being filed in Federal court against Bastide, Baker, Doyle, Garcia and Bradford. INS handled the aliens they had taken into custody.

On Saturday, day five since the arrests, Chase returned to Minnesota from New York where he'd just attended Jack's funeral. He was on his way back to Masquerade to see Ann at the hospital. He hadn't seen or talked to his mother since he and Caz had taken her statement. Caz had informed him his mother had been released from the hospital on Thursday and he would go home and see her second.

Chase had never spent a second of his life worrying about anything. In the past week he'd had more misgivings and anxiety
attacks than anyone person deserved in a lifetime. The first thing
he had to do was ask for Ann's forgiveness and some how he'd
explain and make her understand the terror he'd felt last Saturday.
He tried not to *what if* the scenario that might play itself out with
her and realized he was nervous for the first time in his life.

Chase steered the rental car into the hospital's parking lot and
got out. He entered the hospital and went to the information desk.

"Ann Longworth's room number, please."

"I'm sorry, sir, but she checked herself out of the hospital on
Wednesday."

"Checked out?"

"You're Angela Franklin's son, the FBI agent involved in the
embezzlement at the children's Agency, aren't you?"

Chase nodded. Small towns, he thought, where everyone knew
everyone else's business.

"Agent Franklin, I'm sorry about what happened to your partner."

Chase stared at the women for a minute. "Can you tell me
why the doctor released Ann Longworth when she had severe injuries?"

"She left of her own accord, Agent Franklin, and against the
doctor's orders."

He should've gone home first. "May, I use your phone?"

"Certainly, just dial nine to get an outside line."

Chase picked up the receiver from the phone the woman had
offered him and called his mother. After talking to her, he learned
Ann had gone back to St. Paul without saying goodbye.

Damn her!

CHAPTER NINETEEN

Seven months had passed and Ann waited as the 727 touched down at Minneapolis/St. Paul International. She'd sold her car deciding in favor of the ease of flying back to Minnesota in the midst of January's winter. Her bleak existence matched the falling snow as she stared out of the aircraft's tiny window during the plane's descent. The fresh, new fluff blanketed and concealed the plowed piles of winter's grayed snow.

It took another hour before Ann had retrieved her luggage and climbed into a cab. After stopping to retrieve her mail and get a take-out salad, the cab driver assisted her with luggage, mail and a large package the post office had held for her. Ann paid the cab driver and closed her apartment door. She saw the emblem on one envelope and knew she held in her hand a Federal subpoena to testify against her abductors. She'd given a statement to an unknown FBI agent, left Masquerade, then went to Deputy Chief Edwards and resigned her position with the Minnesota State Fraud Division after ten years of service

Ann never made contact with Angela Franklin. Out of emotional necessity, she headed for Washington State. At the time, it was the furthest escape she could think of to just run away. She drove and used cash to keep Chase from tracking her down. Unfortunately, her thoughts went with her.

The flashing, red light on her recorder caught her eye and she ignored it. She chose not to listen to any messages and flipped through the box of mail instead. The large package had accompanied the stacked up mail and excluded a return address.

Shifting her eyes around the empty apartment, Ann recalled it took some neighborly help to dump and get rid of everything belonging to Geoffrey. All that remained was the bedroom set, her TV and VCR, a rocker, some personal things and a few books. She wasn't sure why she had continued to pay the rent on this place, but now she would give it up and move on, following her testimony.

Ann couldn't confront Chase or Angela and after checking out of the hospital last summer, she went back to Angela's house packed up her personal belongings and her Trans Am and left Masquerade. Her actions followed actually two, she recalled, unknown federal agents coming to the hospital and taking what turned into a five-hour statement. Oh, they were both nice enough, no question about it, but neither ever mentioned Chase, and she didn't have the courage to ask how he was doing. She'd heard the news about Jack Trevor, but she didn't know how to offer her condolences either.

Upon driving to the northwest coast, Ann writhed with her own slow death over Christie's homicide. She analyzed and examined minutely the murder and her own abduction during the recovery of her injuries. She'd played Geoffrey's words over and over trying to change what she actually heard. She relived and replayed the brief second she heard his words, had battled miserably with her misdeed, and tried like hell to forget the hours that followed after she walked into Angela's house the day of her birthday. She'd scrutinized everything to the point of making herself sick. None of it made any sense, and yet, recalling conversations, it all made sense. During the six plus months she spent in the State of Washington, Ann traveled every inch of mountains and sea to change the final outcome. Geoffrey said Chase was her brother and Christie, Mandi and Jack were still dead. She couldn't change any of it no matter how hard she tried.

The only conclusions she reached had been she would never know her father. And the esteemed Angela Franklin must have had an affair before Chase's birth and Ann had been the result. In her methodical mind, this didn't fit with anything Angela had told her. Ann continued as she had for the past seven months to assess everything carefully and during her flight back, she convinced herself to put it all behind her. She'd never see any of them again anyway. The past couldn't be altered. Now she held the subpoena that would force her to look into his emotionless, brown eyes. Dragging her luggage into the bedroom, Ann avoided looking at the bed knowing sleep always forced the never-ending nightmare. The violent dreams of her pending death that had loomed every night mixing with the reality of abandonment had changed after the FBI arrests. Repeatedly now, Ann dreamt she was still locked inside a brick maze and being hunted. Always taking place during the night, she was running, running away, trying to escape from Chase inside the crazy maze. She'd wake up soaked with perspiration. Her blankets and sheet had found a way to twist around her shaking body after tearing themselves from the corners of the mattress. Like clockwork, Ann would lie there in fear not moving, her lungs heaving as she gasped and panted for air. In the silent darkness she'd listen, hearing nothing. Only after being fully awake, would she find the nerve to unravel her body from the torn bedding, slowly, quietly, then reach and turn on the bedside lamp and glance around the room believing Chase would be there ready to handcuff her and lock her up in jail. Like a bad habit, she would climb out of bed and check every room and closet in the efficiency she had rented in Washington. She'd done it so many times, Ann believed the ritual had become a way of life. In the beginning the dreams depicted true events of her kidnapping. Now she had no way of analyzing their meaning, but believed the significance lied in the unchangeable fact—Chase was her brother. Maybe her subconscious mind was punishing her for what they had done on the beach last summer.

Last night had been the first night Ann had slept a dreamless sleep. She woke up for the first time in close to a year feeling nearly rested. Sauntering back to the living room, she glanced at the large cardboard package in front of her, the rest of the mail could wait. Ann slowly ripped off the tape opening the box and gasped as she slid the painting out. She'd forgotten about the seascape from Ships

N Things and nervously looked inside the box for a note. She never mentioned her desire for the painting to anyone and after tipping the large box upside down, a card fell out. She opened it and read *Please call me, Chase*. He'd written down a New York phone number. Ann just stared at the stormy waves wondering how he knew.

Moments later, she walked over tapping the play button of the recorder and returned to the kitchen to eat her salad. The first message came from Scott, wondering what happened to her. The second message was from Angela asking the same. The messages continued between the two and Scott's last message informed her he was in the playoffs and she had to call him. His voice sounded almost desperate. There were several messages from sales people. One even trying to sell siding to an apartment renter. *Yeah right, that'll work*, she thought.

The twenty-third message came from Chief Deputy Edwards and was dated three days ago. He wanted her to call him back as soon as possible. One more message came from Angela sounding frantically worried. Why didn't she have the damn phone disconnected before she left, or at least shut off the recorder? One more salesman and the twenty-sixth message, Ann dropped the fork in her hand hearing Chase's voice.

He wavered at first, he hemmed and hawed, then questioned why hadn't she returned the acknowledgment receipt of the subpoena they'd sent her. He said the trial begins on Monday and Ann knew she'd have to face him in Federal Court. At least Chase didn't ask what had happened to her, musing he didn't *give a tinker's damn*. She'd gone over the gut-wrenching words zillions of times. And Geoffrey had said the split second before she'd lost consciousness Chase was gonna come looking for his sister.

Ann flinched, dropping her fork a second time when a thunderous pounding met with her apartment door. How could anyone know she'd returned? It had only been thirty minutes since she set foot inside the apartment. Gradually, Ann made her way toward the door and peered through the peephole instantly groaning. Chase stood on the other side of the door. *How did he know?*

"Ann, I know you're in there. I've had someone watching your apartment. Now open this fricking door before I kick the damn thing in!"

His tone prone to patience, resounded angrily as he continued hitting the door. Ann unbolted the deadlock, leaving the chain on and cracked open the door. "I'll get the receipt for your subpoena, just hold on."

As she stepped away from the door, the sound of splintering wood and the door hitting the wall made her lurch forward. "What the hell are you doing?"

He growled and marched toward her. "Something I should have done last July!" Chase grabbed Ann by the wrist, pulling her close to him and kissed her.

Stunned at first, Ann balled her fists and began thrashing violently against his chest, then shoved him away. The words came out in a blood-curdling scream. "Don't *you* ever touch me again." She backed away and instantly swiped her mouth in disgust with the back of her hand.

God, she really did hate him. Chase held his hands palms up and stared into her blue eyes. The smoke color had paled and lacked her spirit and spunk. She'd lost weight, too much he felt and looking at her now, she appeared frail and lifeless. Stepping back, he asked, "Where have you been for the last seven months?"

She spoke in a suffocated whisper. "What do you care?"

Her smothered voice seemed as dark and empty as the space they stood in and Chase scanned the living room. The blinds were closed, but he still saw carpet markings were furniture once sat. "You're moving?"

Ann followed his eyes around the room and went into the kitchen without speaking.

He followed her and sat down on one of two chairs at a small table. A plate of salad sat there. "You know, I can understand the hatred you've acquired for me, but how is it you could just up and leave without a word to my mother? Not to mention, Scott and Max are worried about you as well."

Ann didn't look at him, she couldn't. She bit her bottom lip when a dull ache tugged on her heart. *She didn't hate him.* He obviously didn't know.

"Look at me when I'm talking to you."

Ann turned and faced him. His puzzled gaze shot bullets at her and his anger burned through her. The set of his chin suggested his stubbornness. She'd forgotten his handsome face, how compelling his presence was, and how his rugged and vital power had attracted her. Shaking her head slightly to clear away the immoral feelings, she turned away without answering.

She heard the movement behind her and didn't move. He was standing inches from her and touched her arm. The words came out in a whisper. "Chase, don't." Ann stepped around him retreating to the living room and began pacing.

Chase followed her again and instantly knew she held another secret. Wrenching her fingers, biting her bottom lip were a few of the signs he had relived too many times and lost count. He understood her lack of trust and the blatant hollowness in her eyes. Good Lord! He'd never considered Ann might still be in love with Doyle. For seven months he had done everything within his power to keep his mind off of her and Trev. She had disappeared and he believed he'd lost her forever. He got the call almost an hour ago when she finally returned from wherever she had fled to. Right now his heart was thumping out some disorganized rhythm. He had wanted to start things over with her, and she was hiding behind those eyes of hers.

"You're still in love with him, aren't you?"

Ann swung around and her head flew up in shock. In a weak and tremulous whisper while her fingers trembled, she said, "What in God's name are you talking about?"

Chase studied her momentarily, and asked again though he couldn't say the name. "You still love him."

Ann had signed the receipt for the subpoena and choked on a

laugh. "Here's your receipt, please, just go away. I'll be in court on Monday to testify."

If she didn't still love him, had she met someone else? She had avoided answering him and Chase didn't take the paper. Instead, he crossed his arms as he spread his legs and planted his feet. "I'm not leaving until you look me in the eye and tell me that you never felt something for me. Did you, or did you not feel something for me?"

Ann turned her back on Chase. She inhaled deeply and let the air slither out of her lungs. "I was never in love with Geoffrey."

Chase swung Ann around holding her at arm's length. Her eyes filled with panic at his mere touch and it didn't stem from any hatred of him. "Annie, that's not what I asked you."

She shifted her eyes to his hands gripping her arms.

The smoky color that had stolen his heart darkened and jolted him and Chase let go of her.

Ann backed away from Chase clamping her arms securely around her upper body. If Angela didn't want him to know, she wasn't going to be the one to tell him. Unhooking her arms, her fingers went to her temples and with closed eyes, Ann massaged a thrashing headache.

Ten thousand knots of desperation fusing with bafflement gnawed on him in the pit of his stomach. He didn't recognize his own pleading voice and said, "Annie, I'm sorry about what happened at the hospital." *God, he couldn't stand seeing her like this.* "I'll go away, if you really want me to."

She didn't stop kneading her temples, nor did she open her eyes. "Chase, it's not your fault and you can't be forgiven for *things* you know nothing about."

His chin dropped as his mouth opened to rebuttal. "What the Sam hell are you talking about? I don't understand. Tell me what's wrong?"

Ann dropped her arms to her sides and exhaled. She bit on her bottom lip shifting her stare to the floor. "I can't tell you. You'll have to ask your mother."

Ask my mother. "Ask my mother what?"

"Please," she cried, "just leave."

"Un-uh. You're going to tell me."

Tears were filling the brim of her eyes. "Chase. It's not my place to tell you."

He stepped toward Ann and took her wrist pulling her into the kitchen making her sit down. Sitting down across from her and blocking her escape, Chase said, "If there's something I need to know concerning the trial next week, I'm not leaving until you tell me what it is."

Slumped in the chair, she stared down at her hands and fingers wrestling tightly with each other.

"Ann, what do you know that I don't?"

Tears began streaming down her cheeks. "I can't believe you don't know already."

"Know what?" Reaching for a box of Kleenex on the counter and handing her one, he said, "Tell me." He set the box on the table in front of Ann.

Ann dabbed at her cheeks. "I assume the distance between you and your mother is because of me."

Totally annoyed, Chase ground his words out between clenched teeth. "My mother and I resolved our differences the day after *he* took you from me. Now, tell me what's going on."

Ann whipped out another tissue and blew her nose. "Chase, Geoffrey told me you're my brother," she cried into the Kleenex.

His eyes damn near popped out of his head as the words blew out of her mouth. Chase stood up and paced the tiny floor to work off his anger trying to decide where to begin with her. His misplaced orphan wasn't getting away a second time and he almost laughed at the absurdity of her statement. "Orphan Annie, I assure you, you are *not* my sister."

"But—"

His anger ruled the moment. "Ann, shut-up and listen to me! If you had bothered to stick around instead of sneaking out of the hospital and running off to God only knows where, you would have learned *all* the facts!"

Ann stood up with her jaw squared off to meet him in a confrontation. Chase blocked her passage rigidly placing her back in the chair like she was a bothersome fly.

"Annie, you're going to sit there and listen to me, if it takes all damn night! After you hear the whole truth, I'll leave," he sneered deliberately, "that is, if you still want me to leave."

She glared upward at his crossed arms and insulting grin and knew she had no other alternative. She crossed her arms out of spite.

"Orphan Annie," he purposely taunted, "if you had bothered to stay in the hospital, you would have known I came to see you. Imagine my surprise finding you'd disappeared again. Only this time, I knew it was of your own doing when hospital staff advised me you checked yourself out. I realize it took me several days to sort out all the arrests and get the paperwork done, but you were my first and only priority once we had the charges filed.

"Chase—"

He held up a hand. "I'm not done and you *are* going to listen without asking your incessant questions. Your name at birth was Annarose Leigh-Arvon Longworth."

Ann gaped in surprise. How had he learned of the second part of her middle name? She had dropped the Arvon part because she didn't like it and it meant nothing.

"You were born July 10, 1960, which by the way if you will recall on your last birthday, you were in that ship shop in Masquerade. That painting in there was supposed to be your birthday present, but you know why you didn't get it. I saw you in there looking at it and went inside after you left. The reason I blew up at the hospital that day was because I'd gone to Mom's house to ream you a new ass for confronting Garcia, which Caz did inform me of. When I saw blood everywhere I went bizerk believing it was your blood."

She tilted her head sending him a questioning look.

"I know you changed your name several years ago, why, isn't important. Your father was a drunk named Harlan Gerald Longworth. His excessive drinking is what killed him. He staggered out of a bar into a passing car. I believe you were three at the time that happened. Your father had signed away all parental rights to you before your birth."

She started to ask a question.

Halting her with his hand, he barked, "Don't interrupt me! Your mother was Letitia Marie Phelps. She was born here in Minnesota and died in childbirth at the age of twenty-seven in Chicago. She met your father while working at Devil's Point."

The shock of hearing his words siphoned the blood from Ann's veins.

"Yes, Devil's point. Your mother and her brother had a fight over the fact that she had been charmed, so to speak, out of her pants by your father. After the fight, your mother ran away from home when she was twenty-six. She left behind one sister, Annaleigh Rose Phelps whom she loved and cherished with all her heart. And by the way, who was killed in a boating accident but not before marrying David Welston and becoming Annaleigh Rose Welston. Annaleigh had one child, a son, Scott David Welston and her brother is Maxwell *Arvon* Phelps."

Chase stopped momentarily and watched Ann chewing the hell out of her quivering lip. Tears were streaming new trails down the side of her cheeks. "Annie, Max is your uncle and Scott is your cousin. And for God's sake, I am *not* your brother!"

Tears blinded her, placing strain on her voice. Even if she had wanted to speak, she couldn't. Ann grabbed more tissues and blew her nose.

"Max came to see you in the hospital the day you were abducted. Between my first suspicions of you, and Max filling in the details, I uncovered the information about your past." Everyone's been worried sick about you for the past seven months. In fact, I doubt I can take another phone call from my mother, Max, Scott or the AG's office harassing the hell out of me to find out where you disappeared to."

Sobs had taken over her body uncontrollably. Tissues were piling up on the small kitchen table and Ann still couldn't speak.

"Seems the Chief Deputy wants you back. I promised everyone as soon as Jack was buried and the trial was wrapped up, I'd hunt you down for all of them. The best I could do for the time being was have your place checked daily by the locals. I knew you wouldn't flagrantly walk out on a pending trail."

"Chase . . ." Ann couldn't get the words out and realized she was crying for the second time in her life. Through her sobs, she asked, "Did you tell all of them about me?"

"Yes, they all know Max is your uncle and frankly have all been blaming me for your disappearance."

As if thirty years of tears needed to be released, Ann's sobbing magnified until she couldn't control the tremors.

Chase swept her out of the chair, blanketing his arms around her securely. Tenderly he rocked her. "Annie, I thought I'd lost you forever."

As her sobs began to subside, Ann had no desire to back away from his embrace.

Chase tightened his grip and kissed the top of her head. The sweet smell of her hair was no longer a fading memory. "Annie, I was so scared when he stole you away. I thought I would go out of my mind."

Her breathing began returning to normal and Ann leaned back telling him, "Chase, I have to go to Masquerade and see Max. But how did you ever find me after they took me?"

Refusing to let go of her, Chase gazed into Ann's eyes. After checking his watch, he said, "It's Friday afternoon and we've got until the trial starts on Monday. Since I'm in no mood to share you with anyone, I'll call Scott and Max and my mother and tell them I've found you."

She grabbed another Kleenex and wiped her nose. The facts were overwhelming and Ann's head was swimming in pain from her headache. "If you do that, you know they're all gonna want to come here."

Chase knew Ann was right. "I know how to handle them. Right now, let's work on that headache of yours. I know exactly how to get rid of it," and he began massaging her temples and then the back of her neck.

God, there was magic in his fingers, Ann thought.

Chase gazed into Ann's eyes. "Better?"

She nodded her head not wanting him to stop.

"Annie, come with me to my hotel room and let me wine and dine you privately. I'll explain everything you want to know."

"I need a shower and clean clothes." She was still trembling and waited, watching the play of emotions filling his face.

"Annie," he brushed a gentle kiss across her forehead and grinned, "I told you once never say that to a man who seriously wants to assist," and his mouth played with hers.

His lips softly caressed then swallowed her up until her sobs had completely dissipated. Ann gave herself freely to the passion igniting between them. She responded and her arms came up, wrapping around his neck.

Her mouth was warm and sweet and he no longer feared the untamed response she brought out in him. He released her lips gazing into her unrestricted eyes. The secrets were gone and the fire had returned. The fire he knew held his heart prisoner. He felt uncivilized and without discipline claimed her lips again. Chase hugged Ann craving the touch of stroking her flesh through infinity.

Raising his mouth from hers, Chase nibbled on Ann's earlobe inhaling the scent of her flesh. He wanted to recreate everything from their night on the beach and nipped a path down her neck and back up to her honey flavored lips.

Her mind whirled and Ann believed this was going to lead them both to a place she wasn't ready for, not here in this apartment, she thought, and pulled away.

Chase read her eyes well and it hit him why her apartment

was void of furniture. "I'll wait, go take your shower." He grinned thinking certain things he'd really like, before he chose to descend on Ann's lips one more time.

CHAPTER TWENTY

When Chase made contact with his mother and Max, they both started crying and insisted he had to bring Ann *home* to Masquerade. Out of selfishness, Chase more or less lied and told them they had to discuss Monday's trial, but he would bring her home next weekend. When he got in touch with Scott, his life-long friend told him he'd better be best man at the wedding and it could take place the day after the Super Bowl.

Sitting in his hotel room, Chase liked the wayward strand toppling across Ann's forehead. "Are you still having nightmares?"

"How'd you know?"

"You told me, Scott told me, my mother told me and you look like you haven't slept in a month of Sundays."

"Last night was the first night since his supposed death that I haven't had one. At first, the dreams were almost identical to the way I'd been abducted. After awhile they changed and you became the one I was running from."

"To some degree your dreams were accurate. Ann, I've spent every day trying to find you ever since I discovered you left."

"I assumed when you sent those other agents to take my statement, you knew what I knew and didn't want to see me. You have to have some kind of understanding for what I was going through after what I'd been told."

"I do now, but I didn't then and I made the assumption you were mad at me because of everything I said and did to you at the hospital that day."

"That didn't help, but it had nothing to do with my reason for leaving."

Trying to lighten the mood, Chase said, "If I offer you wine, will there be a repeat of that night on the deck?"

"Not if you don't jab a gun into my guts and scare the crap out of me," she quipped flashing him a grin.

With a hearty laugh, he said, "Now that's the Annie I remember."

Ann couldn't stop herself from looking at him. A handsome face, she mused, kindled with passionate beauty. Traces of humor glinted from his eyes and she noticed for the first time, "You shaved your mustache."

He handed her a glass of wine and teased, "And you're supposed to be a trained observer."

"Not anymore."

"I'll grow it back, Annie, if you prefer."

Ann accepted the glass while staring at his whiskerless face and decided he was devilishly handsome with or without it. "I like. I also like the painting, thank you."

"You're welcome." Chase picked up his glass and said, "Here's to you, Annie."

"Me? What for?"

He chuckled thinking it hadn't taken long for tradition to pick up where they left off. He actually missed her inquiring mind. "You did our work for us."

"I had to prove your accusation of me wrong."

"At a high risk to your own life?"

She shrugged. "Chase, I know I was wrong not to tell you about Geoffrey, but when I first discovered his name on Madison's monogrammed calendar, I didn't believe it." Looking at him over the brim of her glass, she added, "I didn't want to believe I'd been so vulnerable with love. When it was too late, I thought I was a goner. How did you ever find me?"

"With the aid of my mother."

"Angela? I made sure she knew as little as possible." Ann looked away distinctly remembering. "But, it didn't help Christie, did it?"

"What happened to Christie wasn't your fault."

"Perhaps you're right, but I shouldn't have backed down. I

should've made her go back to St. Paul." She took several deep breaths. "She'd still be alive if I had made her go back."

"Maybe," he handed her a tissue as tears welled in her eyes, "but the way my mother tells it, you didn't have a chance in hell against the two of them."

Ann's head came up.

"Sweetheart, she admitted they ganged up on you and had no intention of giving in or backing down. Believe me, you don't argue with Angela Franklin. And my mother hasn't forgotten the ramifications either. But the fault and blame belong solely to the one's who committed the brutal crime."

After blowing her nose, Ann asked, "How did she help you find me?"

Chase stood and refilled both their glasses before he started and then sat down again. "I've read your statement and you know most of it. Because of the trial I can only tell you what you were directly involved with, but by the time it's all over you'll know everything."

"Okay."

"My mother woke up and saw who had kidnapped you. We thought it was Garcia, but her description of what she saw didn't fit. During our questioning, she told Caz and me you had piles of paperwork in your briefcase and had figured out how monies were being embezzled. I went digging and found your paperwork, the computer printout and the monogrammed calendar pages. That's when I discovered Doyle was still alive. We had a photo of him which my mother did identify as your abductor."

"How did you know where to find me?"

"We'd already discovered the dance hall where they were counterfeiting money. Caz called the electric company and discovered the juice had been pumped back in at the dance hall and the house of the old man who originally owned the two places."

"How did Madison gain access to the D-E-C-S files to change the deposits?"

"Believe it or not she was paying someone in their office. Her attorney advised her to cooperate with us and we have that person in custody also."

"What was Susan Bradford's roll in this?"

The questions were methodical like she was performing duty. He didn't care since the questions had been part of what made him fall in love with her and said, "You had it all figured out. All we had to do was run her prints to find out she wasn't who she said she was. We took a chance and arrested her as bait based solely on your taped interview before we executed our search warrants at the dance hall and the house. Her father happens to be a drug cartel from San Luis Potosi, Mexico who'd decided upon a career change. We wanted her father as badly as we wanted everyone else. What you didn't know is that Bradford and Doyle are brother and sister and actually have the same mother, Madison Baker, and the same father."

"Oh my God! Madison is Susan's mother, too?"

Chase nodded remembering Baker's statement. "She'd been lovers with Bastide for thirty-four years. She had Godefredo first and two years later, Caccila or Susan Bradford as you know her. Bastide had arranged for his son to be given a million dollars in order to start his airline business. Together Garcia and Doyle were flying under radar smuggling drugs and counterfeit money. When Baker learned the orphanage had passed the Minnesota Legislature is when she made contact with Bastide on a lucrative business deal she called it.

Ann recalled what Geoffrey had told her of their initial meeting. She also thought over Geoffrey's last words again. *I'm gonna go looking for my sister . . . he's gonna come looking for his sister.* Under the influence of several whacks to one's head the words could definitely be misconstrued, but contain extremely opposite meanings.

Her eyes had enlarged to baseballs and she'd started chewing her bottom lip. "Ann, what is it?"

Ann wavered and swallowed more wine, then explained the discrepancy and her blunder.

Chase stood up stepping closer and brushed a finger along her cheek. He thought of how he believed he would have given Cindy the world in exchange for her love. He couldn't give Ann the world served on a silver platter because she had his heart and everything that went with it. No, he accepted, he couldn't substitute materialistic things for love. In fact it wasn't even an exchange, but the giving of his undying devotion to only one, and Ann was the one. What he didn't know with Cindy, he had learned from Ann and it all centered on the gift of love. It took the day his partner was buried, but he finally understood when he saw John Caleb shedding tears with Trev's brothers and sisters. And, right now, he didn't have a clue if Ann felt the same about him.

"Tell me what happened to Jack."

Holding her chin in his hand, he'd also learned from Ann he couldn't keep secrets. Chase tugged Ann out of the recliner and kissed her amorously. "Come with me and sit," and he took her hand pulling her toward the bed.

Chase yanked his boots off and poured himself bourbon, then lit up cigarettes for both of them. "You want more wine?"

Ann took the cigarette and said, "No."

He drank the bourbon, then inhaled deeply on his cigarette letting smoke filter out slowly. "Jack and I were partners for ten years. We'd been everywhere together, we argued like brothers, and we were devoted to the other as partners. Five and a half years ago we were on a case involving diamond smuggling from Africa into Cuba and then Miami." He inhaled again. "During that case I was shot down in the jungles of Cuba where Jack carried me for five miles to a hospital. We didn't know it until it was too late, but we'd been set up and walked into a slaughter that day."

Tenderly Ann, asked, "Does your mother know?"

"No. I never talk about the job let alone the hazards. Besides, the incident started a trail of bad luck in my life." He crushed out his cigarette and held her hand caressing her palm. "Shortly afterward, my father died as you already know and things had never been that great anyway between my mother and I. Not to long following my father's death, I met Cindy and we stayed together until last year. In fact, it ended six weeks before I met you. I really thought I was in love with her, Ann. She'd moved in with me. We got a different place together because Cindy didn't care for my masculine apartment. Somewhere in there she agreed to marry me. Guess if you're forced to agree, it's not meant to be. About a month after moving into the new place," Chase finished the bourbon in his glass, "I came home in the morning after an all night stakeout and found out how devoted Cindy was to me. She was in bed with another man."

Ann put out her cigarette without saying anything.

"We weren't engaged long enough to tell my mother. I ended it, paid off the lease on the apartment and moved in with Trev until I could find another place. I swore off all women after that. Then, this transfer came along and Trev and I volunteered. The papers came through for Japan while we were working this case."

Ann swallowed a lump in her throat. She'd forgotten he was leaving the country.

"Jack wanted it badly and never made it. He took a bullet from an AK47. It entered through the sleeve of his vest and lodged in his heart."

Ann covered his hand for a moment, "Chase, I'm so very sorry," and she held his face between her hands before planting a kiss on him.

His hand slid behind her neck pulling her in and their tongues swirled in unison. Her response had given him everything he needed to do away with his pain. After ten years, he never would have believed it possible.

Reluctantly, their foreheads leaned against each other. "Annie, I've never done this much talking in my entire life. But you and Cindy both taught me secrets can't be part of any relationship. I won't speak freely of the grisly gore I see in my job, but I'll always answer your questions, if you'll only ask me. I haven't been able to get you out of my system since you stole my heart last summer."

Ann stood up alienating the two of them. He'd filled in all the blanks of her barren past as well as his own. He gave her all the answers she'd spent her entire life in pursuit of. He'd actually given her relatives and a family. Her name finally had significance! Was he also telling her he loved her? He hadn't said he loved her. She'd never allowed or given herself a chance to wonder if she loved him. How would she know this wasn't another mistake? "When do you leave for Japan?"

"I don't."

Her heart skipped like an old vinyl record and she swung around to look at him. "You're staying in New York?"

He stood up, pushing his hands into his pockets as discipline not to reach over and touch her. He had to see all of her to weigh her reactions. "No, I'm still transferring," and he saw the excitement quickly fade from her oval features. "Annie, I've stared death in the face every day for too many years and it's time for a change. After the trial, I'll be assigned to the Minneapolis Bureau permanently."

"Here?"

He nodded, lightly taking her hand when her eyes brightened. "And, I am going to convince you before Monday morning how much I love you. You'll never feel vulnerable to love again. I love *you*, Annie."

Her heart did that blasted flipping thing and Ann could barely contain her excitement. She didn't know how she knew, or why. She didn't even know when she figured it out, but Ann just knew she believed in Chase with all her heart. And somewhere in the middle, she discovered the depth of her love for him.

"I love you, Annie."

She jumped into his arms throwing her arms around his neck and began kissing him. Her action had thrust him backward where they both fell onto the bed and she was on top of him. "I love you more, Chase Edward Franklin."

Wrapping his arms around her, Chase said, "Annie, marry me."

"When?" she asked placing kisses on his jaw and neck.

His grin turned to laughter, eagerly wanting to appease her. "Right now."

"Let's go," she stated.

Ann had convinced him, caressed his mouth and kissed him with a motive that encouraged his willing participation.

Printed in the United States
4518